DWELLER UNDER THE ROOTS

BOOKS BY MARK HOBSON

Fiction

World Quake

World Quake 2

Grey Stones

A Murmuration of Starlings

Wolf Angel

A State of Sin

Dweller Under The Roots

Now May Men Weep

DWELLER UNDER THE ROOTS
A Folk Horror Tale

By
Mark Hobson

COPYRIGHT © 2024 MARK HOBSON
ALL RIGHTS RESERVED.
THE MORAL RIGHT OF THE AUTHOR HAS BEEN ASSERTED.

PUBLISHED BY HARCOURT PUBLISHERS

HARCOURT
PUBLISHERS

EXCEPT WHERE ACTUAL HISTORICAL EVENTS AND CHARACTERS ARE BEING USED FOR THE STORYLINE OF THIS BOOK, ALL SITUATIONS IN THIS PUBLICATION ARE FICTITIOUS, AND ANY RESEMBLANCE TO LIVING PERSONS IS PURELY COINCIDENTAL.

BOOK COVER DESIGN BY KEN DAWSON

For Sophie, Emily, Jacob, Leo,

and Esme the dog.

Nestled above the remote village is a wildwood forest. It is so impenetrable that moonlight surrenders to the shadows like a servile vassal. Here, the wind gibbers like old crones, and a thick fog rises out of the cold earth, its tendrils curling promiscuously through tree branches.

Through this forest winds a crooked path. It twists and turns over ground knotted with roots.

One way in and one way out.

Once, many years past, people came here. Some came to hunt, others came to walk the old coffin route, and still more came to pay homage. But that was then, and this is now. Now, they stay away.

A tumbledown cottage with ivy walls and broken windows sits at the end of the crooked path. Nobody has lived here for a long time. Children and adults tell stories of wraiths and ogres, of nightmarish things that materialize one moment only to vanish the next.

The cottage should be empty. But tonight, an orange light flickers weakly beneath the door. Within those walls, a man fears for his life and his sanity.

Lee Harris leans his shoulder against the door, desperately attempting to keep the seething, crawling things in the garden from bursting inside and overwhelming him. In his feverish work, he glances up at the ceiling and hears more of them slithering over the cottage roof and worming down the chimney. An overpowering mephitic smell pushes through the walls; Lee cannot banish from his mind the image of the small child whose fearsome visage is a mass of earthworms.

He asks himself again: what led him to this place, deep in the cancerous heart of the forest? What led him to the horrors of this night?

PART ONE

The world is bound with secret knots

ATHANASIUS KIRCHER
MAGNETICUM NATURAE REGNUM
1667

CHAPTER 1

IT STARTED ONE WEEK BEFORE when Jacko Page had said, "The job's a piece of piss. We'll be in and out of there before you know it."

Jacko, Chris Keeble, and Lee Harris were inside Jacko's car repair workshop tucked into the railway arches on Hudson's Passage. They'd gathered here after scoping out the tiny post office during the morning.

"It'll be easy, man," Jacko insisted. "The Postmaster and his missus are getting on. In another year or two, they'll have a nice big pension coming their way. They won't give us any trouble, trust me."

Jacko Page was a small man who spoke so softly you had to lean in to listen to him. He was an ex-squaddie and was as hard as they come. Most of the time, this reassured Lee, but sometimes it frightened him half to death. Because when Jacko got an idea in his head, there was no talking him out of it. Usually, he was right about these things.

Still… Lee had doubts about the scheme and voiced these concerns.

"What if they do? Give us trouble?" he asked.

"They won't. At their age, they aren't going to play the big hero. Besides, it's not really their money we'll be taking. And they'll be insured."

"Jacko's right," Chris Keeble piped up from where he stood in the workshop's inspection pit. "They'll do all right out of it."

He wiped his hands on his blue mechanic's overalls and climbed up the steps to join his mates.

"Anyway, this place isn't doing so well. Is it, Jacko?" Chris said.

Jacko sighed and pulled a face. "Things are tough," he admitted reluctantly. "I have lots of overheads, and the bank is on my back about late loan repayments."

Lee looked around the workshop. Typically, there would be three or four cars in here getting fixed and several more waiting outside. Today, there was just a single hatchback being spray-painted electric blue. It was no secret that Jacko's business was struggling.

"It's okay for you, Lee," said Chris with a worried frown on his forehead. "You have a decent job at the supermarket. But Jacko said only the other day that he might have to let me go."

Jacko patted Chris on the shoulder. "I'm sure it won't come to that. But the place could certainly do with a cash injection."

He turned to Lee and gave him his best James Dean grin.

"Of course, there'll be a nice pile of readies in it for you, too."

Dweller Under The Roots

It wouldn't be the first job they'd pulled. The three had hit the service stations on the motorway several times in the last few years, allowing them a quick getaway to Manchester or Leeds. And up to now, a combination of careful planning and Jacko's military training meant they'd drawn zero attention from the law. It was a lucrative sideline, and the benefits outweighed the risks. But robbing the local post office was too risky for Lee. The chances of being caught were too great. Even wearing balaclavas, someone might recognize their voices or mannerisms or wonder at all the cash they'd suddenly come into.

Jacko's counterargument was that stealing money from service stations or ATMs was proving increasingly difficult. To foil robberies, most used radio-controlled devices that released blue dye all over the notes within moments of being stolen. A small provincial post office in a one-street town in the English countryside made for an easier target. They'd seen for themselves the set-up: a large safe in the cash office stuffed full of money – tens of thousands of pounds in Sterling and foreign currency just sitting there on the shelf, not to mention the money in the cash tills. One poorly positioned security camera, a dozy elderly couple nattering to their customers, no fancy shutters on the door. And next door was a covered ginnel leading to a patch of waste ground at the back. All told, the place had minimal security and a nice place to park their getaway cars. As soon as they had the money, they would split up and drive to separate locations, where they would lie low for a bit until the dust had settled.

Lee's sober protestations felt lacklustre compared to the money they were talking about. Not millions, admittedly, but they were set to gain ten or twenty grand each, which would set them up nicely.

He listened as Jacko and Chris talked over their game plan:

How they'd make their escape (Jacko would provide three cars from the scrapyard at Cooper Bridge).

How long they would keep their heads down (a few days, or maybe a week, should be long enough).

The best way to launder the proceeds of the robbery (use the betting machines in the local bookies by placing small bets and cashing out the remainder in clean money).

Jacko's gritty determination was having the desired effect because, by the time they worked out the details, Lee couldn't help but feel the buzz of adrenalin coursing through his veins. His friend, Lee reflected, might be a little mental, especially when he'd had a few beers and was regaling them with stories of his time in the army, but he was pretty unflappable in a crisis. The term self-possessed described him perfectly. If anything went wrong, Jacko would know what to do.

"Right, so that's sorted, then," Jacko said, breaking into Lee's thoughts.

"When do we do it?" asked Chris.

"Tomorrow. In the afternoon, before they empty the safe for the weekend."

Jacko moved across to one of the workbenches and dragged it to one side. There was a hole in the wall behind it. Reaching in, he pulled out a canvas holdall and placed it on top. Lee and Chris gathered around as he unzipped it. Inside were an assortment of handguns and sawn-off shotguns.

"Give these a clean, Chris. While he's doing that, I want you, Lee, to pop along to Tiny Bob's market stall and buy some burner phones."

He stuffed a few twenties into Lee's hand.

"See that Tiny Bob keeps his mouth shut, mind you. Tell him we know all about his little sideline if he starts asking questions."

Tiny Bob was actually twenty stone of colossal blubber. As a result of his size and a diet of chip butties, he used an O2 cylinder to help with his breathing. One day a week, Tiny Bob left his tatty council house to work on his market stall. A few years back, he used to flog pirate DVDs, but since On-Demand arrived, nobody watched DVDs anymore, and now he flogged second-hand mobile phones.

Lee patiently listened to Tiny Bob's endless sales patter, his voice making a wet whistling sound through the oxygen mask. He blathered about how, for an extra ten quid, he could sync Lee's old phone. Or perhaps he wanted to upgrade from Android to Apple? "Give me a few days, and I'll get my hands on some second-hand state-of-the-art next-generation gear, buddy."

Lee, wondering why he would want to be a buddy to a weirdo who enjoyed watching the kids on Dance Moms, held up his hand to cut him off mid-flow.

"Just three of these workaday ones will do," Lee said, pointing at a plain burner phone.

"Very retro," said Tiny Bob, sucking through his oxygen mask. "I like your style."

"How much credit do they have?"

"They come preloaded with five quid, but I can add more."

"Stick another tenner on each, will you?"

"Not a problem," Tiny Bob wheezed like an old Dyson Vac. "Are they for something special?"

Lee didn't reply. He just glanced off to the side, and after several seconds, Tiny Bob got the message.

"None of my business. Discretion is my middle name."

Tiny Bob leaned forward, his tummy spilling over the stall like melting lard. He passed the carrier bag over.

"Do you want to score some Charlie?" he asked conspiratorially, winking at Lee. "You seem stressed out, buddy."

"I'm fine." Lee snatched the bag and shoved the notes into Tiny Bob's chubby hand.

Back at the workshop, Jacko had shut the garage doors to keep out prying eyes, so Lee had to use the side entry. Inside, he found them readying the three getaway cars. Lee was an excellent driver, but he knew Jack Shit about engines and made coffee while they worked. Occasionally, Chris would sit behind the wheel and press the accelerator while Jacko tinkered under the bonnet, tuning the revs. They made a few adjustments to the cars' suspensions. There wasn't time for a Cut and Shut, so they cloned the reg numbers by adding false license plates and used wire wool to rub off the chassis numbers. They planned on scorching the cars after the robbery, but it was better to be safe than sorry.

It was early evening by the time they finished. Jacko said they should spend the next day going about their regular routine; Lee would go to work as usual (he'd ask his boss for some time off that he was owed), and Jacko and Chris would open the car repair workshop. Everything should appear normal.

They stepped outside and locked up. Jacko grabbed a quick smoke and ground his cig out on the pavement.

"If either of you have any questions," he told them, "now's the time to ask."

Lee and Chris shook their heads.

"Champion."

•   •   •

So that was the plan.

But this is what really happened.

Parking the cars on the waste ground, they rolled their balaclavas down over their faces and climbed out. Lee glanced at his watch; it was approaching half past four, and the sun was giving up its token resistance to the dusk.

Stuffed down his waistbelt and hidden under the hem of his plain jacket was an old gun, the kind his grandad might have used in the war. Lee had loaded it with three rounds. He'd only ever fired the thing once when they did a bit of target practice on the moor last summer. Chris had a similar weapon. Their guns were just for backup in case something unexpected happened. Jacko, who would lead things, was armed with a sawn-off shotgun. It was a nasty-looking thing, and the sight of it shoved in his face would frighten the Postmaster so severely that he'd do exactly what he was told unless he wanted his face blasted with pellets. Jacko had a low bullshit threshold; the others knew he'd use it if it came down to it.

Lee prayed it wouldn't come to that. Again, he was riddled with doubts. He had a horrible void in his stomach. Things didn't feel right. It felt too rushed, like Jacko hadn't planned the robbery as thoroughly as usual. It was as though an opportunity for an easy job had fallen into their laps, and their leader couldn't resist taking it, which wasn't like him.

It was too late to pull out, so Lee moistened his dry lips and followed his mates up the cobbled ginnel.

They exited the passage onto the High Street, turned sharply to the right, and Jacko shouldered open the post office door.

There was just one customer inside, a geeky teenage girl who turned sharply as the door banged. Her mouth fell open on seeing three men wearing balaclavas come charging in, giving Lee a glimpse of a multi-coloured brace. When she saw the shotgun, she squealed like a mouse, dropped the brown parcel she held, and slid down the wall.

Jacko marched up to the counter, levelled the shotgun at the Postmaster, and thrust a handful of plastic bags across, making it clear what the Postmaster needed to do.

Meanwhile, Chris watched the door while Lee watched the girl. She was whimpering quietly, so Lee pressed a finger to his lips, and she fell silent.

The Postmaster and his wife emptied the tills, stuffing notes into the carrier bags.

"Do you want the loose change?" the Postmaster asked in a querulous voice.

"Just the pound coins and the two-pound coins," Jacko growled.

"Is that all?"

"Well, I don't want any fucking stamps, do I Grandad? Open the safe and fill those bags."

The elderly man turned and moved hesitantly towards the door to the cash office.

"Come on, get a move on!" Jacko commanded.

But before the Postmaster had gone any further, the cash office door opened, and a burly chap stepped out. He had biceps and shoulders the size of a medieval archer's and legs thicker than Canadian Redwoods. Wearing sweatpants and a t-shirt, he looked like he'd just returned from a workout at the gym.

He towered over the Postmaster, glowering at Jacko, Chris, and Lee. Lee felt his stomach contents do a liquid backflip.

"Who the hell do you think you are?" the burly chap snarled at Jacko, stomping to the counter.

"Just give him the money, Son," the Postmaster urged.

"Not likely, Dad." And he reached over the counter and snatched the shotgun.

"Mad bastard!" shouted Jacko, and Lee watched in alarm as a crazy tug-of-war developed, both men refusing to yield.

The Postmaster's son was so brawny that he hauled Jacko off his feet and over the counter.

"Help him!" shouted Chris from the door, but Lee was rooted to the spot. The teenage girl started to scream, and the Postmaster's wife scrabbled to get away and sent display stands toppling.

A deafening report shattered the air, stunning everyone into silence. The top of the burly chap's head disappeared in a spray of red mist. Then he went ramrod straight like he was standing to attention before crashing over. Claret jetted from the gaping wound.

The girl went into hysterics. The elderly couple were kneeling and tugging at their son's lifeless body. Lee's head was ringing from the gunshots' reverberations.

"Fuckfuckfuckfuckfuck!" Jacko, usually calm, was as near to being panic-stricken as Lee had ever seen him. But to his credit, he quickly regained control of himself. Ramming the still-smoking shotgun under his coat, he grabbed the bags filled with cash from the tills, slid back over the counter, and pushed Lee towards the main door. Chris was already through them, and Lee and Jacko followed him around the corner and down the ginnel.

CHAPTER 2

"WHAT DO WE DO? WHAT do we do?" shouted Chris once they reached the cars.

"We stick to the bloody plan, don't we."

"But Jacko, you just killed a man."

Jacko turned on Chris and grabbed him by the lapels with one hand. "You need to get your shit together. Quickly."

He shoved him roughly away. Lee could see Jacko's eyes through the balaclava opening. They were blazing with anger and determination.

Jacko nodded to himself, saying again, "We stick to the plan. You know where to go. Keep your heads down and talk to nobody."

Then he pushed the bags of cash into Lee's chest.

"When you get to your safe house, find somewhere to hide this."

"Why me?" Lee asked in alarm.

"Because I have enough on my plate getting rid of the shotgun, don't I?"

Lee wasn't happy about driving around with a shedload of hot money, but he was wise enough to keep his trap shut.

"What are you both waiting for?" Jacko asked. "Get your effing skates on. And don't use your phones. Wait until I contact you first."

Then he was flinging open the driver's door to his car and seconds later was motoring away and leaving a spray of gravel in his wake. Lee and Chris exchanged a glance and then followed suit. Lee gunned the engine to his Defender, and the vehicle roared up the narrow track behind the row of shops with Chris hot on his heels.

The three cars raced by the canal, fishtailing on the unstable ground. They blasted under a stone bridge and followed the track as it swung right, up a short incline, and came out onto the High Street. Here, they went three separate ways, and Lee joined the lines of traffic weaving through the small town centre.

He could hear police sirens from somewhere, and Lee remembered that he was still wearing his balaclava. He furtively slipped it off and shoved it into the glove compartment with the money and the gun.

At a set of lights, Lee pulled up behind a builder's van towing a small cement mixer. He waited for the lights to change. The sirens grew louder, and a few seconds later, he saw an oncoming police car forcing a path through the rush hour traffic. Vehicles moved aside to let it through, and when the police car was near him, Lee shifted the Defender onto the curb to make room. He felt sweat trickle down his brow. The police driver gave him a thumbs up and hurried through the gap, and Lee breathed a sigh of relief.

The lights changed, and Lee followed the builder's van. He briefly thought about the unfortunate chap Jacko had blasted. What a terrible stroke of bad luck for the man and the three of them. What were the chances of the Postmaster's son being in the post office just as they burst in to rob the joint? The silly fool had tried to be a Have-A-Go-Hero, and now he was dead, lying in a pool of blood and brain matter with his parents tugging at his corpse.

It was a complete fuck-up. Killing someone changed everything. Now, the rozzers would pull out all the stops to catch them and slap them with a murder charge. For armed robbery and homicide, they'd be put away for twenty-five years minimum, Lee reckoned.

Lee felt himself starting to shake from delayed shock. It took all his effort to keep the car on the road. The builders turned into the pub car park at the Rose and Crown. Lee picked up speed as traffic thinned out on the edge of town.

When he saw the signs for Hardcastle Crags, Lee spun the wheel and stamped down the accelerator, engaging the vehicle's 4x4 as the roadway steepened sharply. The town was nestled at the bottom of a deep valley and overlooked by woodland, and as the car entered a tunnel of trees, the premature twilight forced Lee to turn on his headlamps.

The road climbed higher and higher. A moped came into view, its single light shining like a bulbous eyeball. The rider weaved over the white lines before swerving safely across to their side of the narrow road, but the near miss alarmed Lee enough to cut his speed. He longed to be at the safe house as soon as possible, but if he drew too much attention to himself or crashed into a tree or a ditch, he could forget about lying low and keeping below the radar.

He switched on the car radio and tuned through a few local stations, but it was too early for the robbery to have made the news. Lee forced himself to relax. He hit the button to lower his window, and the freshening autumn breeze felt soothing on his face.

Jacko was right. They just needed to stick to the plan and await events. There was no need to panic. Everything might still work out okay.

The road straightened at Midgehole, a tiny hamlet of holiday lets and picnic spots. He drove by a row of terrace houses and then a field that sloped down to Hebden Beck. There was a bus stop and the shell of a burnt-out country house that had caught fire long ago, and a few hundred yards further along was the small car park where tourists would leave their cars and campervans before hitting the hiking trails. Lee drove on, the road again twisting and turning around the landscape. The route became a narrow and badly potholed byway. Then, a rugged trackway with a grass strip down the middle between tyre ruts. The dense woods closed in tightly on both sides.

When he was a teenager, he and his friends from school sometimes hung out in the woods near Gibson Mill, but they'd never ventured much further than the old trestle bridge across the narrow chasm at Blake Dean. Certainly, they'd never come to this place. He was sure he'd remember if they had. Lee looked at the trees to either side, but the trunks were packed so tightly together, and their roots and branches so gnarled and twisted, the shadows so impenetrable, he could barely see more than a few feet into the woods, even when he switched to full beam.

Lee slowed to a crawl. If he'd followed Jacko's directions properly, the turning leading to the safe house should be coming up. Shortly after, he spotted the mark: a white stripe painted on a tree trunk. Just past it was a pair of stubby gateposts covered in lichen, and Lee swung the car between them. The tyres vibrated as he drove over a cattle grid, and the twin headlamps probed the darkness like an insect's antennae, lighting up a track barely scratched out of the ground.

Lee leaned over the wheel and strained his eyes through the windscreen as the car edged forward. The way ahead narrowed even further, and the Defender pushed through a screen of overgrown foliage. The branches scraped the car's bodywork and sprung back as it passed through.

Then Lee saw the crumbling walls and sagging roof of an old, tumbledown cottage. In the car's headlamps, he observed that much of the tiny abode was cloaked in a tangle of ivy, the vines so dense they almost obscured the lower windows and the door. A row of dormer windows looked down at him from the crooked roofline, bookended on the left and right by chimney stacks. An overgrown garden at the front presented a formidable ingress to the front door, with all manner of traps and obstacles. A separate building to the left of the cottage looked in even worse condition. Lee thought it must have been an old stable block at one time. He prayed it wasn't an outdoor toilet.

Please, he begged, let there at least be indoor plumbing and electricity.

Lee swung the car over to the side of the track and took a moment to consider this place would be his home for the next few days, maybe longer after the bungled robbery. The nearest village might only have been a handful of miles away, but the cottage was so isolated it might as well have been a thousand. Lee reminded himself that was the whole point, but his heart sank all the same.

Before stepping out, he turned the Defender around. He switched off the engine and lights and looked back the way he'd just come. He could no longer see the track and woods, just a tenebrous blackness, which carried a heavy weight of ill-boding that nearly made Lee cry out. A shiver passed through him like someone had dropped an ice cube down his back.

Then Lee cursed under his breath. He needed to get a grip. The woods and cottage may be sinister, but they were his sanctuary, his hideout.

Reaching over, he opened the glove compartment and retrieved the gun and the money. Jacko had also provided a heavy-duty rubber flashlight and a set of door keys. Taking them, Lee left the Defender and used the flashlight to navigate a path through the tangled garden. The weeds and brambles endeavoured to entangle his feet. At one time, Lee mused, there must have been a garden path and maybe a vegetable patch somewhere under here, but nature had long since reclaimed the plot.

He stopped before the door. Shining the light on the keyhole, he inserted the key and twisted it. Much to his surprise, it turned smoothly, and the door swung inwards.

Reaching inside, Lee felt on the wall for a light switch and flicked it down.

Weak light illuminated the cottage's parlour, and Lee breathed a little easier.

Then his gaze wandered around the interior. Jacko had warned him the place was a bit on the rustic side, and he wasn't wrong. The furnishings – what little there was – had seen better days. Under the parlour's only window were a rickety table and two wooden chairs. A rocking chair and an armchair with holes in its upholstery sat before an empty fireplace. A blanket box tucked into the corner also served as a small table.

On the opposite wall was a range covered in half a century of grime, with a thin pipe snaking in a zigzag up the wall and through the second chimney breast. A staircase disappeared through a trap door to the upper floor. Under the stairs, Lee saw another doorway.

Closing the cottage's front door and snicking on the bolt, he shoved the flashlight down his belt and crossed the bare floor to investigate. Flicking on more Bakelite light switches revealed a kitchen with a mangle, a massive sink with a deep basin, a single wooden stool, and a door that must lead down to the cellar. On a shelf was a radio with an aerial. Lee randomly opened a few cupboards, seeing Jacko had stocked up on food. His friend had also left a small camping stove with butane gas. Finally, on the unit was a six-pack of beer.

Climbing the stairs, he spent a few more moments exploring. There was a loft room containing a single bed, a sleeping bag, and a holdall jammed with a set of jeans, a sweater, and some spare underwear. In an alcove was a bookshelf holding an assortment of dog-eared books to pass the time. Last but not least, at the end of a short hallway, Lee discovered a tiny toilet cubicle – thank God – and a sink. He tested the taps; a steady trickle of cold water came out.

He checked the windows, and satisfied that everything was in order, Lee returned to the parlour. It might not be the Ritz, he mused, but it could be worse. Leaving the gun on the table, he considered where he could hide the money.

Walking across the room, he opened the blanket box, but on second thoughts, he decided it was too obvious a hiding place. Maybe he could pull up one of the floorboards? Lee wandered around, testing them with his feet to see if any were loose, but as he did, he glanced up and spotted one of the stone bricks on the outside wall was jutting out a few inches. Lee stepped across. He grabbed it to find it was loose. Jiggling it about, Lee pulled the brick out. There was a hollow space behind. Taking the flashlight from his belt, Lee shone the beam into the hole and reached inside. His fingertips dislodged something, making it rattle. Taking hold, Lee pulled the object out.

Lee yelped in surprise. It was a small, mummified animal, a cat by the looks of it, now a dried and shrivelled-up husk. He tried to fling it away, but his fingers were caught between the thin rib bones, and it refused to come off. Dashing over to the front door, Lee unbolted and yanked it open, stepped outside, and shook his arm more vigorously. The dead cat flew away into the undergrowth.

Jeez, he thought, wiping his hand on his jacket. The poor mite must have somehow become trapped behind the wall and died there. God knows how long ago.

Dweller Under The Roots

Inhaling a shuddering breath to calm his over-frazzled nerves, Lee went back inside. Taking the money, he returned to the hole, and after checking there were no further surprises, he pushed the plastic carrier bags into the opening, wedging them down the back, making sure they were packed tightly. Bending to retrieve the brick, Lee jiggled it into position and banged it with the heel of his hand until it was flush with the others. Standing back, he cast his eyes over his handiwork. Satisfied, he prepared himself for bed.

CHAPTER 3

LEE PEELED OPEN HIS EYES and glanced around at his unfamiliar surroundings. He'd been dreaming about his old man, of a trip to Windermere years ago when they'd spent the day seated side by side on the lakeshore, fishing for roach, tossing handfuls of maggots into the water, and drinking a flask of Oxo. It was Lee's last happy memory of his dad because soon after, his parents divorced, and Dad started drinking heavily. After a decade of boozing, the old fellow's liver packed in. Now he was six feet under and only came to say hello in dreams.

Lee rubbed away the last residual image of the dream and sat up. His head felt stuffy, like he'd had a skinful of beer – which he hadn't. The previous evening, he'd kicked off his shoes and socks, climbed into bed, and dropped straight off to sleep.

Moaning at the dull ache behind his eyes, Lee looked at his watch.

Dweller Under The Roots

It was after eleven. He'd overslept. He'd meant to rise early and have a better recce of his surroundings, but already the day was half done. Cursing under his breath, Lee got to his feet. Crouching low at the loft room's little window, he peeled back the lace curtain and peered outside.

The sky – what little he could see of it through the canopy – was overcast, lending the woodland a heavy, oppressive feel. The bedroom overlooked the back of the cottage. From the window, Lee spied a crooked path between elms and oaks. The trees were so jam-packed in serried ranks that they encroached onto the path after a hundred feet. Lee wondered where the crooked path led to.

Shrugging, he turned away. He needed to piss and then have something to eat.

Something crunched under his bare feet, making Lee stop halfway to the door and look down. The rug was covered in brown powder, tiny heaps of it. Puzzled, Lee bent over. There was some other stuff there too, flecks of black tarry substance. He ran his fingertips in the powder, thinking it might be soil, but when he sniffed them, Lee thought he detected a familiar briny smell like seaweed.

Perplexed, Lee shook his head. He was sure it hadn't been there the night before. Now, it was all over the soles of his feet. He'd have to wash them later.

He was in a hurry to empty his bladder, and by the time he'd peed and flushed the clanky old toilet and made himself a bacon sandwich, Lee had forgotten all about it.

• • •

Lee made himself a second strong cup of instant coffee to drive out the headache, and while he drank his brew, he cleared away the breakfast dishes. His thoughts inevitably returned to yesterday. He wondered what leads the police had. Jacko, himself, and Chris had carried out the robbery in the middle of a busy town centre (so they could slip away in the rush hour), meaning there might be dozens of potential witnesses. Still, the sum total of what they'd seen might be negligible. People tended to see different versions of the same event, and over time, their stories changed. Their memories played tricks on them; their recollections became clouded, or they picked up on what others said and reworked their accounts. Before long, they'd metamorphosed into something else entirely.

Then there was CCTV. Cameras everywhere, spying on people 24/7. Would they provide the police with a breakthrough? Maybe, Lee conceded. More likely, they showed a snarl of traffic winding through the streets, their three getaway cars hidden amongst hundreds of vehicles. They'd used false plates as well.

So, Lee thought to himself, they'd done nothing to give away their identities. They'd got clean away. Assuming Chris and Jacko were both holed up in their bolt holes, Lee reminded himself.

He fished out the small burner phone from his front pocket and wondered whether to turn it on and check for messages. Lee decided it was too early and risky, although eventually, he would have to chance it.

Dweller Under The Roots

At midday, he turned on the radio. The robbery was the top story on the news bulletin. They named the murder victim – Kenny something or other – and the police said they were working on several leads, but as of yet, they'd made no arrests. The robbers were described as armed and dangerous.

Whether any of that was true was questionable, but for now, the seeming lack of a breakthrough put Lee's mind at rest.

Lee decided to take a proper look around to take his mind off things, starting with the one place inside the cottage he'd not yet explored.

He opened the cellar door and peered down a flight of wooden stairs. They disappeared into the darkness. Lee felt around for a light switch but failed to find one, so, leaving the door slightly ajar, he went to the parlour to get the flashlight. When he returned to the kitchen, he saw the cellar door had swung wide open. The black opening seemed to study him, and Lee shook off the odd motion, unsure where the idea had sprung from. A cool breeze kissed his bare arms as he went down the steps.

Halfway down, Lee flicked on the flashlight and soon spotted a pull cord dangling from the cellar's ceiling. He tugged at it. Feeble, pale light washed weakly over the subfloor space. A peculiar smell of vinegar assailed Lee's nostrils.

Turning off the flashlight, he went down the last few steps and scanned his surroundings.

He appeared to be in an old root cellar. The floor and walls were of bare, hardpacked earth, and down the middle was a row of dilapidated timber shelves holding dozens of wooden crates. They contained lumpy and mouldy produce, some so rotten they had fermented. Lee saw furred-over turnips, winter squashes covered in thick goo, perished beets and carrots. Dangling from the shelves were strings of shrivelled onions. Boxes of English Cox apples had spoiled so severely they looked like knobbly, congealed jelly.

Lee strolled to the end of the line, feeling the coldness of the underground storage cellar seep into his bones.

The end shelf held large glass and earthenware jars with curled-up labels and wooden stoppers strung with dusty cobwebs. Lee approached one of them and peered at it. The cellar was darker at this end where the light didn't penetrate, so he switched on his flashlight and directed its beam at the glass vessel. It was filled with amber liquid, and suspended in it was a weird, twisted root in the shape of spindly limbs. Lee wiped the grime off the label, but the writing was illegible. Beside it was a smaller bottle full of rusty nails with pieces of red string wrapped around them.

Lee turned the corner to start up the other side, the flashlight playing over the timber shelves.

Suddenly, he stopped in his tracks, and what he saw next made him gag and nearly bring up his breakfast. The shelves here were covered in a glistening, slick carpet of white slime. Lee stared in incomprehension for several heartbeats, trying to work out what he was looking at. Then he saw hundreds of slugs and snails clinging and slithering up the shelving unit or oozing their slime trails over the wooden crates and their contents. Dozens more inched over the earth floor towards the light from the cellar door, leaving horrible sludgy gum in their wake.

Lee cried out and rammed his knuckles into his mouth to avoid puking. He'd never seen anything so revolting in his life. The nasty little creatures must have been down here for years, breeding and feeding off the mouldy produce. Some slugs were even eating each other, little cannibal critters munching away with their microscopic teeth and jaws, shitting yellow puss all around.

Lee backed away, checking his shoes, and ludicrously fearing they might have sneaked up on him (how difficult must it be to outrun a snail or a slug?), he hurried around the end of the shelves and back the way he'd come, and then scooted up the cellar stairs two at a time, yanking the pull cord as he went. He slammed the cellar door shut and stood in the kitchen, his skin crawling. There was a gap at the bottom of the door, and Lee envisaged the creatures sliding up the stairs and squeezing their squelchy bodies across the kitchen floor.

"Shit, shit!" Lee exclaimed, plucking a tea towel off its hook, twirling it around, making it into a rope, and ramming it under the bottom of the cellar door. It would have to do. Hopefully, the things preferred the damp cellar and would stay down there and leave him alone.

After his experience, Lee desperately needed some fresh air. Jacko had warned them to stay out of view, but Lee reckoned that the chances of being spotted in these backwoods were minimal. He should be okay if he stayed near the cottage and didn't wander too far.

Shrugging on his jacket and pocketing the gun, he opened the front door and poked his head out. He looked around and listened intently. The way was clear, and the woods peaceful, with just a woodpigeon calling from somewhere in the distance. Lee left the doorway and forged a path through the garden. The car was still where he'd left it last night.

He moved around the cottage, inspecting the plots of land and the surroundings, breathing in the crisp air. At the back of the building, Lee looked up at the loft room window, and then his eyes were drawn towards the crooked path he'd seen earlier. From ground level, the pathway seemed to barely penetrate the crush of trees. If anything, the woodland seemed to have inched closer, creating a tangled barrier of horizontal branches and interlaced outgrowths that formed a solid wall a mere fifty feet along the crooked path. Roots snaked over the ground, waiting to trip anyone foolish enough to venture along it. Lee had no intention of trying.

He continued with his inspection, and as he walked, Lee decided the cottage was a good choice for a hideout. Jacko had done his homework. It was secluded, falling to pieces, perhaps, but hidden away from prying eyes. Lee wondered how Jacko had come across it and who its previous owner was. The dwelling must have been empty for a long time because its timeworn appearance suggested very little had changed for decades. Whoever once lived here experienced a down-at-heel, impoverished life.

He turned the corner and approached the small outbuilding detached from the cottage. There was a row of small windows on the back wall, shattered where the putty had crumbled away. A rusty oil drum acting as a water butt rested on two bricks, and Lee used it to lever himself off the ground so that he could look inside. A strong stink of animal urine made him pull away. Instead, he wandered around to the front. There was no door, just an opening that led inside, where Lee found two animal stalls with peeling whitewashed walls and soggy straw on the floor. The smell was even worse, and he thought wild animals probably used it on cold or wet nights. Holding a hand over his nose and mouth, Lee gave the building a customary check and then turned to leave.

Just on the inside of the entrance was a blue tarp. Lee dragged the corner aside to reveal a log pile and a long-handled axe. Taking the axe and a couple of logs, he set about chopping them into kindling for the range and fireplace.

He worked methodically for ten minutes and was soon bathed in sweat. Some of the wood was severely rotted – further proof the cottage had been abandoned for years – but the logs in the pile's center were mostly dry. He worked the axe head to slice away the damp bark and chopped the remainder into slim pieces for the range and quarter sections for the fireplace grate. With a few bits of scrunched-up newspaper to start a fire, he'd soon have a roaring blaze. The cottage would feel more homely, and nobody'd be around to spot smoke coming out the chimney.

When he was done, Lee replaced the axe, pulled the tarp back into place, and gathered up the kindling beneath his arm.

All of a sudden, from somewhere deep within the woods, came high-pitched laughter. Lee froze. It was a dreadful sound and flooded his brain with raw terror. He shivered like an insect was crawling up his spine, making his shoulder blades contract. He dropped the kindling and held his breath.

It came again, a macabre cackle. Not the laughter of someone experiencing joy, but more like something you'd hear in an asylum. Lee let out a sudden curse. Snapping out of his paralysis, he took the gun and jogged around the back of the stable block towards the source of the noise.

The woods fell quiet for a few seconds. The only sound Lee could hear was his heart beating in his chest.

When the laughter came for a third time, it was further away and finished with an awful chittering warble that undulated through the woodland and rebounded from tree trunk to tree trunk. It didn't even sound human. There was a heartbeat of stillness before hundreds of birds took flight, chirping wildly as they ascended through the upper branches, sending autumnal leaves floating to the earth.

Lee stood stock still, his limbs palsied, the gun hanging uselessly from his fingertips, and his eyes scanned the trees. The crooked path twisted away from the cottage, and unless his imagination was playing tricks on him, the barrier of branches seemed thinner, the way more inviting.

His eyes were drawn down the track, and he took an involuntary step forwards as though something was pulling him. Then he gasped, his breath escaping in a rush, breaking the spell.

Lee beat a hasty retreat to the cottage, gathering up the firewood on the way.

CHAPTER 4

LEE STOOD WITH HIS BACK against the door and drew in a shuddering breath to steady his nerves. His thoughts felt scattered all over the place.

Just what the hell had happened? That horrible laughter from the woods had seriously freaked him out, coming fast on the back of his fright in the cellar, that's what. Lee asked himself again: was the sound even human because the nerve-shredding cacophony had a raw, feral quality? It could have been fox cubs, he tried to reason. Lee had heard some once, a vixen and her young making a horrendous racket late one night, sounding like a cross between a child's terrified shriek and a dog in distress. Or, if it was human, it might have been teenagers larking about.

Whatever its source, Lee could still hear its echoes ricocheting in his head.

There was no denying that it had given him the willies.

He dumped the bundle of firewood onto the blanket box and went to the kitchen for a glass of water. He gulped it down quickly, refilled it, and sipped more slowly, counting to ten. Lee turned on the radio, thinking some music might add a touch of normalcy to the place, but all he got was crackling static. Not surprising. Reception out here in the sticks must be hit-and-miss. Oh boy, what he'd give to be back home watching the Saturday afternoon football right now!

He returned to the parlour, glancing at the cellar door as he passed. The rolled-up tea towel was still in place, keeping the slugs and snails out. That was one piece of good news, Lee reflected.

Feeling crabby at the unfortunate circumstances that led to him sheltering here, Lee asked himself: was it all worthwhile? Well, there was one way to find out. Going over to the wall, he pulled out the loose brick and retrieved the bags of money from their hiding place. Lowering himself into the armchair, Lee tipped their contents onto the floor. Heaps of notes and coins fell everywhere.

Lee sorted through them, gathering the fivers, tenners, and twenties into bundles and counting them. He did the same with the coins.

A few minutes later, he sat back, his sour mood not improving.

There was just over five hundred and sixty quid. That's all they had to show for their effort. Split three ways, the cash from the post office tills came to a measly sum. So much for the tens of thousands of pounds Jacko promised. A man was dead, blasted at point-blank range with a sawn-off shotgun, and there was a national manhunt underway, and all for a few hundred quid.

What a fucking shitshow.

Dweller Under The Roots

Not for the first time, Lee thought his life was a joke. The sequence of choices he'd made over the past twenty-odd years, leading up to the here and now, was pure happenchance. Had Lee not become friends with Chris Keeble at school, then he'd never have subsequently fallen in with Jacko Page, and his life would have panned out differently. Instead of being holed up with the fucking Rozzers after him, he might have been working as the manager at the supermarket or selling home insurance, living in a nice suburban semi with a wife and kids.

He, Chris, and Tiny Bob had been in the same class at Junior School. They lived just a few streets apart, so they hung out together in the evenings and weekends: three cheeky scallywags who plagued the council estate. In truth, Lee and Chris shared a closer bond than Tiny Bob, who was more of a hanger-on. Even then, Bob was chubby and a little peculiar. Constantly sucking on a gobstopper, Tiny Bob had weird habits that grew more bizarre as he reached puberty. For instance, if he ever became stressed (which was often), he'd stand in the playground and headbutt the wall, starting with gentle impacts before quickly ramping up to full-strength strikes, his forehead repeatedly smacking the brickwork until Lee or Chris would pull him away with blood running down his face.

On another occasion, after an argument with Mr Brooks, the woodwork teacher, Tiny Bob had stormed out of the school only to return with a box of matches to set light to the storeroom. Luckily, someone spotted the small blaze before it spread too far, but the fire brigade evacuated the whole school as a precaution, and all the pupils and staff were sent home early. (For a week or so afterwards, Tiny Bob was a bit of a hero with the other kids, which only encouraged his crazy stunts.)

Pissing into the teachers' petrol tanks was a favourite one. Blocking up the toilets and flooding the changing rooms was another.

Stealing the petty cash from the school tuck shop was more rewarding and the gang's first taste at theft.

But then Tiny Bob became hooked on glue sniffing, which frightened the hell out of Lee and Chris after they watched him go on a rampage while sky high. Another time, Tiny Bob finished up in the hospital after a seizure, and when he came out, it was like something had broken inside him. He developed a fascination with knives, gathering up roadkill and dissecting them, and that's when Lee's parents and Chris' parents had enough and told them, from now on, they should steer clear of Tiny Bob. Lee and Chris didn't need telling twice.

A few months later, the two boys went to Secondary School, and Tiny Bob ended up in a unit for children with special needs. Their paths didn't cross for years.

It was at secondary school that Lee and Chris first met Jacko Page. Jacko was several years older than them. Jacko had deep-set eyes and cheeks scarred with acne, and he smoked Marlboros and sneaked vodka into class, which made him the coolest kid around.

Strangely, Jacko didn't seem to have many friends. He was softly-spoken and wise beyond his years, with a laid-back outlook that seemed to intimidate the other kids. While everyone else was struggling with rampant hormones, Jacko would quietly watch from afar, perhaps puzzled as to why those around him found life so stressful. Nothing ever fazed Jacko Page. The other boys lacked the confidence to befriend him, and the girls (who all secretly fancied him) were too timid to ask him out.

Aloof and self-possessed. That was Jacko.

Everyone wanted to be like Jacko.

So it was a surprise when Jacko took the first step and approached two kids in their first year of Secondary School - Lee Harris and Chris Keeble - and teamed up with them.

It was the last day before the summer break. Lee and Chris had somehow navigated their way through their first year and were looking forward to six weeks of larking about. Next term, things would be different. They'd no longer be the new kids in school: a fresh batch of eleven-year-olds would be starting after the holidays, a set of weedy, nervous pups ripe for the taking.

The last day was sports day when the whole school turned out in force on the bottom field to watch the track and field events, the egg and spoon races, the wheelbarrow races, and the three-legged races. Even the teachers took part.

Lee and Chris had been tasked with fetching chairs down from the school's IT and Computer Science block, ferrying them to the sports field. They were on their third relay, loafing along the hallway and gently ribbing each other, when a voice spoke out of the shadows.

"They can't make you do that, you know? It's slave labour."

Lee and Chris put down the chairs and watched as a familiar figure stepped forward, his shirt hanging out, necktie pulled to one side.

"You have rights," Jacko Page said softly.

"We don't mind," Chris had replied.

"Really? I've been watching you going back and forth for the last half hour. While you both sweat your bollocks off, you're missing out on all the fun. Just so they can sit on their arses."

Lee and Chris had shared a glance.

"Unless you put your foot down, they'll have you doing that all day. And then they'll have you carry them back again. Trust me, I've been there."

Lee, whose back and arms were aching, wondered if Jacko Page might have a point. He could hear cheers and shrieks of joy wafting through the open door at the end of the hallway. He also thought this was the most he'd heard Jacko say in the past twelve months.

"What can we do about it?" Lee asked while wishing there was something they could do about it.

Jacko was shaking his head, the thumbs of both hands hooked in his belt loops. He walked over, and they could smell nicotine on his breath and his clothes.

"You could just refuse. Put those chairs back and say that you ain't doing it anymore."

"What, and end up with a detention?"

"A detention for what? Refusing to fetch and carry while the teachers lounge around in the sun? You're here to learn, not take shit from them."

Jacko looked down the length of the hallway. There was nobody around.

"Come on, I'll help you," he said and grabbed both chairs by their plastic backs, swung around, and then marched towards the IT Classroom. Lee caught his friend's uncertain look, shrugged, and followed Jacko. After a moment, Chris did the same.

The classroom blinds were down, leaving it dim inside. They could make out rows of desks covered with laptops and IT hardware. Jacko Page had slung the chairs into a corner and was standing, hands on hips, looking at them. He had a stern look on his face, and for half a heartbeat, Lee thought Jacko had tricked them into this act of disobedience. Then, the frown disappeared and was replaced by a lop-sided grin.

"Do you boys want to earn a bit of money," he asked in a sly drawl.

Lee and Chris stared back blankly.

"Well, do you? I'm not talking a few quid on top of your pocket money. I'm talking a couple of hundred nicker each. Maybe more."

"Two hundred pounds?" blurted Chris.

"Keep your voice down. Yes, two hundred quid each for a few minutes of work. Well?" Jacko demanded.

"Yes," Lee and Chris both said simultaneously.

"That's what I thought. I've had my eye on you two for a few months, and I can tell two clever boys when I see them."

Jacko turned away, opened a cabinet door, and produced three small backpacks. He stuffed one each into their hands.

"Right, then," he said, talking quickly. "Let's fill these bags with as many laptops as possible. Look sharp, now."

Lee turned to look at the dozens of expensive laptops, thinking about the money they could make by flogging them. He also considered the trouble they'd be in if caught. Jacko must have read his mind.

"Don't worry. It's the last day of term. Everyone is outside having fun in the sun, and after they've finished their silly races, everyone – including the teachers – will be in a hurry to dash off. The kids to the park, and the grown-ups to the pub. They have demob fever."

"What's demob fever?" Lee asked.

"It doesn't matter," Jacko replied, scooping up computers and pushing them into his backpack. "All I'm saying is, nobody will be coming in here. Maybe not until after the summer break. Which gives us a free run to help ourselves."

Jacko gave them a wink.

"Get a wiggle on, boys."

They spent the next few minutes going from desk to desk, sliding laptops into their bags while keeping one eye on the door. By the time they'd finished, they had five or six each. They slung the heavy backpacks onto their backs.

"Next, we put them into our lockers. Then, when the final bell rings, we grab the bags and our other things and walk right out of here, nice and casual-like. Then we meet up later and devise a way to turn these beauties into hard cash."

So that's how their partnership, their little illegal enterprise, started: by stealing school laptops and making a bundle of money. Nobody suspected them of a thing. They put the theft down to intruders, and the school paid for new laptops out of their generous budget.

Their little gang spent the summer stealing and thieving around the estate and the town. Sometimes, they nicked a few wallets and purses or broke into cars and took CD players and stereos. On one occasion, they forced their way into the garages behind the youth centre on Foundry Street and rode off with a quad bike (the owner spotted them from his apartment window and gave chase in his car, but a bit of neat driving from Jacko soon shook him off their tail).

After the summer break, Lee, Chris and Jacko turned their thoughts to nicking what they could, when they could, from school: they targeted classrooms, lockers, the staff room, and the gym equipment storeroom. Jacko knew lots of people, so fencing the swag was simple. Lee worried his parents might wonder where he was suddenly getting all his extra money from (even though Jacko warned them not to splash the cash too freely), but his mum and dad were in the middle of splitting. Dad was hitting the booze, and they barely paid their son any attention.

Then, at the end of the school year, one year to the day since they got together, Jacko finished school and decided to join the army, so the little threesome of thieves became a twosome. Lee and Chris, so used to following Jacko's lead, drifted aimlessly through their remaining time at school, and their criminal venture fizzled out.

It was another six or seven years before they bumped into Jacko down the snooker club. He'd been discharged from the army for stealing from the commissariat stores and set up a car repair business (he'd trained in the vehicle pool department, fixing military vehicles). But as Jacko told Lee and Chris over the snooker game, he found Civvie Street a struggle. Nothing could replace the rush of life in the Forces. Well, almost nothing.

Jacko confided in them that he was considering picking up where they'd left off. But now, instead of pick-pocketing or nicking cars, Jacko planned on moving up a level. There were heaps of cash to be made. It was there for the taking. Were they interested?

• • •

Lee came out of his reverie. For a while there, he'd been lost in thought. His trip down memory lane stirred different emotions, not all bad. They'd had some good times (as well as a few lucky escapes from the law). But maybe this latest episode – that was putting it lightly; it was murder, pure and simple – was the wake-up call they all needed. If they could extricate themselves from this bind, then Lee was done with this life of crime. If that meant parting ways with Jacko and Chris, calling a permanent end to their partnership, then so be it.

From now on, he wanted to earn an honest crust.

He could only speak for himself, but when Jacko got in touch, Lee would make it clear that he wanted out. He would give Jacko another day or two, and Lee would phone him if he'd not heard from him.

His mind made up, Lee scooped up the money, bagged it up, and strode over to the hole in the brickwork. Lee reached in, but a sudden sharp pain made him yelp. He dropped the bags behind the wall and snatched his hand back.

There were three scratch lines across the back of his hand. Lee stared at them in shock and amazement. He tried telling himself he must have caught it on the edge of the bricks because the alternative was plain stupid. Quickly, he pushed the brick back into position and then hurried into the kitchen to run his hand under the tap.

The cold water took away the sting. Lee examined the small bumpy weals left behind. He shook his head. This place was getting to him. Its remote location wasn't helping. He needed to get a grip and stop being so damned tense all the time.

Lee turned off the tap and automatically reached for a tea towel to dry his hand. He stopped. The tea towel was back on its hook beside the sink when it should have been scrunched under the cellar door.

With dread seeping through him like cold, black oil, Lee carefully turned around.

The cellar door was wide open again. He hadn't noticed. He hadn't noticed the coldness seeping up the stairs, either. Nor the squelchy sounds coming from below.

Lee gave a childish whimper and thought he might shit himself. Then a hot iron of fury burned in the pit of his stomach because he'd be damned if he'd stand here like a frightened spinster, cowering before a cellar filled with slugs. Slugs, for crying out loud!

Yelling, Lee slammed the cellar door shut, dragged over the stool, and shoved it under the handle, thinking in his madness that ought to keep the creatures out.

God, what was wrong with him?

Lee abandoned his idea of making a fire. Sitting in the armchair and toasting his feet on the crackling flames sounded inviting, but given the strange incidents, it had lost some of its appeal. Instead, he made himself a hot drink, grabbed a blanket from the blanket box, and sought refuge in his bedroom. It would be nighttime soon.

In the loft room, Lee noticed the brown powder again. He could see where he'd walked through it. Once more, he wondered how the stuff had ended up in here. The cottage must be riddled with holes in the walls or gaps in the slate roof so that it could have trickled or blown in. He'd clear it away first thing tomorrow.

Sitting upright in bed, Lee sipped his drink. Things would feel different in the morning. The cottage was just a cottage made of bricks and mortar. It might have been tucked away and unlived in for decades, and the woods were mysterious and eerie. But weren't they always like that, especially after dark? He'd never been one for camping trips because he'd always liked his creature comforts. That's what the problem was; Lee was out of his comfort zone. The creepy crawlies and the woodland creatures couldn't hurt him. As for the cellar door? Perhaps the latch was loose, it had come open, and the tea towel had fallen down the stairs. There could have been more than one hanging on the hook.

His excuses sounded flimsy even to himself. But hell, what else could he do but try and come up with rational explanations?

Lee had always been partial to a good book and needed something to distract him and settle his mind. He crawled to the end of the bed to examine the dog-eared paperbacks and hardbacks on the bookshelf. There were a few of the classics (not his thing), one entitled DODMEN AND THEIR SIGHTING STAVES (a quick flick through showed it to contain lots of hand-drawn sketches of men holding strange-looking sticks. They reminded Lee of The Cerne Abbas Giant, but without the big phallus. Next to it was a thick book called THE HISTORY OF THE HOLY WELL OF SYMONDS YAT, then one with the title ARCHAEOLOGICAL FINDS: PREHISTORIC CAMPS OF RADNOR FOREST (that sounded like a bore-fest) and lying flat at the end of the shelf, A VAGABOND ON THE GREEN ROADS OF ENGLAND.

What a great choice, mused Lee. The cottage's previous owner had an eclectic taste in reading matter, that was for sure. He grabbed one of the classics, opened it at random, squirmed down inside the sleeping bag, and began reading.

After just a few minutes, he put the book down. On impulse, Lee unzipped himself and reached for the book lying flat on the bookshelf.

He turned it over in his hands. The cover was dull brown. On the front, in green, a face stared back at him. The face was surrounded by leaves, making it look like someone peering through a hedge. It had a moustache, a goatee, and thick bushy eyebrows, all green. The face bore a stern expression.

Below it, the title was in faded script - A VAGABOND ON THE GREEN ROADS OF ENGLAND. There was no author's name. Lee opened it, the movement releasing a cloud of dust. He turned the pages, looking for a publication date. 1920. Old then, but not of genuine antiquity. Still, it might be worth a bob or two, he thought, unable to help himself.

Lee spent several minutes skimming over it. There was no description or foreword, but from what he could tell, it was a kind of journal slash autobiography slash travelogue written by a tramp named Percival (no surname) describing his journeys along ancient and forgotten trackways and bridlepaths around England early in the twentieth century. He would walk these old arteries that once connected rural communities and hilltop villages, sleeping in hedgerows and digging up wild potatoes or turnips. During his travels, Percival spoke with country folk, listening to their fables and stories, yarns and folktales, and bedtime stories, chronicling them in his book. Sometimes, Percival would throw in his own adventures and odd happenings. However, going off their bizarre nature, Lee wondered if the old fellow hadn't partaken of a few psychedelic mushrooms along the way because he spoke in flowery passages of changelings and sprites, faeries and water kelpies (Lee had never heard of them) and coffin routes.

Out of curiosity, Lee turned to the index and wasn't surprised when he found one entry listed for Hardcastle Crags. Lee thumbed back to the indicated section. Percival preferred the old Anglo-Saxon name of Tarr Dair, which roughly translated as Black Valley, instead of the more modern Hardcastle Crags about the stacks of millstone grit, once a feature of the landscape. Here, Percival walked the old pilgrim's route connecting Monks Bretton Priory some miles to the south with Bolton Priory further north. The track crossed Daisy Beck at a point named the Withypool Steps. Lee knew them; they were a set of stepstones and the only remains of a clapper bridge that travellers and traders once crossed on foot.

As well as being a route used by holy men and traders, the trackway passing through Tarr Dair was also an old corpse road. Centuries ago, according to Percival, the dead were carried from remote rural communities through the countryside to the parish church of Christ on the Mountain at Pecket Well, sited at the head of the valley. Mourners would lug wicker or seagrass coffins for miles, stopping at Butter Cross Stone to rest. Folklore had it that the corpse road was a twisting trackway because spirits could only travel in straight lines, so a meandering route prevented them from returning to haunt the living. The dead were carried with their feet pointing away from the family home for the same reason. Nor could they cross running water. Some country folk claimed that if a body were carried across a field, the field would never again produce a good crop. The passage finished with the words:

Paths of the dead would cross mountains and valleys, stepstones and bog causeways and stiles, and other betwixt and between locations to hinder the free passage of the spirits. Sometimes, the way would travel right through the centre of a house.

Lee slammed the book shut and flung it down the end of the bed. Seriously, reading all this mumbo jumbo wasn't helping with his nerves. Lee told himself that, other than the fact they were only a thirty-minute walk away from Withypool Steps, nothing else linked the cottage with this silly book written by this foolish man named Percival.

Lee switched off the light and settled down for the night.

CHAPTER 5

SOMETIME DURING THE NIGHT, LEE woke with a bad cramping pain in his stomach and a spinning head. He thought he might be coming down with something, either a cold or some bacterium from the cat scratch (when did he accept it was the result of a feline attack, his sleepy head asked?). Too drowsy to dwell on things, Lee rolled over, pulled the sleeping bag and blanket over his shoulder, and went back to sleep.

By the time he woke at dawn, the griping cramps had passed. Lee sat on the edge of the bed and ran a hand over his face, his palm scratching the two-day stubble. He thought about yesterday, about the noises in the woods, the horrible things in the cellar, and all the other weird stuff, and determined he needed to get his shit together. There'd be no more jumping at shadows or thinking scary thoughts. It would take more than a dead cat to give him the heebie-jeebies. He'd feel much better after having a wash, a shave, and a stack of pancakes layered with thick syrup—breakfast for Kings.

The book was still on the end of the bed. Lee plucked it up, tossed it back onto the shelf, and tidied away the sleeping bag. Then he quickly dressed, rolled up the rug with its layer of black powder, and carried it down the stairs and through the front door. He placed it against the cottage wall, meaning to sling it in the outbuilding later.

Out of curiosity, Lee approached the tangled bushes where he'd thrown the cat on his first night. He poked around with his foot for a second, and sure enough, the mummified remains of the animal were still there, looking all shrivelled and leathery but definitely dead. So, no deceased feline had found its way back behind the cottage wall, then, Lee mused. He looked again at the scratches on his hand, shrugged, and went inside to find his razor.

Notwithstanding his new mood of defiance, it was with a trace of vigilance when Lee walked into the kitchen a short time later. The stool was still wedged under the cellar door's handle. Lee grinned sheepishly, bemused at how easily he'd become spooked.

He soon had the pancakes on the go and half a mug of steaming tea down his throat. As he waited by the butane stove, he flicked on the radio just in time to catch the tail end of the lead story.

...Postmaster and his wife appealed for help catching their son's murderers, promising a substantial reward for anyone who could provide information leading to a conviction.

Mark Hobson

Lee turned up the volume.

Although police have refused to confirm what leads they are working on, they did reveal they have switched the focus of the manhunt to Manchester, leading to speculation that the armed robbers may have escaped along the M62 motorway. Detectives in charge of the case again stressed that the three suspects were armed and dangerous and that the public should not approach them. Instead, if they spot the robbers, they should contact the police immediately.

Lee turned the radio off. While he used a fish slicer to stack his pancakes on a plate, he thought about what he'd heard. If the police were concentrating their search on Manchester, that meant Lee, Chris and Jacko had successfully slipped through the net during the rush hour without being spotted. It also meant the police weren't linking it with local criminals.

Lee carried his mug of tea and pancakes through to the parlour. Sitting at the small table, he gazed through the window as he shovelled in mouthfuls of food. After a minute, he put down his knife and fork and pulled the small mobile phone out of his jeans pocket.

Switching it on was a risk. The police could track mobile phones through their signal, but surely only if they knew the number. Additionally, cheap burner phones were only good for texting or making calls, not for going online, so they couldn't pinpoint suspects through GPS. If Chris or Jacko were still safe in hiding, Lee couldn't see how the police would be able to home in on his phone. And if they were looking in the wrong place anyway.

It was a risk worth taking, Lee concluded. He took the plunge and powered the phone up. He put it on the table and resumed his breakfast, but the burner buzzed loudly just twenty seconds later. Lee picked it up and studied the small display.

ONE TEXT MESSAGE

Lee checked the time that it was sent. Shortly before midnight. He opened it:

WILL PHONE U SUN EVENING. STAY COOL. WE NAILED IT. J

Lee reread the message. Today was a Sunday, so Lee only had a few hours to wait for Jacko's call, but the message seemed to corroborate the news update on the radio: that they'd got away with things by the skin of their teeth. He'd learn more when they spoke, but if all was well, Lee planned on telling Jacko that the post office hit was his last job. Whether his friend liked it or not.

Lee turned the phone off and returned it to his hip pocket. He finished breakfast.

• • •

When he stepped outside again, Lee noticed the wind was picking up. It stirred the leaves and made them whisper. If he wasn't mistaken, a change in the weather was on the way; there was already rain in the air.

Following the positive tidings, Lee felt better than he had since arriving two nights ago. He wasn't on edge or glancing over his shoulder for once. He might soon be getting out of here with a bit of luck. Lee grabbed the rolled-up rug and carried it under his arm to the outbuilding.

It was dingy inside, with scarcely any light pushing through the entrance and windows. The stale smell caused Lee to wrinkle his nose again. He dumped the rug in one of the empty animal stalls. Avoiding the filth, he moved deeper inside to look around.

Across from the stalls was a workbench and vice. The top was covered in old wood shavings and various tools, such as a mallet, chisels, a few carpentry planes, a marking gauge, and a hand drill. On the wall hung try squares, claw hammers, callipers, and spirit levels. Everything was strung with sooty cobwebs. Lee picked up a few of the items, blowing away the dirt. The place reminded him of those industrial museums where everything was like in the olden days when people worked in textile mills as weavers or sweatered in timber yards. If you ignored the fire exit signs and the giftshops, they were like stepping back in time. This was the real thing. Apart from the cobwebs, it was like the previous owner had just laid down their tools and vanished, leaving everything as it was. In a way, it made Lee sad.

Propped up against the back wall below the line of windows, he found several planks of wood. An idea briefly flashed through Lee's mind. He could use the wood to plug the gap beneath the cellar door and keep those slugs and snails out of the kitchen. But he quickly dismissed the notion; there was no point anymore – Lee planned on leaving in another night or two.

He turned to go but stopped when the floor sagged an inch under his feet. Lee looked down and scraped away the damp and matted straw. There was a trapdoor secured with a rusty bolt. He wondered where it led. Maybe it was another way into the root cellar. But then, why was it locked from the outside? Wherever it went, he'd be fucked if he was going down there to find out.

A movement through one of the small windows caught his eye, pulling his thoughts elsewhere. Lee looked up in time to see a tree branch swaying halfway along the crooked path. He saw someone in a red coat skulking behind a trunk.

"Shit," Lee intoned under his breath and stepped away from the window. From the shadows, he watched silently as the person slipped through the trees, heading away from the cottage.

He was pretty sure whoever it was had been watching him. He was also pretty sure it was a woman.

Lee kicked himself. Somebody knew he was here. It might only have been a dog walker or someone enjoying a stroll through the woods. Equally, it might be someone with bad intentions. Either way, it complicated things for Lee. He should have been more careful.

Lee waited until he was sure the coast was clear and slipped outside. He needed to head back to the cottage and think about this. Lee had almost reached the door when a scream in the near distance erupted from the woods. It startled him so badly that he nearly lost his balance. The high-pitched shriek ended with a warbling cry.

"Help! Someone, please help!"

CHAPTER 6

"CHRIST ALIVE!" LEE SPLUTTERED, FEELING like ice-cold fingers had just squeezed his heart.

No way could he mistake that for an animal. The scream was definitely human in origin. Nor was it kids fooling around. There was a panicky quality to the cry from somebody suffering extreme pain or mind-snapping fear.

It must be the woman he'd just seen – there was no other explanation. It had come from behind the cottage, where he'd seen her disappearing down the crooked path.

Lee's self-preservation instincts screamed at him to get inside and bolt the door, or better still, jump into the car and drive away. If he'd been spotted, and someone was hurt or in trouble, it would mean the police inevitably turning up.

But then something odd happened. For once in Lee's life, he put somebody else first instead of only looking after Number One. If the lady, whoever she was – dog walker, rambler, nosey-parker – was harmed or in danger, he couldn't just stand aside and do nothing. Helping a person in distress wouldn't make up for all the shitty things he'd done in his life, but it would be a start. The rise of the new Lee Harris.

Then, the selfish part of his character elbowed its way back in as if alarmed at this rare moment of big-heartedness, but also working out the simple fact: helping the woman might be a way of avoiding the police getting involved. One moment of charity might save him a big headache.

"Balls," Lee intoned under his breath, thinking quickly. Then he pushed open the cottage door, and in double-quick time, Lee grabbed the flashlight and the gun and was back outside in short order. Slipping the flashlight into his back pocket, Lee wriggled the weapon behind his trouser belt and pulled his sweater down, ensuring it was hidden; turning up with a firearm wouldn't be wise.

Scott glanced at the sky. Gentle raindrops pattered down from the canopy of russet-coloured leaves, damping his face. The weather was turning, alright. He would give it half an hour, and if he couldn't locate the woman, he would come back.

Lee headed around the corner, squeezed down the narrow gap between the outbuilding and the cottage, and passed over the rear garden to the crooked path. He hesitated because, once again, the woodland trail left him feeling unsettled. Yesterday, the way seemed passable, the trees not so dense, but today the tangled branches and exposed roots looked thicker than ever. They presented a daunting obstacle. It had to be in his mind. Woods didn't creep closer overnight, he told himself.

Refusing to surrender to infantile cop-outs, Lee squared his shoulders and launched himself down the path. He forged ahead, his keen eyes looking out for the woman. The way jinked left and right, and at each turn, the pathway narrowed more and more. Soon, the branches were snagging on the sweater's sleeves. At the point where the path burrowed deeper into the woodland, Lee paused to look back at the cottage. He could just see it through interlaced branches. The tumbledown dwelling suddenly seemed appealing and cosy despite its missing slates and crumbling brickwork.

Muttering curses to himself, Lee turned away and dove into the sunless underworld.

The worst of the rain was blunted beneath the high canopy. In the shade, hundreds of biting insects bothered him, and he scratched at his neck. Lee leaned back and looked up. The tops of the trees swayed sideways, making the trunks creak and bump together. Lee found it dizzying. He also felt distracted because even when he strained his ears, there were no sounds of birdsong or wildlife rustling around in the undergrowth. Apart from the annoying pests biting him, the woodland seemed lifeless. Then why did he feel like he was being watched?

Lee concentrated on picking his way over exposed roots, using the flashlight in the darker areas. The path dipped and rose or snaked around trees. Twigs snapped beneath his trainers. Fungi covered the fallen branches alongside the trail. He recognized some wild edible mushrooms, but others had white gills, bulbous stems, or red caps, which Lee thought would be poisonous or psychedelic. He also saw some that looked like rashes of purple spores clinging to rotted bark and still more that swayed in the breeze like kelp in a sea's current.

He listened for any further screams or cries for help or sought out glimpses of the woman's red coat, but Lee hadn't heard nor seen any signs of her since entering the woods. He could try calling out but was reluctant to give his presence away, preferring a more furtive approach. He hoped to slip through the trees for a clandestine look if he came across her. That way, if there was nothing amiss and the woman posed no threat or didn't need assistance, Lee could edge away and go back. He also didn't wish to startle her by jumping out of the undergrowth.

The trees crowded in even closer. So thick was the ground cover that someone could be standing within a few feet of him, watching, and he wouldn't even know. The thought wasn't a pleasant one. Lee slowed to a stop and told himself it was time to abandon this daft venture. After all, there was little to gain and lots to lose.

He turned around and was shocked to see the path he had just trodden along disappear after a few feet. An embrasure of branches barred the way. Which was impossible. He'd just come that way! A shudder went through him from head to toe, followed by a surge of panic that flooded his brain. Jesus! If he became lost in here.

Lee reached out and thrust his hands into the interweaved limbs and outgrowths. Brambles cut his skin, but he ignored their sharp edges and made an opening, elbowing it wider and ramming his torso inside the gap he made.

A face so old and scored with rough and deep lines that it resembled tree bark peered back at him from within the entwined branches. Lee cried out reflexively and fled in the opposite direction. He crashed through the woods along the trail, telling himself that it wasn't a face; it was just an ancient tree bole that resembled one, or a barn owl: anything but a face.

He thought he heard sounds of pursuit, a rustling of trodden leaves, and a wheezing breath. The noises – if they weren't in his head – drew alongside him, keeping pace.

This couldn't be happening, Lee's mind screamed. Stuff like this only happened in bad horror movies.

Lee risked a look to the right and instantly wished he hadn't. There was someone there, alright, and it wasn't the woman in the red coat. Running just feet from him was a person so stooped that their shoulder blades rose up above the crown of the head. As badly contorted and hunched as they were, it was incredible they could move so fast. And why weren't the trees impeding them? And the face. Oh, God, the face.

Lee thought it might be a mask carved out of wood, but he knew the face was real when the mouth tilted up in a slanted smile. The eyes were like hard-boiled eggs, white and bulging from their sockets.

The tangled strangeness of the situation left Lee dizzy. He was crying, and phlegm was trailing out of his mouth. He whipped his head back around because the thing pursuing him was too much for his eyes to bear, and at that moment, Lee crashed out of the thick woodland into a small clearing. A stone cross was at the centre, thrust towards the sky, and etched on its surface was a stick man holding two staffs, like the pictures that reminded him of The Cerne Abbas Giant. Dodmen, Lee remembered they were called.

Then his foot caught in an exposed tree root, and Lee tripped and stumbled headfirst into the stone cross, knocking himself out.

Later, Lee couldn't decide if he was dreaming or experiencing some weird, abstract vision triggered by concussion. It might even have been an out-of-body experience. He'd vaguely heard of astral projection, of how people induced such a deep state of meditation they claimed they could detach a part of themselves from their earthly self through sheer willpower. This astral form could function separately from the host body and observe the physical world. Some people experienced out-of-body experiences while dangerously ill, but whether this was the human spirit leaving their bedridden bodies or some chemical imbalance in their brains wasn't clear.

Lee always thought it was a load of guff, until now.

Lying on the ground, drifting in and out of consciousness, Lee felt something tug itself free of his solar plexus. The sensation was like riding a rollercoaster when your stomach briefly rose into your throat. Only this time it kept climbing, and suddenly Lee's viewpoint was two or three metres up in the air and suspended over his still form.

He tried crying out in alarm, but his astral form couldn't generate words. Below him, Lee heard his terrestrial 'doppelganger' murmur in its sleep.

This new realm he found himself in was much the same as the other world, except it was dusk, and the trees all around were younger. Lee felt himself propelled away from his sleeping body, floating softly above the ground. He re-entered the treeline and glided along the crooked path.

After the initial fear, the sensation of free-floating became pleasant. It was like being filled with helium, and Lee bobbed along like a blimp that had escaped its mooring lines. His senses were much more heightened, with every sight, sound, and smell jacked-up to the max.

Lee didn't know where he was headed. He had some control over what direction he went, a certain degree of free will, but equally, he sensed that something or someone was pulling him down that path, further away from the cottage to an unknown destination. Lee wasn't afraid. He'd forgotten all about the distressed woman and the hunched person in the woods.

The strange half-world below the umbrella of trees grew stygian. Mushrooms and spores glowed in the dark, in wonderful purple, blue and green hues, marking the path. Their luminosity lit the leaves and fallen branches, growing so intense it seemed to Lee like he was travelling along a tunnel of pure light. He'd never seen anything so beautiful.

So mesmerized was he by the otherworldly spectacle that Lee could banish the sheer madness of things. In any case, tucked away in the back of his thoughts was the persistent idea this was all happening in his head.

Without warning, the trees ended. At the same instant that he exited from the woods, daylight crackled back into place, and Lee hovered at the treeline, looking out at a commanding landscape. Now little more than a gash scratched out of the earth, the trackway snaked away from the woods. It crossed a stream where horizontal stone slabs formed a makeshift footbridge. Was this Daisy Beck and the ancient clapper bridge he'd read about last night? Indeed, the geography seemed familiar simultaneously as it looked different. There were fewer signs of man's impact on the landscape. Lee saw no dwellings or stone walls marking field boundaries. Instead, the ground ascended in a series of gently rolling hills. Halfway up the long slope, there was a large boulder overhanging the trackway. On the top side of the boulder was a V-shaped notch, which lined up perfectly with a strange hump, a mound, on the horizon a quarter mile away. Lee had a strong sense of deja vu because he was again convinced that he knew the area and that the mound would one day mark the spot occupied by the parish church of Christ on the Mountain at Pecket Well. Lee turned around (or, at least, levitated about) and peered into the woods at his back. The path lit by the glowing fungi lined up perfectly with the clapper bridge, the notch, and the mound.

A tingle passed through his astral form, a sixth sense once more telling him that someone was watching him. Lee wheeled around and saw the figure of a man atop the rock, his silhouette standing out against the sky. In one hand, he held a long staff that was planted in the notch. He reminded Lee of a shepherd with a crook; all he needed to complete the picture was a herd of sheep pressing around his legs. With his other hand, he beckoned to Lee.

Something told Lee that he ought not to go any further. That should he answer the compulsion to follow this man, this Dodman, that he might never return to his host body lying unconscious on the forest floor. That an invisible thread would be broken forever.

Dweller Under The Roots

Lee faltered on the edge of indecision.
Until a voice called gently to him.

"Hey, mister. Are you alright?"

Lee groaned feebly at the throbbing ache coming from his head. It caused him to reach up and probe the spot. The instant his fingers made contact, the agony increased. His hand flopped back down by his side.

It was raining more steadily. The droplets of water sprinkling onto his face helped wash away Lee's grogginess, and he peeled open his eyes.

A face peered down at him. Thank God it wasn't the wrinkled-up and ugly kisser belonging to the old crone. This one was quite fetching. Blonde hair framed an open countenance containing blue eyes and a small, slightly upturned nose with tiny nostrils. The face tilted in concern.

"You've taken a nasty blow to your head," the woman crouching over him said. This didn't stop her from jabbing hard at the sore spot on his scalp.

"Argh! Watch it!" Lee cried out and sat up. The world around him swam crazily as another dizzy spell hit him, but he was still able to notice the red coat she was wearing.

Lee looked around. He was sitting on the ground, surrounded by trees. Nearby was a stone cross. The flashlight lay in the grass.

Things came back to him in stages. The robbery. The hideout in the cottage. The woman watching him from the pathway and her cries for help. Lee recalled in more detail the bent and twisted person with the face of a harpy chasing after him and his subsequent fall. There was also a stretch in Lee's memories filled with strange lights and mystical landscapes. Lee also recalled a dream about flying, although his memory of that was more vague and hazier. The whole lot meshed together in Lee's addled brain, making him unsure of what was real and what was a figment of his imagination caused by his smacking his head against the stone cross. They may have been old and abandoned flashbacks from years ago.

He looked again at the woman before him. She didn't seem harmed or frightened. Other than a worried frown on her brow, she appeared fine. Lee was the one in a state, and his appearance probably left much to be desired. He noticed splotches of blood on the front of his sweater for the first time.

She must have seen him looking because she took a hanky from her red coat and dabbed softly at his scalp, using the rainwater to clean away the blood.

"I don't think the cut is too deep. But it probably needs washing with TCP. You'll have an ugly yellow and purple bruise there for a week or two."

She had a local accent, Lee noticed. Not soft like from Leeds, but a tamped-down country accent, with a twang of old Yorkshire. She was probably descended from farming stock several generations back. She really was quite stunning, with a determined thrust of her small chin.

Then Lee realized she was studying him with equal interest, and he blushed with embarrassment.

She pulled out a mobile and swiped the screen, asking, "Is there anyone I can call?"

"No," Lee said loudly and grasped her thin wrist.

He felt her flinch, and he relaxed his hold.

"No," he repeated more quietly.

"Okay," the woman said, stretching the word out and retrieving her hand from his grip. She returned the phone to her pocket and pulled up her hood; the rain was drumming down into the clearing.

"I'll live. Thank you for helping me. I'm sorry, I didn't get your name?"

"Amelia."

She looked at him patiently, and he thought about making a name up, but before he knew what he was doing, he replied, "I'm called Lee."

"Hello, Lee," and she smiled.

Lee rubbed the back of his neck and tried to massage away the stiffness.

"So, Lee. What are you doing way out here in the woods? I've never seen you around before. Usually, I have the place to myself."

He glanced up at her, wondering if she was grilling him for information, but she had an earnest expression, and her keen eyes darted around his face.

"I, erm, thought I heard someone call out. Like they were crying, sort of thing."

"A child?"

"No, I don't think so." Lee blinked his eyes several times, trying to arrange his thoughts. "I don't know what I mean."

"That's silly. Maybe you hit your head harder than I realized. Well, whatever you were doing stumbling around in these woods, Lee, you can't just sit there. There's a storm coming."

Lee squinted his eyes and studied the looming clouds overhead. There was barely a breeze, but the air had an earthy smell that foretold thunderstorms.

"I'd best get going."

"Where do you live?" Amelia enquired. "There's nothing around here for miles, apart from the old…" Her voice trailed away.

"Oh, in that direction," Lee answered, pointing vaguely into the woods.

He struggled to his feet and felt suddenly sick and lightheaded, and if it weren't for Amelia grabbing his arm, Lee was sure he'd have keeled over.

"Take it slowly. Let it pass."

Lee set his feet apart and waited for the queasiness to fade.

"Thank you," he told her again, but the world resumed spinning when he took a step. Lee bent over at the waist and gripped his knees, but tilting his head worsened the pain.

"This is no good," Amelia said. "You can hardly stand up, let alone walk."

She stooped down and picked up his flashlight.

"You'll have to come back to my place. It's only ten minutes away. I can take a closer look at your head injury."

Lee wanted to tell her it wasn't necessary, that he could manage, because talking with this stranger was unsound. Yet Lee found he wasn't in a hurry to part company. Just the opposite: he felt compelled to be with her. And he wasn't sure he'd be able to find his way back to the cottage, path or no path. One tree was starting to look like any other.

Amelia must have sensed his hesitation.

"Lee, if you fell and hurt yourself again, I'd never be able to live with myself. These woods can be dangerous and confusing. After you've rested, and once the storm passes, I'll see you home safely."

Amelia looped an arm through his.

"Now come on."

She steered him away from the clearing.

"Shouldn't we stick to the path?"

"That way takes longer. I know a shortcut."

Lee let her lead him deeper into the woods. He stealthily slipped his free hand beneath his sweater, feeling reassured when he found the gun was still there. All the while, he kept a close look out for the bent figure with the serpentine spine and the hideous face.

CHAPTER 7

EVERYTHING ABOUT THIS SITUATION WAS wrong, Lee figured. He should never have come looking for her. He ought to be holed up in the safe house, keeping to himself and waiting for Jacko's call. Instead, he was severely concussed and being led further and further away from the cottage by this mysterious woman named Amelia.

As they headed between the trees, Lee snatched occasional looks at her profile. He wondered just who she was. He was sure she was the same person he'd caught spying on him. The same person he'd heard crying out for help. But Amelia appeared unharmed. She also seemed utterly relaxed at finding a lone man in the woods. If anything, she radiated a gentle serenity that he found infectious.

Still, her calm manner couldn't completely dispel Lee's unease. Somewhere in these woods lurked the creepy, ghoul-like character with the ugly mug carved out of bark. Just saying that to himself made Lee question his sanity. Had he really seen that face staring back at him between the branches? Or was it a figment of his wild imagination? As they walked (stumbled, in Lee's case) through the woodland, he replayed the sequence of events in his head. The blow he'd received when he'd fallen into the stone cross didn't help with his efforts because much of what had happened over the last hour was scrambled up, and he once again came away uncertain of what he'd dreamt and what was real.

Maybe it would come back to him later, but Lee wasn't sure of anything right now.

On top of all that, he was starting to feel nauseous again.

Therefore, he was relieved when Amelia led him out of the woods into the open after just a few minutes.

"Here we are," she said.

Leaving the shelter of the trees, they found themselves exposed to the inclement weather. Heavy rain lashed their faces. The wind was picking up again. Lee looked around. They were in a bleak valley with steep, grassy slopes.

"I know where we are," Lee said. "Blake Dean. Where the old trestle bridge crossed. Miners used it to ferry granite from the mine to the reservoir higher up on the moor when constructing the dams. I used to play around here when I was a teenager."

"You know the area well, then. Have you lived here all your life?"

"Yes, hereabouts," Lee replied, trying to be evasive without sounding like he was being evasive.

The trestle bridge was long gone, dismantled many decades ago to recycle the timber. All that remained was the base of two concrete supports. Lee could make out the dark tunnel entrance to the pit head near the top of one slope.

A small stream ran down the middle of the valley, where shallow water gushed over smooth, rounded stones. Eventually, the stream joined with Hebden Beck and wound down the lower part of the valley to Colden Clough and Gibson Mill. They'd exited on the northern fringes of the woods, a good three or four miles from the cottage. Lee hadn't realized he'd wandered so far.

Luckily, there was no old crone and no Dodman standing on a boulder and holding a staff, like from his dream. Besides, that was away to the east.

"This way," he heard Amelia say and looked to where she pointed.

Next to the stream was a flat plot of land. Resting on it was a large static caravan, one of those big fancy ones with a little fence around the front, sets of wooden stairs to the front and rear doors, and a big butane tank tucked in around the back. On the roof was a satellite dish. Leaning against one wall was a moped.

"You live here?" Lee asked.

"Of course."

"By yourself?"

Amelia flashed him a big smile and said, "Come on, before we both get soaked."

She guided him over the bumpy ground and up the steps at the front. Behind the fence was a small decking area with folded-up sunchairs and a barbeque pit. A brightly coloured curtain screened the window beside the door so that Lee couldn't see inside. Amelia opened the front door (she didn't use a key, Lee saw: probably there was no need for one out here in the wilds, he realized) and shepherded him over the threshold.

Lee brushed the rain out of his hair and then checked out the caravan's inside.

He whistled gently.

It wasn't what he was expecting. Rather than the cramped and slightly rundown and damp caravans Lee remembered from family holidays to Skegness, this was large, palatial, and very well-appointed. While he stood looking at the upholstered couches, the glass-topped dining table with matching chairs, the Smart TV over an electric fireplace, the fitted carpets, the lampshades, the framed photos and magazine rack and coffee table, and, further down the caravan's main body, an expensive-looking fitted kitchen, Amelia removed her red coat and threw back the curtains.

"Very nice," Lee purred, briefly forgetting about his sore head. "This is amazing."

"I can't complain."

He turned to look at her, raising one eyebrow.

"You live here, like, all year round?"

"Why not?" Amelia asked him, seemingly enjoying his reaction. "It serves me perfectly well enough."

"I'd say," Lee said, thinking what a shithole the cottage was in comparison to this palace.

"I don't own the place. It belongs to a friend. He let me stay after I split with my ex last year. He holds deeds to the land and has a permanent residency permit, so he says I can use this for as long as I want. But I don't intend on staying here for the rest of my life, Lee."

Lee whistled softly once more.

"Why can't I have friends like that?" he said.

"It's my bolthole until I get my life back on track."

Not so different from the cottage, after all, Lee thought to himself.

"Do you mind if I use your bathroom?"

"Straight down the hall on the right."

Lee wiped his shoes on the mat and stepped across the front lounge and through the kitchen, noting the wine glasses and the spotlessly clean surfaces. Down the short hall, he passed a bedroom containing two single beds. To his front, through an open door, was the main bedroom, which included a huge double bed. Lee swung to his right into a spacious bathroom which actually had a square bath, as well as a toilet and sink.

He pushed the door shut and turned on the taps. Hurriedly, Lee lifted the hem of his sweater and pulled out the gun, and then, bending over, he rolled down one sock and shoved the weapon inside.

"So, how many people does this baby hold?" he asked as he worked.

"It's a six berth," Amelia called. "There are three bedrooms and two bathrooms. There's also a couch bed if it's needed."

"That's cool," Lee replied, rolling the sock over the weapon and pulling down his trouser leg. "But don't you miss your family and friends?"

"A little. When we split up, my boyfriend said nasty things about me, making my life hell. So, I came here to escape all the drama. The peace and quiet are good for me."

Lee turned off the taps and looked at himself in the mirror. His head was a mess. Congealed blood smeared his scalp and hair, and one of his eyes was bloodshot.

"Still, it must get a bit boring, right?" he said, turning away from his reflection and twisting the door handle. "There are only so many times you can explore the woods."

Lee opened the bathroom door to find Amelia standing right outside. He jumped.

"Lots of questions, Lee," she said quietly, looking directly at him.

Lee shrugged helplessly.

After a heartbeat, Amelia smiled and said, "Let's look at your wound."

He followed Amelia back to the kitchen. On the dining table rested a small first-aid kit.

"Park yourself down, Lee from hereabouts," she told him and pulled out a chair for herself.

He watched as she opened the first-aid kit and rummaged around inside, removing sticking plasters, sterile gauze dressings, and rolls of adhesive tape.

"I'm no Florence Nightingale, so this will have to be rudimentary."

Taking an antiseptic wipe, she cleaned the cut and swabbed up as much blood as possible. Next, she applied some TCP, which stung and made him flinch, and then opened a pack of thin suture strips.

"Try and sit still while I close up the wound."

Lee did as he was told. Amelia leaned in close as she positioned the strips over the cut, allowing him to breathe in the woody musk she was wearing. She caught him looking into her eyes, shook her head, and continued with her task.

Then she leaned back to look at the fruits of her labour.

"I really shouldn't give up my day job," she told him, pulling a face.

"I'll look handsome with a scar."

"If you say so."

His head was still throbbing, like the worst kind of hangover.

"Do you have painkillers in your box of tricks?"

"Yes, but it's best to take no ibuprofen because they might mask more serious symptoms. And stay off the coffee for a few days because too much might flood your brain with stimulants. I'm worried that you might have a mild concussion."

Lee saluted like a good boy scout.

"However, you do get a sticker for being a brave little boy," and she reached across the table and pressed one onto his sweater.

Over their heads, the rain was coming down heavier than ever, drumming onto the caravan's roof in a continuous roar. It lashed against the windows, and the gusty wind rocked the walls.

Lee glanced at the kitchen clock; it was coming up to six in the evening – he must have been out of it for quite some time. The storm meant he wouldn't be going anywhere anytime soon, and once it got dark, the woods would be too dangerous to find his way back to the cottage anyway.

He thought again of the telephone call from Jacko. Taking out the small phone, he switched it on and checked for missed calls. If – when – the call came, he'd need to take it in private. He placed the phone on the dining table within easy reach.

"Are you waiting on a call?" Amelia enquired, nodding at the phone.

"Just a mate. It's nothing important."

"Just as well, because reception can be sticky out here, even on a fine day."

She glanced out the window at the weather and then turned back to look at Lee.

"While we wait to ship you out, why don't you tell me about yourself? What do you do for a living?"

Lee puffed out his cheeks and then wrinkled his nose.

"Nothing very exciting. I work in a garage."

This was half true because when he wasn't working on the checkouts down the supermarket, Lee did help out around Jacko's repair shop; nothing mechanical, just sweeping up and making the tea. It was simpler to mix truth with lies, he'd learned. That way, it was easier to remember the made-up stuff.

"A grease monkey who likes getting back to nature. There can't be many of those around. Particularly ones with flashlights and cheap-as-chips phones. That mobile is like something out of the Stone Age."

Lee laughed awkwardly.

Amelia leaned forward. She stuck out her bottom lip.

"You're not a drug dealer, are you? Or a burglar, scoping out your next job?"

"Don't be daft," Lee said and squirmed in his seat, his eyes shifting to the phone again.

"Where did you say you lived?"

"I didn't."

"Well, you'll have to clue me in a little, Lee. When this rain stops," and she looked up at the roof, "if it ever does stop, either we walk there, or I give you a lift on my moped. So, 'fess up, boy."

Lee chewed on his lip for a second.

"You can just drop me off somewhere."

Just then, Amelia started to giggle, taking Lee by surprise. She sighed dramatically like it was all too much for her.

"Ah, Lee. I shouldn't tease you. I saw you earlier at the old cottage in the woods, trifling around in the woodshed."

"So, it was you?"

"It was indeed. I was snooping on my new neighbour. I guess a red coat isn't the best kind of camouflage because you clocked me, and being the considerate person I am, I vamoosed out of there rather sharply."

Lee grinned, finding her wily inquisitiveness enchanting.

"And then I followed you," he said back.

"After hearing these mysterious cries for help that you mentioned. Which wasn't me, I stress. Wrong person. I'm sorry that you ended up with me instead."

"I'm not."

"Not what?"

"Sorry that you found me."

Amelia pouted again, saying, "Well, I couldn't just leave you lying on the ground."

She rocked back in her chair because their faces had come very close.

"Are you living there? In the cottage? Or doing the place up? Heaven knows it needs a makeover."

Lee dawdled with a reply, so Amelia answered for him.

"Something like that," she said, mimicking his voice. "A man of mystery. I can see women going for that."

She came to her feet and gathered up the first-aid supplies.

"Time for a brew, methinks," she said.

•   •   •

When Amelia returned with the tea and a packet of hobnobs, Lee asked what she knew about the cottage and the woodland.

"What do you mean precisely?" she asked back over the rim of her cup.

"Oh, you know. The history of the area, that sort of thing."

"A history buff, a nature lover, as well as being good at fixing engines. Glory be."

Amelia sipped her drink.

"I thought you said you've lived hereabouts all your life?"

"Yes, just not here here," Lee said. "More down in the town than in the sticks."

"But you played around these parts as a child. All the kids come up here at some point, drinking cider and courting. I know I did, much to my parents' horror."

"I did all of that, too," answered Lee. "But we mostly knocked around Gibson Mill. I only came to where the old bridge used to be on a few occasions and never in this part of the woods."

Lee thought about something she said.

"Your parents didn't like you coming here, then?"

"They were worried about the company I was keeping. And the boys, of course. But those weren't the only reasons."

Lee waited for her to continue.

"You must have heard the stories," she said calmly.

"What stories are those?"

"The ghost stories, silly."

Lee nearly spilled his tea.

"Everyone has heard the ghost stories, Lee."

"Err, not me."

"Really? I thought it was part of the local lore. Even my parents talked about them. They used to try and put me off from coming up here by telling me all kinds of scary tales and legends."

"It didn't work because here you are all these years later."

"Not that many years later, mister."

Lee listened to the rain beat down. Talking about this kind of thing during a wild and stormy night probably wasn't wise.

"What kind of scary tales did they tell you?" he asked nonetheless.

"Oh, the usual thing. Of how, on foggy nights, strange shadowy phantoms stalk the woods. They appear one minute and are gone the next. Or some people talk of mysterious lights – orbs – that dance through the tree branches. Your standard, off-the-wall ghosties and ghoulies gibberish. Everyone knows someone who claims to have witnessed something."

Lee remembered his dream of the glowing mushrooms.

Amelia went on.

"A school friend of mine once swore blind that she heard animal hooves stomping around one evening when she was here with her boyfriend. At first, they thought it was a horse or a deer, but then the noises started pounding from above their heads, from high amongst the tree trunks. And there was this vile smell, she said, like you get at the zoo or the circus, only a hundred times worse."

"What did they do?"

"They ran from the woods crying and bawling and didn't stop until they were home. She never went back there again."

Lee couldn't blame her.

"But as I said, it's all gibberish. Silly tales with which to scare children."

After his own experience, Lee wasn't so quick to dismiss them. But he kept this thought to himself.

Instead, he asked Amelia about the cottage. Did she know anything about the previous owner?

"I'm afraid not. The place has been abandoned for as long as anyone can remember. I think it fell into ruin between the wars. Why are you asking all this, Lee?"

"No reason. Just curious, I guess."

Amelia finished her drink and then nodded towards the sounds of the storm outside.

"It looks like I was right about the wind and the rain never stopping. I'm not risking riding my bike in this weather, Lee. So unless you fancy a walk in the dark and getting wet through in the process, you're welcome to stay the night. There are plenty of spare beds. Or you can crash on the couch."

Although it pained him to admit it, Lee knew Amelia was right. Not for the first time, he wondered at the wisdom of following her into the woods. But he couldn't turn back the clock.

Besides, the caravan was preferable to the old cottage and its many mysteries.

•   •   •

Lee rested on one of the single beds, staring up at the ceiling and listening to the storm beating the hell out of the caravan. Thank God it was securely anchored to the ground otherwise he was sure it would have toppled over by now. Inside, it was snug, warm, and comfortable.

But he couldn't sleep. Not after hearing Amelia tell him of the ghostly sightings. Even if they were just old wives' tales.

He thought of the old tramp, Percival. He'd travelled these parts, collecting and recording details of ancient fables for his book. Lee wondered if the rumours of apparitions and dancing lights passed down through the generations were all a part of the same mythos. Crazy superstitions that may have been grounded in fact but had become bedtime stories told at Halloween. Wasn't that the case with all such legends?

Lee rolled over onto his side and picked his phone off the bedside cabinet. He checked the screen and saw no missed calls or messages from Jacko. It was nearly midnight, and although Lee told himself things were probably fine, he couldn't help but worry something had gone wrong.

His head throbbed, adding to his woes.

Dweller Under The Roots

Lee climbed out of bed and padded down to the kitchen. Turning on a magnetic strip light over the sink, he filled a tumbler with water and gulped it down in one go. The wind was howling like a banshee, prowling around the caravan like it was searching for a way in. Peeling back the curtain, Lee hunched down and peered outside into the night. He couldn't see much, mostly leaves and small twigs blowing around. Lee snapped the curtain back into place, turned the light off, and quietly returned to bed.

He paused outside the bedroom door because he could hear murmuring coming from Amelia's room.

Lee thought she must be talking in her sleep. He tip-toed to her door and pressed his ear to the wood. He was mistaken: although indistinct through the partition, the words had a literate quality. They weren't the messy, mixed up, monosyllabic dialect of someone slumbering, but rather definite speech forms. He just couldn't make out what she was saying.

He strained his ears to hear better but to no avail.

Just then, her voice stopped mid-sentence, and the sudden stillness had Lee holding his breath. He thought he heard the floor creak, so he hurried back to his room in case Amelia caught him eavesdropping. He crawled under the sheets.

CHAPTER 8

Lee was woken by sunlight pouring into the bedroom. He couldn't remember falling asleep, but he must have drifted off at some point, lulled by the whine of the wind. He felt surprisingly refreshed. His headache had gone.

Sitting up, he saw the curtains were parted, and the door was ajar. Amelia must have popped in to check on him. He could hear her clattering about in the kitchen.

Climbing out of bed, Lee glanced through the window. The storm had blown itself out, replaced with clear skies and early-morning sun. The only signs of the foul weather were a detritus of windswept twigs and leaves lying all around.

Slipping on his shoes and retrieving the gun from where he'd hidden it under the bed, Lee went down the hall, stretching and yawning.

Amelia was setting out the breakfast table. There was toast in the rack, bowls of raisin bran, and a pot of tea.

"Good morning," she said brightly.

"Buongiorno."

"Did you sleep well?"

"Eventually. The storm made for an eventful night."

"They always sound worse through the thin walls and ceiling. But I reckon the woods will be full of fallen branches and other debris, so we'll take the moped back to your place. First, let's enjoy breakfast."

Lee took his seat and spread butter on a slice of toast while Amelia munched on a bowl of bran.

"There's fresh grapefruit juice in the fridge if you like."

"Tea is fine."

He drank some. It was strong. He added extra sugar.

While they ate and chatted, Lee cast his mind back to last night. He decided not to mention hearing her talking. Firstly, because it didn't look good, admitting he'd been snooping on her after she was kind enough to let him stay over. Secondly, it was none of his business; Amelia might simply have been chatting to a friend on the phone.

Spending a night away from the creepy cottage, in comfy surroundings and pleasant company, had done him a world of good, regardless of the perils involved. But it was back to reality, the cold light of day quickly reminding him of the fix he was in. As soon as he was alone in the cottage, Lee would phone Jacko and find out what was happening.

He noticed the TV in the front lounge was tuned to some programme about people flogging antiques. Lee glanced at the time. Jesus! It was already mid-morning. They should get their skates on.

He started to gulp down his tea and shovel in mouthfuls of food. Amelia noticed.

"Either you're starving or in a rush to leave. Am I boring you?"

Lee couldn't reply because he had a mouthful of bran. He mumbled incoherently.

"What was that?" Amelia asked.

Lee tried again but with the same results.

Amelia held up a hand to stop his attempts, saying, "Never mind, I'd rather not know the answer."

She pushed away from the table.

"We'll be on our merry way in five minutes."

Lee clung onto Amelia's back as they rode the moped along the twisting country lane. The overnight rain had left the road surface slick, and the motorcycle threatened to slip on the sharper bends, but Amelia was a good rider and kept her speed down.

They skirted the large tract of woodland, heading east and then south. As they went, Lee looked into the inky blackness occasionally, but the crowded trees stubbornly refused to reveal their secrets. The woods covered a much larger area than he realized, expanding well beyond Hardcastle Crags and all the way to the edge of the high moors. He could easily picture ramblers losing their way.

They soon reached the hamlet of Midgehole, and when he saw the scorched shell of the big mansion, Lee leaned forward and shouted over the buzz of the engine.

"What is that place?"

Amelia turned to look, her crash helmet bumping against his.

"It used to be a children's home and then a borstal," she yelled back, returning her gaze to the roadway. "Then it was empty for a bit before some squatters moved in. One night, they accidentally set the place on fire while cooking up their crystal meth."

"When was this?"

"Yonks ago."

"Was anyone hurt?" Lee asked, craning his neck as they whizzed past the old ruin.

"I don't think so. Hang on, I'm going to put my foot down."

Lee held on tight as they picked up speed to 30 mph.

Now they motored along the same route Lee had followed the night of the robbery: past the tourists' car park and along the twisting lane, which grew narrower and narrower. They passed no other vehicles. The way soon morphed into a slender grass strip that tapered into the trees.

Lee could feel his buoyant mood fall away as they neared the turning to the cottage, like the proximity of the brooding building was leaching away his joy. He wondered if there were such things as vampire houses that sucked the life out of their occupants.

They passed the trunk with the white stripe, and he told Amelia to slow down. Then she steered between the lichen-covered gateposts and over the cattle grid (which made his teeth rattle), and they had to duck their heads to avoid the screen of low branches.

The cottage seemed to loom over them even though it wasn't a grand building, and Lee felt a cold sweat on his forehead. Amelia weaved over the bumpy track, pulled up alongside his Defender, and switched off the moped's engine.

For about a minute, they sat on the bike and just looked.

Lee felt drained of energy. He wondered if Amelia was the same.

Eventually, she removed her helmet and said in a flat voice, "Home Sweet Home."

Lee climbed off the moped and handed her his helmet.

"Thanks for the ride," he said, trying to summon a smile. "And for rescuing me."

Still looking at the house intensely, Amelia said quietly, "No problem."

"I'd best get inside."

And he turned to go before swinging back around.

"Would you like to come in?"

He hoped he didn't sound too desperate because that's how he felt. Lee had a sudden aversion to being inside by himself.

"It's not much," he added. "It's filthy, squalid, and draughty, but I can show you around if you like. Return the compliment, kind of thing."

Amelia scraped her eyes off the tumbledown cottage and looked over at him.

"You're not really selling it, Lee. But how can I turn down such an invitation?"

Lee quietly breathed a sigh of relief.

Amelia put the crash helmets over the moped's handlebars and walked behind Lee as he weaved around the weeds and brambles out front. As he neared the front door, he sensed Amelia hanging back and turned around to see her standing and looking at the bushes where he'd tossed the dead cat. He went back and joined her. The animal's mummified remains were hidden from sight, so it was curious that she'd stopped at that spot.

He was about to ask if she'd changed her mind when she grinned and resumed walking.

Lee unlocked the front door and ushered her inside, noticing another slight hesitation as she crossed the doorstep.

Had she been in here before, he wondered? If she had, maybe she remembered the awful feeling the place gave you.

"I see what you mean," Amelia said, looking around. "It's, erm, quaint."

"I did warn you."

She walked to the middle of the room and peered up at the ceiling beams.

"It will take a lot of time and money to fix the place. Those joists are riddled with woodworm, for starters."

"Are they?" He followed her gaze and saw the thousands of pinprick holes in the dark beams. He felt terrible at going along with the pretence of giving the cottage a makeover, but what choice did he have?

"If they are termites, then you have real problems. A termite infestation is miles worse than woodworm damage. And they're harder to detect."

Lee didn't even know if Britain suffered from termites.

"The ceiling could cave in."

"Thanks," Lee said, adopting a glum expression.

"Is it this bad in all of the rooms?"

"The upstairs is a little better. The bedroom is snug, and the toilet just about flushes. You get used to the place."

Amelia looked like she didn't believe him for a second. She went over to the range and opened the glass door.

"At least you have firewood for cooking and heating."

She entered the kitchen and Lee took a second to look across at the wall where he'd bricked up the money. He hoped she didn't notice the loose brick.

"Whoah!" she called out. "What the deuce is going on here, Lee?"

"What is it?" he asked and urgently followed her.

She stood in the centre of the kitchen, pointing where the stool was wedged under the cellar door's handle.

"Please tell me you have a rational reason for doing that," she said.

"The cellar door keeps swinging open, and there's a cold draught," Lee replied, hoping he sounded plausible.

Amelia dragged the stool away, and needless to say, the cellar door stayed shut. She waggled her eyebrows at him.

"Looks okay now," she said.

"Maybe the latch was loose or something."

"What's down there? Do you have somebody chained up?"

"Damn, my secret is out – I'm the local nutter."

"Well, I might as well have a nosey," Amelia said and stepped towards the cellar stairs.

"Wait, you can't!"

"Why not?"

"Because it's all cobwebby and dark. The bulb barely throws out any light."

"It's a good job one of us remembered to bring this then, isn't it," Amelia told him, producing the flashlight from her jacket pocket. "And I'm not afraid of a few spiders."

She went down two steps and looked back over her shoulder.

"Are you coming?"

"I've already checked it out. There's nothing much to see. I'll wait here."

Amelia looked him up and down from head to toe like she was getting the measure of him.

"Sissy," she concluded and then dove into the shadows.

He soon lost sight of her. Her footsteps sounded from the stairwell, and then there was a click as she turned on the flashlight, then a second one as she yanked the pull cord. Weak light bled over the cellar floor, but Amelia had already moved further into the cellar, and Lee couldn't see her from his position.

He imagined he could hear the slugs squelching and sucking a path towards her.

He waited for her to reappear.

Then she cried out in alarm, and Lee knew she'd spotted the awful things, and without thinking, he raced down the stairs to drag her to safety, only to find her standing before the rows of shelves with a delighted look on her.

He looked around in a flash, but the critters had gone. The only sign they'd been here was a mass of slime on the bare floor. Amelia seemed not to notice this or the rotted produce in their crates because she'd discovered the ranks of jars and earthenware containers at the far end of the shelves. While

Lee steadied his racing heart, wondering where the slugs were, she randomly selected vessels.

She wiped cobwebs off one label and squinted at the writing. Her eyesight was better than his because she had no problem reading it.

"GARLIC, CELANDINE, AND HOLLOWLEEK – GOOD FOR STIFF JOINTS AND FEVER."

She returned it to its spot and picked up another jar.

"OX GALL – GOOD FOR THE EYES."

Lee moved alongside and looked over her shoulder. The next bottle she chose held a thin green plant stem.

"VALERIANA OFFICINALIS – A RELAXANT AND A CURE FOR SLEEPLESSNESS. And this one contains Hart's clover and chamomile. It says to make them into a paste and smear it on a blind man's eyes," Amelia said excitedly, showing him a small clay jug.

"THE MANDRAKE PLANT. If you suck the leaves for a month, you can transform yourself into an animal, apparently."

On she went, skipping from shelf to shelf.

"BELLADONNA, OR DEADLY NIGHTSHADE. HELLEBORE, TO CAST INVISIBILITY SPELLS, ONLY TO BE PICKED ON A MOONLESS NIGHT."

Amelia swung around and faced Lee directly.

"You know what this means, don't you, Lee? Once, in the past, a folk healer lived here. It was home to someone who practiced herbal medicine and cast spells. This cellar is where they kept their plants and their potions. I think they used to be called wise men, wise women, or sometimes cunning folk. People would come to them to heal their warts and broken bones and stop their migraines. If people lost a treasured item, the cunning folk would help them find it – for a fee, naturally – or farmers would seek help to ensure a good crop. The wise women practiced midwifery or helped you find love."

Lee shook his head, still torn. A scary dream caused by a concussion; well, he could buy that. But Lee found what Amelia was suggesting hard to subscribe to.

He looked around at the hundreds of containers.

"Sounds creepy to me, Amelia. Conjurers, healers, voodoo magicians, or whatever you want to call them all amount to the same thing - fooling people into thinking they could cure their aches and pains. It was all smoke and mirrors, wasn't it?"

"Oh, Lee. That's an outdated view. These wise folk were enlightened people trying to help their neighbours. They weren't wizards or witches. Besides, many modern medicines have evolved from these old religions and beliefs."

"Applying a bit of aloe vera to your grazed knee is one thing, but casting spells to make a person invisible is something completely different. Anyway, how do you know all this stuff?"

Amelia shrugged. "I don't. I'm just saying. But doesn't it sound exciting?"

"Not to me, it doesn't. It's creepy," Lee repeated.

"Oh, you philistine. Lighten up, Lee. This is so cool. I knew this place had been empty for a long time, but I don't think it's been touched for hundreds of years."

"That's not quite true, Amelia. The cottage may be old and run down, but it has electricity and indoor plumbing. Which means somebody has been living here more recently."

"Oh, yeah. I guess so."

Amelia was only downcast for a handful of seconds, and then she started exploring the rest of the cellar.

Lee, in the meantime, was more concerned about those slugs. Where the hell were they? Hiding in cracks in the walls, maybe.

"Look, there's another door!"

Her cry had him twisting around. She bent over and pointed the flashlight beam into the shadows at the very back of the cellar. When he approached, Lee saw a tiny wooden door about three feet high. The bottom looked like it had been gnawed away by rats, leaving a small opening.

"What do you think is on the other side?"

Lee shrugged in response.

"Let's find out," said Amelia enthusiastically.

"Do we have to?"

Lee was beginning to regret asking her into the cottage. He was worried about missing Jacko's late call.

Amelia ignored him and reached out to lift the door latch, but it was wedged shut. She tugged at it several times, but it wouldn't budge.

"Move to the side and let me have a go," said Lee.

He positioned himself before the door and bent forward to grab the latch in one hand and the handle in the other. Then he pulled. The door remained defiantly shut. He altered his posture slightly, bunched the muscles in his shoulders, and tried again. This time, it sprang open, taking him by surprise. It bounced back against the dirt wall and vibrated. Cold air stroked his face.

Dweller Under The Roots

Amelia shone the flashlight in, revealing a short passage cut through the soil. Tree roots pushed through the walls and roof in fanciful curls.

"What do you think it is? Another exit? Or an escape tunnel?"

"Perhaps," Lee replied. "Or maybe it was added to make life easier for the owner so they wouldn't have to lug their produce up and down the stairs."

"Come on, I want to see where it leads."

Lee had a pretty good idea, but he indulged her and followed her through the tiny opening. On the other side, they both stood up straight. Their heads almost touched the passage's roof. Amelia set off first, moving down the passage and focusing the light beam on the floor and walls.

Every few feet, Lee noticed small recesses at about chest height in the walls, each containing the remnants of melted candle stubs. Wax had run down the walls in yellow rivulets, merging with the slug trails.

After about twenty paces, an opening appeared on their right. It was the entrance to a small and shallow cave. Amelia paused to shine the flashlight inside.

"Yuk! What is that?" she asked, looking uncertain for the first time.

Lee now knew where the thousands of slugs had gone. They were gathered here at this spot, this nest or breeding ground or whatever a slug hidy-hole was called, amassed in one large, sticky accumulation in the damp cave. The blob of goo was so big that Lee imagined he saw it pulsing like a beating heart. It glowed under the flashlight's glare.

"I think I'm going to be sick," Amelia whispered.

"You and me both. Let's keep moving," Lee suggested.

Amelia didn't protest, and she hurried on down the underground tunnel. It jinked to the left and came to an end. Fixed to the wall before them was a set of wooden ladder rungs. Overhead, thin beams of daylight shone down between planks of wood into the passage.

"It's what I thought," Lee murmured.

"Huh?"

"It's a trapdoor. If I'm correct, it should lead into the outbuilding where you saw me yesterday."

"We can get out that way, you mean?"

"No," Lee answered. "It's bolted on the outside. We'll have to retrace our steps."

They set off back, tracking down the tunnel. They hurried past the slug cave and emerged into the root cellar a few moments later. Lee couldn't wait to leave the place behind.

"Hold on a moment while I take some photos," Amelia said, handing him the flashlight and slipping her phone out of her back pocket.

"Do you think that's wise?" Lee asked her.

"I don't think the previous owner will mind, Lee. Not unless you believe in ghosts and curses."

Lee waited as she found the camera setting.

"I have an idea, as well."

"What's that?"

"Just something which might help," she added but said no more.

Amelia spent a few minutes snapping pics, the camera flash lighting up the dim cellar and its bizarre contents like sheet lightning. When she was done, she smiled at him and let him lead her up the cellar stairs to the kitchen. She closed the door behind her. Again, it stayed shut.

"Do you want to see the rest of the place?" Lee asked.

"Might as well."

It didn't take them long. Lee gave her a quick tour of the upstairs, thankful he'd tidied the bed and rolled up his sleeping bag lest she thought he was a slob. Amelia studied the bookshelf, and he thought she might take one of the books and thumb through it, drawn by their subject matter. She didn't. Apart from the cellar and underground tunnel, she appeared indifferent regarding the rest of the cottage.

Back downstairs, it was time for her to go. She gave Lee her number and made him promise to ring if he felt unwell again.

"Remember what I said about not taking painkillers. I'll call around tomorrow to check on you," Amelia informed him, unaware that their paths would probably never cross again. The thought – and the deception – made Lee sad.

Amelia raised herself on her toes and kissed him on the cheek.

Then she hopped onto her moped and rode away, waving over her shoulder as she disappeared through the trees.

CHAPTER 9

LEE LISTENED TO THE SOUND of the moped's engine gradually fade into the distance and then turned and walked over the weed-infested garden to the cottage door, trying not to think about phantoms stalking the woods, animal hooves echoing down from the high branches or plagues of slugs.

As soon as he was inside, Lee slid out his phone, hoping to see a message or a missed call. The screen was blank. He tutted in annoyance. He needed – no, he was desperate – to know the latest news. Irritated with Jacko for not calling him, Lee punched in his friend's number and was seconds from hitting the call button when he hesitated, his thumb hovering over the keypad.

Lee deleted the number and slumped into the armchair with a huff.

Jacko had warned Lee and Chris not to call him but to wait for Jacko to contact them. He'd been quite clear on that. Not because he was their self-appointed leader but because it was too big a risk. How that risk would be reduced because Jacko made first contact was never satisfactorily explained, but Lee and Chris knew to put their faith in Jacko.

It was a day and a half since the text message. A lot could have happened during that time. Jacko could be under arrest, and the police might be bugging his phone.

Lee remained seated in the chair, looking directly at the loose brick where the stolen money was hidden, turning over various possibilities in his mind. Then he lifted his phone and tapped in a different number. It rang and rang. Lee drummed his fingers on the armrest, trying to control his bad mood. Just when he was sure the call would switch to voicemail, someone answered.

"Wassup?" wheezed Tiny Bob.

"Hey, buddy."

"Lee, my man!"

Tiny Bob must be in his council house on Furness Drive because Lee could hear Dance Moms on the TV in the background.

"How's it diddling?" asked Tiny Bob.

"Things are good."

"Ah, I don't do refunds if that's what you're calling about," said Tiny Bob, his sentences coming in short snatches due to his constant breathlessness.

"Don't worry about it," said Lee.

"Another satisfied customer, that's what I like, innit?"

"Listen," Lee spoke quietly, trying to sound all casual-like. "Can you do me a favour?"

"Anything for an old schoolmate. Do you want that mobile upgrade we talked about?"

"Not just at the moment, but soon."

"Well, you just pop along to the market when you decide you want one. I do mates rates, as you know. So, what can I do you for, Lee?"

"I'm trying to get hold of Jacko, but he's not answering."

"Jack-the-Lad is probably shacked up with some woman somewhere," Tiny Bob said, his breathing coming faster for a second or two.

"Yes, you're probably right. Can you try giving him a buzz? I need to get a message to him. But listen, Tiny Bob: is there a way to do it without leaving a trace back to your number?"

Tiny Bob guffawed loudly and then said conspiratorially, "I understand perfectly what you're asking. Don't you worry, Lee – discretion is my middle name. Hang on a jiffy, will you?"

The sound on the TV went down, and then Tiny Bob came back on the line.

"Let me think. I can bounce the call off two mobile masts. That should hide the caller's ID."

"Is it guaranteed to work?"

"Absofuckinglutely. I saw a tutorial about it on YouTube."

Lee wasn't convinced but was out of options and patience.

"Give me the message and consider it done," Tiny Bob added, the words coming out as a high-pitched rattle like someone choking on a piece of chicken. Lee heard a swooshing sound: that would be Tiny Bob's O2 tank kicking in. If he croaked it before contacting Jacko, this whole gamble would be for nothing.

"Tell him I'm leaving town if he hasn't contacted me by tomorrow. Have you got that?"

"Sounds serious," bubbled the voice at the other end. "Have you two had a falling out?"

"No," Lee told him. "But he'll understand the context."

There was a long pause. Was Tiny Bob still conscious? Or even alive?

"What's in this for me, Lee?" he finally asked.

"Put it this way. If you want to avoid a serious beating from Jacko, it will be best to pass on my message. Understood?"

"Gotcha."

Lee ended the call.

That was that, then, he thought to himself. If Jacko Page failed to call back, Lee would be out of here. With the money.

Lee went upstairs to spend a penny and then went to his bedroom. He stood looking at the bookshelf with his hands in his trouser pockets. He really didn't want to get into this any deeper. Still, his conversations with Amelia about the myths and folklore associated with the area and his dream (in the cold light of day, he refused to refer to it as an out-of-body experience) prompted him to learn more. If the cottage once was home to a folk healer, he had to admit to a certain fascination. Knowing a little more about the subject wouldn't harm him, surely? Knowledge was power, as they say.

This time, he chose the one called DODMEN AND THEIR SIGHTING STAVES and carried it downstairs. Settling himself in the armchair, Lee browsed through it.

Mark Hobson

It was a more recent publication than the book about Percival the Tramp and his travels. Written in the early 1970s and edited by an academic with numerous Ph.D.'s, it began:

IT IS DIFFICULT FOR OUR GENERATION TO SUBMIT TO THE MOTION THAT, MANY THOUSANDS OF YEARS AGO, OUR ANCIENT ANCESTORS – MEGALITHIC MAN – WERE NOT THE SIMPLE, UNCULTURED HUNTER-GATHERERS WE ASSUME. THEIR LIVES MAY HAVE BEEN SHORT AND BESET WITH ILLNESS, DISEASE, AND VIOLENCE, BUT THEY WERE FAR FROM UNSOPHISTICATED.

MEGALITHIC MAN HAD ACCESS TO ARCANE KNOWLEDGE, WHICH IS NOW LOST TO US. IT OFFENDS OUR SENSE OF SUPERIORITY TO THINK THAT PERHAPS HE KNEW SOMETHING THAT WE DO NOT. THAT, RATHER THAN MOVING ON A PATH OF ENDLESS PROGRESS, OUR PRESENT LIVES ARE TRAVELLING IN THE WRONG DIRECTION, AWAY FROM INSTEAD OF TOWARDS OUR QUEST TO UNDERSTAND HUMANKIND'S PURPOSE.

THE LANDSCAPE OF MEGALITHIC BRITAIN, UNEARTHED BY ARCHAEOLOGISTS AND SCIENTISTS TODAY, IS CONTINUOUSLY THROWING UP MORE AND MORE SURPRISES FOR US. SOME WE UNDERSTAND, AND SOME CONFOUND US.

ONE OF THESE MYSTERIES IS THE LEY SYSTEM AND ITS PURPOSE.

LEY LINES ARE A VAST NETWORK OF STRAIGHT LINES THAT JOIN THE MEGALITHIC SITES OF ANCIENT BRITAIN. THEY CRISSCROSS THE LANDSCAPE, CONNECTING BARROWS, HENGES, TUMULI, PREHISTORIC CAMPS, AND MOUNDS, MARKED ALONG THEIR ROUTES BY MARKERS SUCH AS STANDING STONES, SIGHT NOTCHES, HOLY WELLS, CAUSEWAYS, AND HILLTOP BEACONS.

THAT THESE ALIGNMENTS EXIST IS NOT IN DOUBT: TRACES OF THEM REMAIN TO THIS DAY, ALTHOUGH OUR MODERN MOTORWAY-BUILDING PROJECTS ARE SLICING THEM APART AND SLOWLY ERODING THEIR

Dweller Under The Roots

PRESENCE. THE ARGUMENTS THAT CONTINUE TO DIVIDE THE SCIENTIFIC COMMUNITY ARE: WHAT ARE LEY LINES? WHY DO THEY EXIST? FOR WHAT PURPOSE DID OUR ANCESTORS SET THEM OUT? OR ARE THEY NATURAL FEATURES OF OUR PLANET?

ARE THEY EARLY BRITISH TRACKWAYS AS SOME PURPORT? OR CHANNELS FOR SOME MYSTERIOUS POWER, AN 'EARTH FORCE' OR PERHAPS A 'BLACK STREAM' OF UNDERGROUND ENERGY?

Lee turned the page to find a map showing a typical ley line. It ran in a straight line, starting from a Roman hill fort in the north and progressing southwest through a markstone in a tiny Somerset village and onwards to a crossroads. This was known as a three-point ley – that is, three significant markers that fall in a straight line a few miles apart. The more markers, the better, or so the text said.

Lee thought of his dream, of how the hilltop mound lined up with the notch atop the boulder, then the clapper bridge over the stream, then along the path of shining light to the stone cross in the clearing. If Lee continued with his imagined line, it would slice right through the cottage's front door. Meaning the place was anchored at the end of a five-point ley.

Percival the Tramp, in his memoirs, talked of corpse roads being paths of the dead.

Corpse roads sounded similar but different from ley lines in that the former followed meandering paths to stop spirits from returning home, whereas ley lines were rifle-barrel straight.

After the map, there were a series of black-and-white photographs of sunken lanes leading towards distant hills, markstones (some had strange vertical grooves on their surface), a motte-and-bailey in Wales, and someplace called the Mixen Tump. Then Lee flicked over and stopped dead because on the page before him was an illustration eerily like the stick man engraved on the stone cross, the spot where he'd taken a tumble.

It showed a colossal chalk figure on a hillside holding what appeared to be a pair of long walking sticks. It dominated the area for miles around. Beneath it ran the description:

THE LONG MAN OF WILMINGTON. A GIANT HILL FIGURE IN EAST SUSSEX, ENGLAND, DATING FROM APPROX. 4,000 BC. IT WAS POSITIONED TO MARK THE STAR CONSTELLATION OF ORION AS IT RISES OVER THE HILLTOP.

Lee sat briefly with the book in his lap and looked at the image. He remembered the man from his dream, his staff wedged into the notch on top of the boulder. A chill passed through him.

He continued reading:

THE LONG MAN OF WILMINGTON, SOMETIMES CALLED THE GREEN MAN, STANDS ASTRIDE A MAJOR LEY LINE RUNNING FROM FRISTON FOREST AND ENDING AT THE BENEDICTINE PRIORY AT WILMINGTON. FOR THIS REASON, MOST LEY HUNTERS REFER TO HIM AS A DODMAN, AN ANCIENT LEY SURVEYOR COMPLETE WITH TWO SIGHTING RODS. DODMEN WORKED IN PAIRS, USING SIGHTING RODS TO MAP OUT EARLY BRITISH TRACKWAYS FOR TRAVELLERS, TRADERS, AND PILGRIMS. LOCAL SHEPHERDS OFTEN SPEAK OF A SECOND GIANT HILL FIGURE – NOW LOST TO TIME AND EROSION: A FEMALE COMPANION FOR THE LONG MAN.

Dweller Under The Roots

THE CONTROVERSY SURROUNDING LEY LINES SHOWS NO SIGNS OF ABATING. ARCHAEOLOGISTS DISMISS THEM AS NOTHING MORE THAN COINCIDENCE, LINES DRAWN ON A MAP THAT JUST HAPPEN TO PASS THROUGH ANCIENT SIGHTS. THEY POINT OUT THAT BRITAIN CONTAINS THOUSANDS OF PREHISTORIC LANDMARKS AND THAT MANY ARE ALIGNED SIMPLY BY CHANCE.

OTHERS PREFER THE 'EARTH FORCE' AND THE 'BLACK STREAM' OF NEGATIVE ENERGY THEORY, IN WHICH MINING, QUARRYING, AND THE EVER-EXPANDING MOTORWAY NETWORK CREATE A MORE MALEVOLENT POWER BY SLICING OPEN THESE ENERGY CHANNELS.

THIS BOOK OUTLINES ALL THESE EXPLANATIONS, WITH CHAPTERS WRITTEN BY PROMINENT EXPERTS IN THEIR RESPECTIVE FIELDS.

Lee's head was throbbing. He put down the book and closed his eyes.

He'd given up trying to second-guess what all of this meant. Perhaps it wasn't a load of old tommyrot, after all. He no longer cared. The only thing he was sure of was that, ever since the bungled robbery, things had gone rapidly sideways. The sooner he was away from here, the sooner his life would return to normal. Lee craved the ordinary right now.

His message to Jacko was no idle threat. Lee was no longer willing to budge on the issue; he planned to hit the road and see where he fetched up once his deadline passed. To start over again somewhere new – maybe Scotland or over the sea in Ireland. Killing someone hadn't been a part of the deal because the guns were only ever meant as a threat; he hadn't signed up to murder. Accordingly, Lee felt justified in taking all the money and just disappearing.

Lee got to his feet and went up the stairs. He needed to sleep off his headache.

On the way up, he stumbled twice. Reaching the landing, his vision swam, and bright colours burst inside his head like he was trapped in a kaleidoscope. Lee grabbed the handrail.

Boy, the blow to his head must have been nasty. He was having a delayed reaction or something because now his vision oscillated, and Lee felt punch-drunk. His stomach started to convulse, and hot bile rushed up his throat. He staggered along the short hallway towards the toilet and just about made it because seconds later, he tossed his cookies into the porcelain bowl.

Lee heaved and retched. His eyes watered as he puked, and painful cramps twisted his guts like someone was scrunching up his intestines in their fist.

By the time he'd emptied his stomach contents, Lee's throat was raw, and his knees shook. He lurched from the toilet and made for the loft room, rolling from wall to wall like a sailor on a floundering ship in heavy seas. Somehow, he made it, and fell face-first onto his bed.

Lee kicked off his shoes and crawled inside the sleeping bag. He was too weak to zip it up. For ten minutes, he lay there and switched from being feverish and agitated one moment to being freezing cold the next. The twin agonies in his head and stomach atrophied his limbs.

Something was seriously wrong, Lee realized.

Whatever he was experiencing, it was more than a mild concussion.

He needed help.

With superhuman effort, Lee delved into his pocket and pulled out his phone. Then he found Amelia's number and dialled.

CHAPTER 10

NIGHTTIME ON FURNESS DRIVE COULD be like a scary exploration of hell. Even for the residents, it was a test of their bottle. Known locally as 'the furnace', its fearsome reputation was thoroughly deserved. Ravaged by crime and anti-social behaviour and often dubbed 'Britain's worst council estate', the tightly packed area of council houses and concrete overpasses was compared to like living in Beirut.

Gang activity, fly-tipping, and arson have become commonplace. The shells of scorched vehicles dot the pieces of waste ground. Teenagers use the estate's many derelict buildings to stash stolen goods and drugs. There is little CCTV, and street lighting is poor, leaving pools of darkness that allow illicit contraband to change hands unseen. Unemployment is rife, so the main way to make money is the drug trade or dog fighting. Dogs roam the streets.

This decaying and neglected neighbourhood was home to every type of toerag and miscreant imaginable, all spawned by a broken society. Numerous attempts to clean the place up failed; a catalogue of wasted urban renewal projects and indifference from the town council. The police had given up, as well. 'The furnace' was a no-go zone for the boys in blue.

The criminals, hooligans, and knaves thrived. One of their numbers was Tiny Bob, a one-time school friend to Lee Harris and Chris Keeble.

Tiny Bob lived in one of the council houses near the end of Furness Drive, where the estate petered out into fields and allotments. It was the quieter end of the road, meaning marginally fewer fireworks pushed through the letterbox and used syringes left in the garden privet. He'd lived here for more than ten years, the rent covered by his Housing Benefit. Two years ago, he applied for a grant to install a stairlift because Tiny Bob was too overweight to climb them unassisted. In fact, he barely left the house, except on market day to run his mobile phone stall and twice fortnightly to attend the Jobcentre.

Tiny Bob was a night owl. Most evenings, he'd stay up late watching TV, wearing baggy jogging bottoms and a vest, eating cold leftovers from his teatime takeaway. He kept his O2 cylinder nearby for when he was short of breath.

It was just before one in the morning when, yawning loudly, he used the remote to turn the TV off. He struggled to his feet. Earlier, Tiny Bob had tried ringing Jacko Page to pass on Lee's message, scrambling the call to hide his ID, but he'd been unable to get through. It would have to wait. Right now, he was too tired. Moreover, he didn't want to get involved in their latest dodgy scheme. Not that they'd let him, anyway; they never included him in their plans.

Tottering from the living room, wheeling the oxygen cylinder in his wake, he collapsed into the electric chair at the foot of the stairs. Pushing the button that started the electric motors, Tiny Bob rode slowly to the upstairs of his house, carrying the cylinder in his lap. Part way up, he needed to clasp the face mask to his mouth and suck on some O2 like a mountaineer climbing Mount Everest.

Once the stair lift reached the landing and whirred to a stop, Tiny Bob heaved himself up and wobbled to his bedroom on bowed legs. He bypassed the bathroom; cleaning his teeth had never been a priority, and being overweight made him constantly constipated (he could go days without a shit, and when he did, it was usually compacted and tarry).

In the bedroom, he undressed slowly. This nightly ritual was an ordeal that left Tiny Bob bathed in sweat and his lungs wheezing like a set of old bagpipes. With a wet fart that rippled the hairs on his back, he plopped his fleshy backside onto the edge of the bed.

Placing the O2 cylinder against the wall where he could reach it, Tiny Bob toppled backwards onto the cushions, drew the covers over his naked body, and turned off the bedside lamp.

It was exceptionally quiet tonight. Even at this late hour, teenagers would usually be tearing around the estate in their souped-up hot rods, or they'd be domestic rows happening somewhere. But not tonight. On this night, a strange stillness had settled over Furness Drive.

Dweller Under The Roots

Tiny Bob found it more unsettling than if a mini-riot was going on. He couldn't relax. The hush was disconcerting. He rolled over onto his side, the bed springs protesting loudly.

He was cold as well. Being a larger man meant he didn't feel the cold so much, except maybe in the middle of January. Tonight, a chill gripped his rotund head and beer belly. Had he left the window open? No, he'd remember if he had.

Just then, the silence was broken by a familiar sound - the ratcheting chatter of the stairlift whirring down its rail to the downstairs hallway. Tiny Bob held his breath (not a good idea in his condition: a few seconds of not breathing meant he might pass out).

Why was the stairlift descending the stairs? Was it malfunctioning? Unlikely – the service engineer had been to check it out only last week.

The noise from the motor stopped for a few seconds before resuming. Now, it was on the way back up.

A horrible fear gripped him. It felt like a solid steel band around his chest, squeezing like some medieval torture instrument.

"Is somebody there?" he called out, the third word more like an expulsion of air.

That must be it, Tiny Bob thought in a panic. He must have an intruder. Somebody who knew about his health problems had decided to break in bold as brass to steal his belongings, knowing he'd be in no fit state to resist. Craven bastards!

"I'm on the phone to the police right this second!" Tiny Bob bawled, and he reached for the lamp.

The bedroom was burnished in weak orange light, the bulb much dimmer than it should be. He looked towards the door.

He'd left it ajar, but the landing was pitch dark, making it impossible to see anything. The stairlift buzzed loudly as it reached the top step and then faded to a quiet hum.

Tiny Bob listened intently as the patter of tiny feet sounded right outside his door.

Kids, for crying out loud. What was the world coming to when young kids broke into your home in the dead of night? But then, some of the little sods around here were nasty juvenile delinquents and hooligans like their parents.

"Go away, d'you hear me?"

Tiny Bob's breath was coming fast, and a clutching, clasping agony squeezed his heart, joined by a brackish taste in his mouth. He scrabbled with a pudgy hand for the O2 cylinder, turning the valve on and finding the rubber face mask. Quickly, he clamped it over his nose and mouth.

The bedroom door slowly opened with a creak, and something passed through into the room. Tiny Bob couldn't quite tell what it was because the edge of the bed blocked his view. All he knew was it was small and dark, slinking like a shadow. The soft footsteps came again, pitter-pattering over the floor. He cringed away, forcing his head and upper body against the headboard.

Then he saw something that made him utter the words, "God Almighty," and the pain in his chest bloomed like a flower's petals, encompassing every part of his vast body. He groaned in agony, his other hand fluttering weakly in the air.

Something was standing in the corner of his bedroom, facing the wall, a small figure of dark and light that flickered in and out of existence like an image from one of those old black-and-white silent movies. The head started to turn slowly around in Tiny Bob's direction. He could hear the neck bone make a dry sound like old hawsers taking up the strain. Tiny Bob's eyes opened so wide they were in danger of popping right out of his head.

The thing in the corner looked at him, and when he saw the face, so deeply etched from age it resembled crumpled parchment, Tiny Bob experienced such terror that it triggered a cardiac arrest. He arched his back, and the bedsheets fell away, revealing his bare flesh. He wet himself, a stream of urine arcing up and splattering onto his colossal belly. Tiny Bob's chest rattled, and the oxygen mask clouded over.

The manifestation in the corner fluttered like it was losing energy, but with each flash of its fading presence, it danced closer. Then it crawled up Tiny Bob's quivering body, clawing a path up his legs, brushing against his groin, and over his chest. One of its claw-like hands squeezed the rubber hose snaking from the O2 cylinder, stopping the airflow.

The spine-chilling face hovered close to his own, and a pair of white eyes bored right into him.

PART TWO

They drew desirable things to themselves from far-off regions

                              HISTORIA NORWEGIAE
                                     15TH CENTURY

CHAPTER 11

THE NEXT TWENTY-FOUR HOURS went by in a blur for Lee. He had no real sense of being. It was like he was no longer anchored to the world but instead was witnessing events through an unfocused mind. The frightening part was that he had no control over what was happening; he was at the mercy of life's capricious nature.

The only thing Lee did know was that he was no longer in the cottage. On the few occasions when he briefly surfaced from his delirious state, he recognized the room where he endured his ordeal. He was in Amelia's caravan, lying flat on his back on the large double bed in the main bedroom. Lee had no idea how she'd fetched him here, but at one point, he thought he heard a man's voice talking across his resting form, so perhaps she'd had some help.

Amelia attended to his needs with tenderness and care, her gentle voice melting through the brain fog enveloping him. Her cool hands caressed his head, soothing away the crippling headaches. She changed his dressing regularly, administered the necessary medicines to bring down his fever, and sat by his side throughout the night and the following day. Without overstating it, she was the epitome of an Angel of Mercy.

A lousy fever wasn't the worst of Lee's problems. A gnawing pain in his stomach competed with the pounding in his head. Any bright light hurt his eyes. And his ears seemed tuned to every little sound or disturbance.

Sometimes, he'd wake up violently thrashing his limbs and feeling agitated, like he'd had a bad dream — but as soon as he woke, he couldn't recall the dreams.

The man came back late in the afternoon (Lee only had an approximate idea of the day's cycle because the setting sun pushed through the curtains). Lee could hear Amelia and him talking in the front lounge. Their voices roused him, and Lee clawed out of the deep ocean of sleep. He wondered who it was. The talking continued for some time, but they spoke in low tones, and Lee couldn't make out the words. Afterwards, he heard bumping noises, like they were shifting furniture around, and shallow laughter. The front door closed a short time later, and footsteps receded from the caravan.

Lee went back to sleep.

The next time he woke, it was to the aromatic smell of freshly cooked food.

He blinked several times as he reacquainted himself with his surroundings.

"Let me help you sit up," Lee heard Amelia say, and she took his torso and drew him into a sitting position.

"Lean forward."

He did as she asked.

Amelia fluffed his cushions and then eased him gently back against the headboard. He watched as she moved away, then returned carrying a lap tray with foldable legs. She set it down over his thighs.

On it was a steaming bowl of stew and a glass of fizzy mineral water.

"You need to eat," Amelia told him. "Food is the best cure for any illness. And the tonic contains nutrients that will give you a gentle boost."

She took a napkin, flapped it loose, and tucked one corner down his top. She perched herself on the edge of the bed.

"Come on, tuck in. I made it especially for you."

She lifted a spoon and scooped out some pieces of meat and gravy, holding the food near his mouth.

"I think I can manage," Lee said, taking the spoon.

Lee tested the first spoonful by dipping his tongue into it. It was nice. No, it was very nice.

He started to eat, only now realizing how hungry he was. Scrub that, he thought: he was famished.

Lee shovelled in mouthful after mouthful, enjoying the apparent pleasure this brought Amelia.

Then he stopped in his tracks.

"Where did these come from?" he asked, indicating his pyjamas. "Where are my things?"

"Don't worry. I washed your clothes and put them into the cupboard."

Lee tried to remember if he'd retrieved the gun from under the other bed before they'd ridden back to the cottage on Amelia's moped. Yes, he distinctly recalled shoving it back down his sock. Therefore, it must have still been on him when he collapsed onto his bed in the loft room. So where was it now? She had to have spotted it when she'd undressed him.

"Your phone is right next to you."

Lee looked. His mobile was on a small dressing table.

She made no mention of the weapon. If she'd found it, Lee was sure she would have booted him straight out the door or called the cops. Lee reasoned that it could have slipped from his sock and become hidden in the sleeping bag. Pinning his hopes that was the case, he went back to the stew.

"You seem better. You have some colour in your cheeks."

"That's twice you've come to the rescue. I owe you."

"When you phoned me, you hardly made sense. All I could hear was incoherent moaning down the line. I thought it was a dirty caller."

"What made you think otherwise?" Lee asked in between slurps.

"Just a feeling that it was you and something was badly wrong."

"A good job that your spidey senses were working."

"So, what happened? When I left, you seemed to have recovered from the blow to your head."

"Delayed reaction, I guess. Or maybe it's that cottage."

"What do you mean?"

"It's just that whenever I'm there, I either feel very low and moody, or poorly."

Lee told her he'd been unwell on his second night there, before he knocked himself out. He left out the bit about the cat scratch.

"But when I'm here, I feel fine," he finished. "Obviously, I wasn't too cracking last night when you brought me over, but right now, I feel pretty good, considering."

Amelia shook her head.

"What?"

"I've heard some lame excuses from men to stay over, but that has to be the most inventive yet."

"I didn't mean it like that," he blustered.

"Knucklehead."

Lee ate more stew. He used a heel of French bread to mop up the gravy. Then something else occurred to him.

"How did you get me here, by the way? If I've got this right, I was compos mentis and too poorly to walk."

"I used your car. It's parked outside. And I had help from someone."

Lee remembered the man from before.

"Who was it?"

"He's called Dave. Dave Minnock. He's the caravan owner. I told you about him."

Another person who knows I'm here, thought Lee. He dismissed the problem for now. He was just grateful for their assistance.

"He's a nice person, and he values my privacy. He came straight around when I called him on the drive over."

Lee lifted the glass and took a sip. It didn't taste very pleasant. It made him grimace.

"What is this, did you say?"

"A nutritional drink. It contains metatones and vitamin B1."

Lee swallowed a bit more and then returned the glass to the tray.

"Well, can you tell this Dave bloke thankyou from me?"

"You can tell him yourself."

Lee raised his eyebrows.

"He's coming over in the morning. He wants to meet you."

"Why?" Lee tried not to sound too blunt.

"Because I happened to mention that you were staying at the old place in the woods, which perked his interest. Dave has lived around these parts all his life. He's like a font of local knowledge and has some interesting things to tell you about the cottage. Things, he says, that might benefit you."

Amelia came to her feet and clapped her hands to punctuate the end of the exchange.

"Right; it's time you had a bath."

Lee peeled off his pyjamas, hung them on the hook behind the door, and sank into the bath with a grateful sigh.

"How does it feel?" Amelia asked through the bathroom door.

"Bloody good."

Indeed, it did. The hot water immediately eased the aches and pains from the concussion and fever. Amelia had added half a bottle of Radox, so white bubbles rose around his ears when he lay back. He could feel their restorative effect.

"Can I come in?"

Lee checked that nothing was visible and then said she could.

Amelia pushed open the door. She'd changed into jeans and a white blouse, and her blonde hair was tied back with a hair tie. She knelt at the side of the bath. There was a concerned look on her face.

"We ought to clean your wound as regularly as possible."

She reached out and carefully peeled away the dressing from his head. Then she found a clean flannel and gently wiped his face and the injury. Lee felt the tension drain from his body, and his neck and shoulder muscles loosened and relaxed.

After she'd cleaned the wound, Amelia wiped the flannel over his chest, moving her hands in circular movements.

"Nice?"

"Very."

She dipped the flannel into the water, squeezed it over his torso, and massaged soap and bubbles into his skin.

"You've been through the wars," she said, lifting one of his hands and indicating the set of scratches there.

"Tell me about it."

Amelia let the flannel float away and rested her chin on the side of the bath. One of her hands hung over the edge, and she dipped her fingers in the water, lazily stirring the bubbles and making a hole in the surface. She looked down at his engorged penis.

• • •

"It's been a long time," Amelia told him as they entered the bedroom. "You're the first since I split with my ex."

Lee murmured in her ear, and he coaxed her back onto the bed and gently pushed inside her.

They both moaned in unison.

CHAPTER 12

WEDNESDAY TURNED OUT TO BE a significant day for many different reasons. It started pleasantly enough. Following their gentle lovemaking the night before, Lee had slept like a babe alongside Amelia. It was the most rest that he'd had for nearly a week, and for once, it was uninterrupted by dreams or feelings of anxiety. Then he was awoken at daybreak by Amelia searching beneath the covers with her hands, cupping him until he grew erect. They made love again, this time with total abandon until they were spent and bathed in sweat. She climbed down off him and rested her head on his chest, closing her eyes.

As they caught their breath, Lee slid his arm around Amelia's slim, pale shoulders and rested his chin on the crown of her head. He breathed in her scent, a mixture of shampoo and her body's natural fragrance.

Lee stole a peep at her face. Never would he have predicted last night's turn of events. Yes, he'd sensed a certain chemistry between them on their first meeting, and the bond that quickly developed, the orbit of their lives looping together, now seemed fated. But their lovemaking was more than just a mutual release. Lee couldn't deny what was right there before him: he profoundly cared for Amelia on a level he'd never felt for another person before. After just a few days, he'd grown massively attached to her.

It was a nice feeling that Lee could quickly get used to, but it ushered in several challenges.

Foremost among them was how to deal with his current plight.

He shouldn't even be here. Lee's plan called for him to pack his stuff and ship out with the money once his ultimatum to Jacko ran out. It didn't call for him to grow closer to Amelia, falling for her. That wasn't in the script. Now that it had happened, Lee couldn't just leave her. In any case, he didn't want to.

Lee guessed he could tell her everything. How would she react if he confessed to the robbery? If he tried to explain how the Postmaster's son died accidentally? And then, to top it off, asking her to go on the run with him? The idea, it was clear to Lee, was crazy.

It felt like fate was continuously throwing a spanner in the works and foiling his intentions.

Lee felt Amelia stir in his arms, and by the time she turned her face up to him, he'd set his troubles aside and smiled at her.

"What are you thinking?" Amelia asked him.

"Nothing much. Just about us."

"Thanks!" and she playfully dug her elbow into his ribs.

"Last night was nice," he said, then added, "satisfying."

"You're so romantic."

"Hey, I didn't hear you complaining."

She nuzzled against his chest and then nodded. "It was fulfilling."

They were quiet for a few minutes, both seemingly content to dawdle before the commencement of a new day—two people in a holding pattern. Then, entirely unprompted, Amelia started to tell Lee of her breakup.

"Ryan was a bastard before the split and an even bigger one afterwards."

Lee squeezed her shoulder and kissed her hair.

"He was generally disgruntled at life and jealous of his brother's success. His pushy parents didn't help, but they only wanted him to do well for himself. He pushed back against them and left home when he turned eighteen."

Amelia pulled the cotton sheet up so only her head was visible.

"Ryan landed a job as a bouncer in a nightclub – that's where I met him, but that's a whole different story – working ridiculous and unsociable hours. Meanwhile, his brother was designing golf courses in the Middle East and earning big bucks. I think deep down, he regarded himself as a disappointment, not only to his family but also to himself."

Lee heard her give a short and bitter laugh.

"It just made him resentful and insecure. He always blamed somebody for his problems, never once admitting it was all his own doing."

"Sounds like a prat. What did you see in him?"

"I've asked myself that a thousand times, Lee. If only I could turn back the clock. Despite his faults, Ryan could be charming in a cheeky way, you know? He had a reputation for being a bad boy, and he had the patter, and stupid me fell for it hook, line and sinker."

"I'm sure it wasn't your fault, Amelia. You're hardly the first woman to carry a torch for a man like that."

Amelia nodded.

"We hooked up and moved in together. Things were okay initially, and soon after, Ryan was promoted to Bar Manager. But then, he started staying out all night after the club shut, or sometimes he'd arrange to go to the pub with his mates, and the inevitable rumours started."

"He was cheating on you?"

"I never had proof, Lee, but that's what people told me. He denied it, naturally. He was an excellent liar, was Ryan. He should have been a politician. As well as the other women, I also learned he was dealing in the club."

"Selling drugs, you mean?"

"Yes. Ryan tried attracting a better clientele by offering VIP packages to local business people, big wigs from the council, and even a few mini-celebs from Manchester. Instead of selling pints of lager and packets of crisps, Ryan realized he could make more money by offering people champagne and coke. I warned him he'd be found out, but Ryan told me to butt out, that I was interfering in the one thing he was successful at."

"Being a dealer in a club is hardly something to boast about," Lee said.

"It was for Ryan, which tells you something about his outlook on life. A few months later, the club was raided by the police and closed down, and Ryan was nicked. Overnight, he went from being the owner of a busy nightclub to having a criminal record and doing community service. Instead of mixing with his rich friends, he was cleaning graffiti off subway walls."

"My heart bleeds," Lee said, feeling hypercritical.

Amelia squirmed up from under the sheet. Her blonde hair tickled Lee's face, but she didn't seem to notice.

"He blamed me, naturally," she continued. "Said I'd undermined him, called me a wet blanket. He even hinted that it was me who tipped off the police. We rowed, and he packed up his things and moved out. He was so distraught that he sought comfort in the bed of one of his ex-employees."

"Sleazebag."

"Neanderthal, more like. He did it partly to hurt me and partly to make me jealous. Ryan thought the best way to win me back was to shag another woman. Can you actually believe that?"

"I hope you didn't forgive him."

"No way! I made it clear we were history. And that dented his pride more than getting arrested – the thought that he'd blown it for good. So he went all out to destroy me. He said it was all my fault, that I was the one who'd been unfaithful, that I'd slung him out and refused to patch things up. He'd turn up at work and cause horrible scenes in front of my boss, and he shared private photos by sending them to my family."

"Private photos?" asked Lee carefully. "Do you mean..?"

Amelia nodded, and Lee saw her cheeks redden.

"What a twat."

"The saddest part is that my family was so ashamed that they refused to involve the police and told me to move away."

"They did what?" Lee sat bolt upright, causing Amelia to slide down his torso. He drew her back up and held her tightly.

"As I said, he went to work on my character, and being the charmer that he is, with a certain way with words and a soppy expression on his face, my family swallowed his story and accepted his version over mine."

"That's priceless. Your parents disowned their own daughter?"

"More or less," Amelia sniffled quietly.

Lee took the corner of the bedsheet and carefully dabbed her damp cheeks.

"The only person who took my side was Dave, Dave Minnock."

"And he let you stay in his caravan so you could try to sort yourself out?"

"Yes. Without Dave, I'd have had a total breakdown. As it was, I was a mess. Dave provided me with a refuge and words of encouragement."

"Did you know him beforehand?" enquired Lee.

"A little."

Amelia wiped away the last of her tears and took a deep breath.

"We moved in the same circles, and a mutual acquaintance put us in touch," she explained. "As soon as he learned of my plight, Dave immediately offered me the use of this place. It's his summer home, which he rarely uses, so he said I should move in rather than have the caravan sitting empty most of the year. He also helped me in other ways."

"Go on."

"When I told Dave about my ex harassing me and making my life a living hell, he said he would go and speak with Ryan. Which he did. One evening, he visited Ryan and had, Dave later told me, a very mature chat with him, man-to-man. I don't know exactly what was said, but Ryan left me alone following their meeting. I haven't heard a peep from him since."

Lee was astonished because, going off Amelia's portrait of her ex-boyfriend, he didn't seem the sort of man to back down so quickly.

"Did he threaten Ryan or something? Or harm him?"

"Dave?" Amelia laughed. "Not in a million years. He's the most peaceful person in the world. Anyway, I spotted Ryan about a month ago while shopping at Sainsbury's. He didn't see me, so out of curiosity, I followed him outside. The odd thing was, Ryan didn't look well. He's lost lots of weight and was white as a sheet. He caught a bus, and in my last glimpse of him, he was just sitting and staring straight ahead, like someone in a trance. It was weird."

Amelia gave a slight shake of her head like the recollection left her feeling perturbed.

"Well, whatever Dave said to Ryan, it did the trick," Lee remarked. "I think I'd like to shake his hand."

Just then, they were interrupted by a knock on the caravan's front door.

"It looks like you might get the chance," Amelia said, slipping out of the bed and scrabbling for her clothes. "That's Dave now."

CHAPTER 13

DAVE MINNOCK'S ARRIVAL TOOK LEE by surprise because he hadn't heard a vehicle pull up outside, therefore he must have come on foot. The knock on the door was loud, indicating a big chap, so Lee was surprised when a compact and snazzily dressed man entered the caravan. Middle-aged, carrying a shoulder bag and wearing a leather jerkin, faded green out-of-fashion corduroy trousers, and a yellow neckerchief, the visitor seemed to bounce on the balls of his feet with excess energy.

Lee stood back and watched Amelia and Dave embrace somewhat extravagantly, like long-parted friends, which was odd considering he'd been here only yesterday. They whispered for a moment, and Lee was just starting to feel awkward when Amelia turned and introduced them both.

Dave Minnock stepped forward, pumped Lee's hand, and gripped his forearm robustly.

"Good to see you on your feet, laddie."

Lee detected a Cumbrian accent and a hint of Scot, suggesting Dave Minnock hailed from just south of the border – perhaps Carlisle.

"Well, I have the two of you to thank for getting me over here."

Dave looked aghast and made a bizarre raspberry sound, saying, "When Milly calls for help, I know it's serious. By extension, the same applies to her friends. Speaking of which, she tells me you require assistance with another matter?"

Lee looked at him nonplussed.

"The old house? The cottage, man? I hear you've been having problems?" he said, making inverted commas with his fingers.

"Erm, you could say that. What precisely has she told you?" Lee asked, cutting his eyes at Amelia.

"I mentioned that you found the place odd and have experienced a few strange incidents, such as doors opening themselves and hearing voices in the woods."

"I'm sure they all have mundane explanations. An old building like that is bound to be full of cold draughts, leaky roofs, and broken plumbing," Lee pointed out.

Amelia shared a look with Dave. "Lee likes to find rational, simplified interpretations for what he's witnessed. Even for strange events that he's seen with his own eyes."

"It's better than going down the other route."

"Even when they tie in with the local folklore I told you about?" Amelia responded and rolled her eyes.

"Be that as it may, these incidents, real or imagined, certainly chime with what I've discovered over the years," said Dave. "I was particularly fascinated with the photographs Amelia sent me."

"What photos are those?"

"You know, Lee? The ones I took in the wise woman's apothecary."

"The root cellar, you mean?"

"Yes, the root cellar."

"Shall we sit down?" Dave suggested, steering them both across to the dining table.

Reluctantly, Lee slid onto the seat beside Amelia while Dave sat opposite them. From his shoulder bag, he produced a laptop. He powered it up.

"I've catalogued much of my work on here," he said by way of explanation.

"Do you study this stuff?"

"Not in any qualified way. I'm no expert in tales of the supernatural, far from it. But I am a very keen amateur historian. A hobbyist and student of tales, myths, and legends connected with this area."

"A bit like Percival," Lee said under his breath.

"Percival the Tramp, do you mean?" Dave enthused, his eyes sharpening. "You've read his book, then?"

"Some of it."

"Marvelous! Percival was an extraordinary man. He was much maligned and ostracised by society during his day. But much of what he said is making more and more sense to modern minds. But we'll come to him later."

Dave spun his laptop around so Lee and Amelia could see the screen. On it was an image.

"Do you two lovebirds know what this is?"

Lee and Amelia leaned forward and scrutinized the image. It appeared to be an old carving depicting a village scene. Lee could see houses and trees, and in the middle, two women surrounded by a circle of figures wearing strange masks with oversized beaks.

"I have no freaking idea," Lee admitted.

"It's what is called a woodcut. They were carvings used by printing presses to produce single-sheet pamphlets. Sometimes, they might contain religious images and be sold to the public. Most date from medieval times, but they actually originated in China thousands of years ago. This particular one is more recent, from the mid eighteen-hundreds."

Dave reached around the laptop and tapped the pair of figures in the middle.

"Do you know who these two are?"

Lee looked. One was tall and one short, both of them in shapeless shifts torn at the hem. Their features were indistinct. On reflection, one might have been a child.

"I ain't got a clue," he said.

"Have you heard of Mother Baxter and Long Meg?" asked Dave.

Lee looked over the top of the laptop and saw Dave's earlier jovial expression had now been replaced by a stern and darker look.

"Should I have?" Lee enquired, thinking that he didn't really want to know because he sensed he wasn't going to like it.

"It's not surprising. The story of Mother Baxter isn't well known, even in these parts. Considering the events I'm about to tell you about occurred right here in this area, it's strange that more people haven't heard of her. It's like the tale has been purposefully forgotten. Consciously suppressed."

Dave clicked on a key, and another photo of another woodcut popped up.

"Here they are again."

Lee and Amelia peered at the image. This one showed four women, each holding what appeared to be tiny poppets. They were conversing with a black devil-shaped monster with enormous bat-like wings. Above them flew a giant dragonfly. Two of the women again had fuzzy faces.

"And once again. This time, Mother Baxter and two companions."

Dave hit the key, and a third picture appeared in black ink. It depicted three figures flying on broomsticks: a woman in a conical hat, the devil again, and a man with a scythe. Townsfolk cowered far below in tilled fields.

"A witch?" said Lee, the word expelling from his mouth in disdain.

"Wise woman," Amelia corrected him. "Cunning folk."

"The term witch means different things to different people, even today. So, you are both correct," Dave offered.

"So, who exactly was Mother Baxter and Long Meg?" Lee asked, sitting back against the leather seat and folding his arms.

"Mother Baxter was a folk healer in modern parlance. She had quite a reputation amongst the villagers and farmers hereabouts for her help to the sick and infirm. According to what I've learned, she also had a more macabre side. She allegedly practiced the dark arts and conversed with imps and daemons from the underworld."

Lee tried and failed to stop a smirk from crossing his face. He glanced from Dave's serious expression to Amelia, tucked in beside the window. He was dismayed to see a frightened shadow behind her intense gaze. He pushed at the inside of his cheek with his tongue, literally having to bite down on any sarcastic remarks.

"Don't worry, Lee. I get that sort of response regularly. You're hardly the first person to be so derisive."

"I didn't say anything."

"You didn't have to," Dave said.

"When was all of this happening?" Lee asked briskly.

"During the mid-nineteenth century."

"Isn't that a little late? I thought witchcraft was big around the time of the English Civil War. The Pendle Witch Trial was in –"

"Sixteen Twelve," said Dave. "And yes, you are correct. Most witch trials and persecutions occurred during the Middle Ages. Pendle is the most famous case in England and Salem in North America. But there were other witch trials in Bideford and Chelmsford. Witchcraft has been practiced for thousands of years in all parts of the world and continues today, although in a very watered-down version."

"And you're going to tell me that this Mother Baxter once lived in the cottage, aren't you?"

Dave didn't reply; he merely looked at Lee sadly.

"What about Long Meg? Who was she, and how does she feature in all this?"

"Long Meg was Mother Baxter's illegitimate daughter. The legend goes that she was born during a thunderstorm with a terribly deformed face. She was also a hunchback."

Lee gritted his teeth, remembering the crooked crone with the malformed features.

"So why the name Long Meg?"

"Coined by the locals, no doubt, as some form of rotten joke. The name stuck: even her mother called her that. Long Meg was also afflicted with the cackling sickness."

"Oh, come on! What on earth is the cackling sickness?"

"Just what it sounds like, Lee," said Dave. "Instead of bawling like most newborns do when they arrive in this world, Long Meg was heard to cackle. For three years, she never cried. Instead, she cackled loudly. Villagers could hear her from afar, particularly at night. Because of that and her infirmities, the other children shunned her, and nasty gossip soon spread. People went to visit Mother Baxter for help with their ailments, but they did everything they could to avoid her infant child."

"That's awful," said Amelia.

"Yes, it is. But even as recently as Victorian England, old beliefs and superstitions ruled people's everyday lives, especially in small communities like Hardcastle Crags. Simple misunderstandings or falsehoods might create an emotional atmosphere and mistrust of people like Mother Baxter and Long Meg. Mistrust might lead to fear, and fear to hatred. Which is precisely what happened in our story."

Lee ran a hand through his hair, his fingers catching on the wound on his temple. He winced and looked at spots of blood on his fingertips. He rubbed away the marks and swatted his hand in the air.

"You've told me this much, so you might as well tell me the rest. What became of Mother Baxter and her poor child?"

"Well, as a folk healer, Mother Baxter's abilities primarily embraced herbal medicine and folk wisdom. As I alluded to, however, they sometimes overlapped into areas of witchcraft and high magic, like alchemy, reciting charms to cause people harm, spiral dancing, things like that."

"What's spiral dancing?" interrupted Amelia.

"Sometimes called the weaver's dance, it's a ritual that pagans have performed since the megalithic era, and more recently by followers of Wicca. By dancing counterclockwise to drums, exponents hope to raise archaic powers and reach the zenith of their abilities."

Amelia chewed on her bottom lip, seemingly turning things over in her mind.

"Mother Baxter's skills were much in demand. The lower classes – I guess you would refer to them as the disadvantaged – could not afford to consult men of medicine, so instead, they turned to Mother Baxter."

"It's like I told you yesterday, Lee," interjected Amelia once more. "If people became ill, had an injury, or sought love, she helped them. Do you remember?"

"Yes. I also distinctly remember you saying these so-called wise men and wise women weren't wizards or witches."

Amelia fell quiet.

"It's difficult to be precise about what occurred because there is limited mention of Mother Baxter in local records," Dave told them both. "It seems she lived an extremely secluded life and had no siblings or close friends. It's not certain that she hailed from here – or if she was English. Even so, word got around, and folk travelled miles seeking her help."

Dave folded his hands on the tabletop.

"Amongst those wishing to avail themselves of Mother Baxter's services were the men building the dams for the reservoirs. The three reservoirs on the High Moor were constructed between 1853 and 1857, and granite for the dams was mined right here," Dave said, pointing at the tunnel mouth on the hillside outside, "then transferred over the Blake Dean trestle bridge on locomotives using the narrow gauge railway."

Dave stirred, and his brown leather jerkin creaked.

"It was hard, demanding work involving long hours for little pay. It was also extremely hazardous. Accidents happened: broken legs, crushed hands, et cetera."

Lee tried to imagine the scene. He pictured the wooden bridge spanning the valley, with steam locomotives trundling back and forth. He heard the sounds of pickaxes striking stones, of men cursing, and pit ponies braying.

"One afternoon, one unfortunate chap suffered a nasty fall near the steam-winding house and was left with a broken spine. He was screaming hell for leather, and the onsite quack could do nothing to alleviate his pain. Desperate, the chap's workmates carried him down from the pithead tunnel, into the woods, and along the crooked path to Mother Baxter's home."

He gave a sad shake of his head.

"Now, curing one's warts or setting a broken femur is one thing, but helping a person with a broken back is something else. According to the scant information I've unearthed, Mother Baxter did everything she could. She was able to help ease the chap's agony – she probably fed him a mixture of absinthe and white willow bark – but how do you treat a broken back, I ask? What did they expect from her? Miracles? None of her herbs and potions would help, so the miners implored her to try something else, anything else. They asked Mother Baxter to apply her knowledge of the dark arts."

Lee felt suddenly weak, his mind brittle. To think this happened in the very cottage he was staying in. A sense of doom started to take hold inside.

"At first, Mother Baxter refused. She told the men it would be useless. So they threatened her. Finally, she agreed. But she would only carry out the dangerous task if they waited outside. They were not to intervene no matter what sounds they heard from within the cottage. Having little option, the other miners filed back through the door and prepared to await events."

Dave steepled his hands and rested his forehead against his fingers, looking down at the tabletop. Lee wasn't sure if this was all hammy and staged or whether he was genuinely disturbed at relating his story.

"Nobody knows what went on inside the cottage that afternoon. For two or three hours, the men milled around in the herb garden as from inside came the sounds of chanting, of wild snorting and – this is the mad part – the stomping of animal hooves and the stink of manure."

Lee and Amelia looked at one another, remembering her old school friend's experience.

"The woods grew dark as dusk arrived early, and odd lights glowed from the pathway, like an avenue of faerie lights," Dave related in flowery prose, like he'd witnessed events firsthand. "Overhead, clouds swirled in majestic patterns even though there was no breeze. It grew icy cold. The men very near lost their nerve and fled. But then, just as they were preparing to bolt, the cottage door opened, and out came their friend: the chap with the broken back."

"He was cured?" Lee asked in awe. "Mother Baxter fixed his broken back?"

Dave looked up with a weird vulpine grin, revealing rows of tiny teeth. Lee could have sworn he saw tears glistening in his eyes.

"If only, laddie," Dave whispered. "If only."

"Well, what happened?"

"The men fled back to their homes, struck dumb with horror. Only one could describe to his wife what he saw emerging from the cottage, and he also sketched this image."

Dave turned the laptop around, scrolled with the mousepad briefly, and then spun it back around. Lee and Amelia flinched in unison.

On the screen was a pencil sketch of some hideous thing, some monster from the miner's terrified mind. It was dressed in rags that clung to its form in tatters. The face was barely human, with what Lee initially thought were antlers coming from its head. On closer inspection, he realized they were gnarled branches. Other than that, nothing was recognizable as belonging to any known species. The flesh was gone from the torso, leaving misshapen rib bones and a long backbone that tapered to a point. Four skeletal arms, two on each side, had tree roots instead of fingers. There were no legs; the creature hovered above the ground.

"The poor fella who sketched this was almost catatonic, but he was able to say the arms moved up and down like a clockwork scarab, and it made a hideous howling sound, deep and resonant."

Through his horror, the image reminded Lee of something from a Ray Harryhausen movie. If the witness was cuckoo, his mind disturbed from what happened, could his account – this sketch – be trusted, Lee asked himself. On the other hand, if it was real, and this creature existed.

Lee never completed his thought because Dave continued with his narrative.

"Following the encounter with this hideous spectre in the woods, word quickly spread. A night curfew was enforced, forbidding villagers from leaving their homes after dark. They stayed away from the woods and no longer visited Mother Baxter for treatment. The few times she and Long Meg visited the hamlet of Hardcastle Crags, people spat at them in the street, and children fled in terror. The man with the broken back was never seen again, and it was presumed he was dead. His widow soon demanded revenge, perhaps fearing her departed husband was cursed to haunt the land forever."

Lee thought he knew where the story was going. He'd heard enough tales of people pronounced for a witch and lynch mobs bearing flaming torches. But he had no idea how wretched events in the past were to become.

CHAPTER 14

"FEAR BREEDS HATRED," DAVE SAID. "It festers like a rotten canker."

As he told them this, he loosened the yellow neckerchief, unravelled it, and used it to wipe condensation from his forehead. Amelia had found a bottle of whiskey and poured them each a good measure, and Dave reached for his glass with shaking fingers.

"The days of The Witchfinder General and The Spanish Inquisition were dark times throughout Europe. All it took was for a neighbour or a naughty child to point the finger, and your fate was sealed. Scant proof of guilt was required: an extra teat on your body or trial by ducking stool. Every woman with a wrinkled face, a hairy lip, a gobbertooth, and a squint eye was suspected as a witch. You'll be familiar with common torture instruments employed to force confessions, like the Scavenger's Daughter, the Wheel of Catherine, and the Judas Cradle."

He took another long swallow of whiskey.

"By the middle of the nineteenth century, all that was supposed to be behind us. Great Britain was the centre of an enlightened world, the beating heart of the Industrial Revolution. Witches being hung or burnt at the stake was for an earlier, less civilized age. That may have been the case in the big cities and towns, but if you lived in the hills and hamlets of northern England and found yourself at the centre of rumour and gossip, malicious whispers and scandalous tittle-tattle, resulting in a man's death and the appearance of some monstrous creature, as Mother Baxter found herself, then…"

Dave left the rest unsaid.

"The locals eventually found the courage to do something about it. One evening, a bunch of them gathered at Gibson Mill, a mixture of pit workers and railroad navvies. They had some dogs with them, and the whole lot crossed the packhorse bridge at Nathan's Folly and slogged through the woods to Mother Baxter's cottage. They probably felt emboldened by their numbers because they marched right up to her door and without knocking, they forced their way inside. The child, Long Meg, fled into the cellar and escaped through some hidden passage, but Mother Baxter wasn't so fortunate. She was shoved outside, paraded before the jeering crowd, and falsely accused of various deeds, amongst them having lured children into her home to draw blood from them. Then her hands were bound, and the rabble dragged into the woods."

Beside him, Lee felt Amelia shudder. He took her hand and she leaned against him.

"The mob tied her to a tree and placed a set of branks over her head."

"What is a set of branks?"

"A scold's bridle," Dave answered Lee. "Often called a witch's bridle. An iron framework that acted as a muzzle with a bit spiked through the tongue to silence the wearer from speaking. They probably feared Mother Baxter might curse them or something. Then they set the dogs onto her–"

"Jeez," said Lee.

"–and watched as they tore Mother Baxter apart. Once they were sure she was dead, they gathered up her remains, and she was buried in some secret spot, most likely at a crossroads somewhere, a practice that stemmed from medieval folklore."

The caravan fell silent for a stretch as Lee and Amelia absorbed the full horror of what had taken place. It was impossible not to visualize the gruesome events, so vivid a picture had Dave painted.

After a minute, Lee rubbed his knuckles against his scalp and surfaced from his thoughts.

"You said Long Meg escaped. What became of her?"

Dave spread his hands.

"Nobody knows. From that day on, she was never seen or heard from again. Some think she sought shelter in an outlying farm many miles distant. Other stories have her fetching up at the children's home at Midgehole – I find that unlikely; because of her flawed appearance, blighted with a deformed face and a twisted spine, she would run the risk of being recognized, and even though she was only a child, Long Meg was as crafty as a fox. Personally, I think she'd have wandered around in the woods or made her way onto the moors and become lost, then had some accident and perished from exposure. Whatever the case, Long Meg is long dead by now."

"In the meantime, the villagers got away with murder," Amelia pointed out in a glum voice.

"Aided by a conspiracy of silence. When it comes to a dreadful record of sin, Mel, the beautiful, smiling countryside beats cities like London and Manchester every single time."

Dave scrolled through his laptop for a few moments, explaining as he did what happened next after Mother Baxter's demise.

"To ensure Mother Baxter could not return," Dave did that inverted commas thing with his fingers again, "the townsfolk took certain precautions. They placed magical items at various spots around the cottage as protection against witchcraft. They acted as a last line of defence."

"What sort of magical items?"

"Things like these," and he turned the screen so they could see a collage of images. "It could have been any number of objects, Lee. Shoes were quite common, placed beneath the hearth. Witch bottles containing urine, hair, pieces of red thread and pins might be buried under the threshold or below the house. Silver coins, mummified cats in walls."

Dave stopped in his tracks because he'd seen the look on Lee's face.

"Have you found any such items?" Dave enquired.

"I might have seen one of these witch bottle things. It was in the cellar. I remember it had pieces of red string wrapped around rusty nails."

Dave nodded sagely and leaned forward over the tabletop. "Did you remove it?"

"No, I didn't even touch it."

"Good… good."

"But there's something else. I found the remains of a dead cat bricked up behind the chimney breast, so I threw it out."

"That's not so good."

"I assumed it must have become trapped and died," Lee explained. "I had no idea that it acted as some anti-witch charm or a safeguard or whatever. Shall I put it back?"

"I don't think it works like that, sadly. Once you've removed the apotropaic object, you'll have immediately left the cottage and yourself wide open to psychic attack from supernatural manifestations."

Lee could feel the inside of his mouth become dry, and he had difficulty swallowing.

"Of course, these things only work if their intended victim is prone to swallow that sort of thing," Dave added. "It's all to do with the power of suggestion. Spells and curses. If one firmly believes a long-dead witch has put a hex on them, then that by itself is enough. An open-minded person might suddenly be convinced they feel unwell or that some bad omen is about to befall them."

"That rules Lee out then," Amelia said quietly, trying to bring some levity to the situation.

"Is there anything else, Lee? Any odd episodes that you can't explain?"

Lee cast his mind back over the few days he'd spent at the cottage. Then he recalled something.

"There was one thing."

"Go on," Amelia and Dave said in unison.

"There was a brown powder on the bedroom floor. At first, I thought it was soil, but when I sniffed it, the stuff smelled of seaweed. I got it all over my feet."

"Sounds like a foot-track spell."

"Come again?"

"A foot-track spell. Placed on the floor by someone who wishes you harm. Their ingredients vary, depending on if they want you dead or maybe to suffer a stroke or be struck down with dementia. They tend to contain elements from animal foetuses, a baby's blood, and soil from the grave of the recently departed. Revolting things like that. You walked through it, you say?"

"Yes."

"Did you feel unwell afterwards?"

"I felt a bit under the weather the following day, suffering bad headaches and belly aches. But they soon passed."

"That's probably because, at the time, you'd have been a total sceptic. Therefore, the spell had little effect on you. Whoever placed it there was testing you, Lee. Probing for weak spots. Your cynicism may have saved you, which I find rather ironic."

"Yeah, it's a right belly laugh," Lee thought aloud.

"If I were you, I'd wash your feet well, just to be on the safe side and alleviate any residual aftereffects."

"I had a bath last night."

"Superb. Try not to worry about it, laddie. We have more important concerns."

"Such as?"

"Such as, what are we to do about Mother Baxter?" Dave said, making spooky sound effects.

•   •   •

"Tell me," Lee said. "How does Percival the Tramp figure in all this, other than writing a book?"

"Ah, now that is another mystery in a sorry tale full of mysteries."

The mystery Dave Minnock was referring to was what linked a homeless vagabond with the gruesome execution of a persecuted folk healer.

Percival's life sounded a romantic one: a drifter leading a nomadic existence plodding around the countryside, sleeping in empty barns or beneath hedgerows, befriending the country folk, and gathering together extraordinary parables for his book, A Vagabond On The Green Roads of England.

"Of all the stories he heard, it was that of Mother Baxter and her daughter that caught Percival's imagination the most," Dave said fondly.

He switched off the laptop and returned it to his shoulder bag.

"A few years after the book came out, Percival returned to investigate further."

"Had his circumstances improved after the launch of his book?"

"Hardly. Percival's book didn't sell well, and he was still living a down-at-heel existence. In the intervening time, the poor chap's health deteriorated. He had "tummy rot" as he liked to tell people, but it was actually bowel cancer. Percival didn't have long to live, so he embarked on one last journey and quest: to seek the truth of what happened here all those years ago."

"And did he?"

"Find the answers he sought?"

Dave shrugged at his own question.

"Percival returned to Hardcastle Crags to discover what turned those men into killers. Was it a case of simple revenge? Or had they become so bent on desperate measures that they'd do whatever it took to rid the place of evil? Sadly, Lee, we'll probably never know because that is where Percival's story ends. He died a short time later and was given a pauper's funeral."

Dave came to his feet and slung the bag over his shoulder.

"He became a part of The Story of Mother Baxter. Kind of fitting, you could say."

Dave slid out from behind the table. At the door, he turned to look at Lee and Amelia. Lee wanted to thank him again for coming to his aid and helping Amelia with her ex, but after everything he'd learned in the last couple of hours, his head was full of other matters.

"What are we going to do about Mother Baxter?" he managed, passing Dave's question back to him.

"That, I don't know."

Dave opened the door.

"But we have to do something," he added over his shoulder as he stepped outside.

CHAPTER 15

"HE CAN'T JUST LEAVE," LEE said, watching Dave Minnock's retreating figure. "If we're going to figure this out, we'll need his expert advice."

"Don't worry. He just needs time to absorb all the facts and develop a strategy. Dave's pool of knowledge is bottomless, but he's also very practical. I'm sure some plan will spring to mind."

"Well, I hope he comes up with something fast."

"Why?"

Lee watched for a moment until Dave disappeared from view across the stream, and then he considered Amelia's upturned face.

"It's just a sense that events are quickly heading towards some big endgame."

Amelia thought about that for a few seconds, then nodded.

"Come on," Lee said. "Let's stretch our legs."

Amelia lent him a parka with a fur-lined hood and slipped on her red trench coat, and they strolled over the rocky ground for several minutes. They shortly found themselves heading towards one of the concrete supports that once bore the trestle bridge. All that remained was a pile of stones. On the ground was a small plaque. Lee bent over and picked it up, but the words had become smudged and rusty. He tossed it aside.

Leaning back, Lee looked skyward and tried to visualize what the wooden bridge looked like as it spanned the valley from one hillside to another.

"D'you fancy a hike?" he asked, pointing at the tunnel mouth clinging to one slope.

"If you're up to it."

"For certain."

"Wait here while I go and fetch the flashlight."

While Amelia hurried back to the caravan, Lee looked around at his surroundings. Today, the area was very peaceful, but around the time the dams were being built, this place would have been bustling with activity. The sound of locomotives loudly venting steam once echoed along the valley, and hundreds of men would make the journey each morning and evening to work and back, sweating, dirty, and tired.

Fast forward a hundred and seventy years, and the contrast couldn't have been more pronounced. The valley was a calm oasis with scant signs of its industrious past. It was quite a beautiful spot with heather and gorse clinging to the valley sides. Other than the two of them, Lee couldn't see a single person.

Or at least, he thought that was the case until a sudden flash on the opposite slope caught his attention. Lee turned his eyes in that direction, squinting. Again, something in the thick gorse along the ridgeline flashed brightly two or three times in succession, like the sun was glinting off something.

It could have been a broken bottle, but equally, it might be reflecting off a pair of binoculars.

Lee shielded his eyes but couldn't be sure at this distance. If there was someone over there, they were keeping their heads down in the gorse bushes. Of course, it might not mean they were observing Lee; it could be an innocent birdwatcher.

Perplexed but not overly anxious, Lee said nothing to Amelia when she rejoined him, and they started up the hillside.

After five minutes, they were both out of breath. The going was more challenging than it looked from the valley bottom, and the hillside steepened the higher they went. The grass was replaced by loose stones and scree, forcing them to crouch over and use their hands. Lee pointed out a more manageable route diagonally across the slope, which should take them to the tunnel.

Eventually, they came out on a natural basalt shelf close to the summit.

With hands on their hips and drawing in lungfuls of air, they looked out over the deep valley.

"Wow," Amelia said in a ragged voice.

It summed up the view perfectly. The stunning vista stretched for miles. In one direction were the purple moorlands extending to Top Withens in Bronte Country, and in the other was the vast woodland sweeping down to

Hebden Bridge. The canopy of trees was too dense to see the cottage, but way off in the distance was the old mansion that had caught fire many moons ago.

They approached the tunnel mouth. The entrance had been boarded up. A warning sign read:

CAUTION – NO ENTRANCE – DANGER OF ROCKFALLS

Ignoring the warning, Lee prised a section of wood aside and peered in. It was too shadowy to see much until Amelia turned on the flashlight. The powerful beam revealed a set of narrow rail lines and sleepers disappearing into the distance.

He turned to her.

"What do you think? Shall we take a look?"

"It looks a little dangerous."

"We'll just go a short way. Agreed?"

After a moment's hesitation, Amelia nodded.

Lee went first, squeezing his frame through the narrow gap. As soon as he was inside, he felt something fluttering wildly just before his face, flying away into the darkness. Lee hoped it was a roosting pigeon and not a bat. Amelia grunted, and he turned to see she was stuck fast in the opening where her coat had caught. He reached back and helped free her.

"We can abandon the idea if you like."

"No way. You're supposed to be the one afraid of the dark, remember?"

She waggled her head and brushed by him.

"You go first, then," he said quietly, and he hurried to catch up.

Dweller Under The Roots

In the tunnel wall was a small steel door, partially ajar. Amelia played the flashlight beam inside, revealing a spacious room on the other side. It appeared to be a blacksmith's workshop with a blackened forge and an anvil. On the wall were various hammers and tongues. In the corner stood a hand bellows; the leather had rotted into thin tatters.

Still present after all this time was a heavy funk of soot and hot metal; it made them wrinkle their noses.

Lee stepped inside and approached something on the floor. He pushed it around with his foot. It was a leather apron and a hood with a square glass visor.

"Hey, look here."

Lee swung around. Amelia was standing by a shelf, rummaging around inside a wooden box.

"It's an antique first aid kit," she told him when he walked over. "There are still various pieces of medical equipment inside. Old scalpels, some forceps. Oh Lord!"

She held up an amputation saw.

"Are those rust marks or blood stains?" Lee asked her, pointing at the blade.

"Urgh!" Amelia cried and dropped the saw back into the box.

"This room must have doubled as the first aid station before the mine was abandoned."

"Looks more like a torture chamber to me."

"You're probably not far wrong, Amelia. Heaven help you if you worked here and had an accident."

"Do you think this is where they treated the miner with the broken back?" Amelia asked.

"I'd guess so."

They spent a few minutes combing around, and then Lee led her back to the main tunnel.

He pointed at the tracks, saying, "Let's see where they lead."

Together, they moved deeper into the dark tunnel, their feet crunching on the stone ballast.

CHAPTER 16

FROM HIS POSITION ON THE far hillside, Dave Minnock watched the two figures disappear into the tunnel mouth. Sighing deeply, he lowered the binoculars. A cloud of midges was buzzing close to his face, but he hardly noticed. His thoughts were turned inwards, dwelling on the talk the three of them had in the caravan.

He'd been happy to share his insights on the legend of Mother Baxter, but there was no doubt Lee's arrival on the scene created a new set of challenges. Chief amongst them was: what exactly was he doing here, and would his presence hinder or help Dave? Another concern: they'd clearly spent the night together because Dave's heightened senses smelt the pheromones and bodily secretions coming off them in waves. Some human emotions, such as passion, lust, and desire, were beneficial, but in Dave's view, tenderness and affection were weaknesses people wallowed in.

He'd have to be watchful.

In the meantime.

Dave clambered to his feet and brushed the dirt off his clothes. Slipping the binoculars into the shoulder bag, he retraced his steps along a narrow sheep trail that wound down through the gorse. After several minutes of difficult walking, he reached the foot of the hill. Skipping across the stream, Dave bypassed the caravan and Lee's car and followed a little-known shortcut through the woodland.

He whistled a merry little tune as he bounded along.

Thirty minutes later, Dave caught the Number 64 bus from the bus stop at Midgehole. He chose a seat near the back behind a lady saddled with a small child. Wiping condensation off the window, he peered at the countryside and houses. The kid, a pesky boy with sticky-out ears, watched him over the seat back, and Dave pulled a few funny faces for him, all the while whispering a few passages from DE OCCULTA HONORIUS. Tonight, the boy's sleep would be disturbed by scary dreams, and his mother would receive some bad news concerning her sister in the morning.

Dave alighted from the bus outside the old Picture House in Hebden Bridge and cut through the park to the footbridge over the river. From there, a pathway led towards York Street, a narrow road crammed with seedy bedsits. Ducking beneath washing lines, Dave pushed past a cluster of wheelie bins into a shabby backyard. He stepped up to a door with peeling red paint and knocked twice.

He heard movement inside, and a shadow moved behind the lace curtain before the door opened, scraping on the uneven floor.

A gaunt man with a pale face and haunted eyes peeked out, blinking against the afternoon light.

"Hello, Ryan."

The man standing in the doorway visibly recoiled in shock when he recognized his visitor. He immediately glanced down at his feet and adopted a cowed posture.

"What do you want?" he stammered in a timid voice.

"Now that's no way to greet a friend," said Dave, smiling. "May I come in?"

The man named Ryan opposed him for a few seconds before nodding almost imperceptibly and standing aside. Dave walked in and refamiliarized himself with the bedsit's interior. It was as he remembered: filthy, furnished with mouldy furniture, and tiny. What few personal possessions Ryan owned were covered in grime or dust. A cheap curtain acted as a wall, the only thing that separated the living room from the bedroom. An underlying stink of male BO permeated the air.

Dave turned when he heard the door close. Ryan stood meekly near the sink, shifting nervously from foot to foot. Dave looked at him, noticing how he could not withstand his gaze.

What a weakling, Dave thought. What a pitiful excuse for a man.

But he had his uses.

"You're nae looking very well," Dave remarked. "You need to look after yourself. Get some food inside you, have a shave, and get some fresh air, that sort of thing. This place could do with a clean as well, Ryan. Otherwise your landlord will be booting you out. And then where will you go?"

Ryan didn't answer. He just shrugged and shuffled across to the sofa.

"How's Amelia?" he asked instead.

"Amelia is none of your concern. I told you that the last time we spoke."

Dave looked around for somewhere to sit, but there was nowhere. It really was a pigsty in here; he counted at least three plates crusted with old meals, and on the mantlepiece was a cup brimming with cigarette butts. He settled for leaning against the windowsill, his hands clasped almost demurely before him.

"It's in your best interests if you pretend you never met her, Ryan. Do you understand?"

Another nod.

"How is your community service going?" Dave asked, changing the subject.

Ryan looked off to one side and mumbled something monosyllabic.

"I didnae hear you."

"It's okay."

"Okay? Is that all you can offer?"

"I'm nearly done. Just two more weeks to go."

"That's good," Dave said, not giving two figs. "Then you can think about getting a proper job, can't you?"

"S'pose."

"There's the spirit! So positive!"

Dave stared at the man on the sofa like a spider might look at a fly. What a contrast he was to the cocksure, arrogant, and bullying prick he once was. The change was staggering. Now

Dweller Under The Roots

Ryan was a mere shadow of his former self, a haunted and frightened maggot, jumping at his own shadow.

"Are your nights still disturbed, Ryan?"

"Uh?" Ryan twitched like someone had shaken his hand with a novelty hand buzzer.

"Your nights? Are you visited during the night hours?"

Ryan seemed unsure of what to say. He opened his mouth like a guppy fish several times, but no words came out.

"Of course you are. It was a silly question. Those things you see when it grows dark and you are here all alone are driving you to the brink of a breakdown, aren't they? And now they follow you around during the daytime as well. There's no respite from them, is there?"

Dave pushed himself off the sill.

"I know this because I summoned them, didn't I? They do my bidding. But you know that anyway. I explained to you that day, after Amelia asked for my help, I explained to you precisely what your punishment would be."

"I haven't contacted her if that's why you're here," Ryan exclaimed in a panic.

"Hush there."

"I haven't gone looking for her or her folks!"

"Hush, I said. There's a good laddie."

Dave touched Ryan's bony shoulder and gave it a warm squeeze.

"Don't get yourself in a tizz."

Ryan drew in a long breath and tried calming himself but couldn't stop shaking in his boots. His face went from white to grey. Dave saw scratches on Ryan's bare arms, which may have been from lice, or they may have been from self-harm.

At any other time, Dave might have felt a touch of pity, but this nasty specimen deserved not a single crumb of charity.

Or at least, he shouldn't do.

But the change in circumstances for Dave meant a shift in fortunes for Ryan. As fate would have it, Dave was about to offer him a second chance. An opportunity Ryan wouldn't be able to turn down.

"Do you want those night daemons to stop, Ryan?"

Ryan's shakes paused, and he looked up, meeting Dave's steady gaze for the first time.

"Those abhorrent things that lurk in your peripheral vision? Your bêtes noires?"

"My what?"

"It's French for black beast. I can make them go away if you like."

"You can do that?" Ryan asked cautiously, maybe sensing a trap.

"It's quite a simple matter. All you'd have to do is recite a mantra, some nonsense like abracadabra, and puff, all that nasty stuff will end just like that," and Dave snapped his fingers.

Dave looked at the young man before him, waiting.

"You'd really make them stop?"

"Scout's honour. And then you can get your life back on track, and our paths need never cross again."

Ryan shot to his feet, and the poor wretch had tears in his eyes as he blurted, "Yes! Yes please!"

Dave's mouth turned up into a smile, which wasn't mirrored in his dark eyes – but Ryan was too excited to notice.

"In return, there is one wee matter I'd like you to attend to. A favour."

Ryan's excitement suddenly plateaued, and he looked like he might crumble in a heap.

"Then, afterwards, I promise you, Ryan, that the two of us are done forever."

Ryan only needed a couple of seconds to make up his mind.

"I'll do it. Whatever you want me to do, I'll do it, Mr Minnock."

CHAPTER 17

AS LEE AND AMELIA PRESSED deeper into the abandoned mine, the light from the tunnel entrance slowly faded.

The walls of grey stone compressed together, and the low ceiling bore down, convincing them they'd be crushed any second. Soon, the white glow from the flashlight became their only source of illumination, and as they tripped and stumbled over the rails, the circle of light bounced around, further disorientating them.

Ahead, the tunnel telescoped into the darkness. Lee sensed they were going downhill because he could feel the ballast slide forwards with each step. A few times, he contemplated going back. But the compulsion to push on just a bit further was strong, hoping the mine might contain helpful clues.

From time to time, sounds reached them. Pinning them down was difficult because sometimes they came from in front, sometimes from the tunnel walls. The noises changed too, from deep, grinding rumbles that had them looking around nervously, to high-pitched tones almost beyond the range of the human ear. Lee again wondered if there was a colony of bats living in there. He tried not to picture them swarming out of the tunnel mouth, their furry bodies and leather wings battering against their faces.

The tunnel narrowed further, increasing Lee's claustrophobia. Above their heads, the timber roof spars sagged down into V-shapes.

Lee came to a stop and placed a hand on Amelia's arm.

"That's far enough."

The walls deadened his voice, giving it the frequency of a Doppler sound wave.

"It's too risky to go any further."

"Yeah, I think you're right," Amelia replied.

They changed direction.

"Wait!" Amelia said and spun back around. "I thought I saw something."

They strained their eyes, attempting to pierce the blackness. Amelia adjusted the flashlight and pointed the cone of white to their front. There was something up ahead, something large and bulky.

"I want to see what it is," she said and continued onwards.

Against his better judgement, Lee trailed after her and caught up just as she reached the object.

The tunnel opened into a larger chamber with a vaulted ceiling. Inside was one of the old steam locomotives. Despite the dangers of lingering here for too long, they walked around it for a closer look. Its drum-shaped sides were dented and rusting, and at the front was a smokestack that curved upwards, reminding Lee of an elephant's trunk. He reflected that its design was very basic, more like a boiler on wheels, but it served its purpose. Attached to the locomotive was a tender piled with coal, and behind that was a line of wagons containing chunks of granite.

"They must have driven it in here, abandoned it just before the mine was shut down, and boarded up the entrance. Afterwards, the tunnel roof sagged, trapping it forever like a sarcophagus. It belongs in a museum," he said, patting the locomotive.

Amelia didn't seem to share his enthusiasm. She was backing away up the tracks, shooting the flashlight around.

"There's something not right here," she said.

"There's something not right about this entire business."

"No, I mean right here. In this spot."

Lee tended to agree. A heavy, oppressive feeling of dread had been building since they first entered the mine, and in a matter of seconds, it shot up several notches.

Across the chamber, he saw a second tunnel entrance burrowing deeper into the hillside. The round opening expelled frigid air like a monstrous mouth breathing very slowly. The darkness there was complete, like a black hole that swallowed the torchlight.

"I don't know about you, but I'm definitely not going in there," she said quietly.

"I concur."

Lee joined her, and together they slowly backed up until they'd left the large chamber with its abandoned steam engine behind, and then turned and began retracing their steps up the gentle gradient. They'd only gone a few paces when a flapping sound had them turning sharply. The flashlight beam glanced off the walls, catching something black flying through the air. Straightaway, Lee knew it was a bat, and he watched in horror as it landed in Amelia's hair.

She screamed and flapped her arms at her head, dropping the torch. There was the tinkling sound of breaking glass, and the world turned pitch black.

"What is it?" she yelled hysterically. "Oh, Lee, get it off! It's in my hair!"

Lee couldn't see a thing. He flung his arms around and felt them dash against her, and he quickly dragged her against him.

"Keep still! Keep still while I help!"

But telling her to be calm while that ugly flying thing clung to her head was pointless. Rather, she grew more panicky. He reached where he thought her head was and flinched when his hands brushed the furry body and skinny limbs. Lee could hear the bat protesting; it didn't make a blood-curdling scream like in the horror movies but chirped incessantly. Ignoring the revulsion welling up inside, he snatched at the creature, ripped it free of her hair, crushed its fragile body in his hands, and flung it away. Then he grabbed Amelia's elbow and crudely propelled her along the tunnel, praying they were heading away from danger.

Thankfully, no more bats pursued them, and after about a minute, they saw faint daylight gleaming off the walls and roof. It guided them to the tunnel entrance, and they gratefully exited through the small opening and jogged across to the rocky shelf, where they collapsed in a heap.

Amelia's hair was a tangled mess where the bat's claws had made a purchase, and she was half crying and half laughing. She buried her face in her hands, groaned loudly, and then said, "What a day I'm having," which made Lee chuckle, which in turn set Amelia off, and they both dissolved in fits of giggles, the pair of them determined not to be beaten by something as stupid as a bat.

"Do you know," she said when she finally regained her breath, "my life was boring until I met you."

"You took the words right out of my mouth."

Lee got to his feet, pulled her up, and suddenly wanted to kiss her. Amelia gave a small gasp as their lips touched. After several seconds, their mouths parted and she whispered, "What was that for?"

Lee shrugged.

"Just an irresistible impulse I was too weak to fight. What can I say?"

"Good. Because it's catching," and Amelia kissed him back with more vigour.

Presently, they walked back down the hill holding hands. On the way, she asked if he'd stay the night.

"What about Dave?" Lee asked.

"He won't be back before tomorrow. It's just that I don't want to be alone tonight. The things Dave told us about the local history have taken away this spot's peacefulness. I used to find it restful here. I was content, you know? But not anymore."

Lee thought about this and asked, "Do you think he knows about the two of us?"

"Dave? I'm sure he does, and I'm equally sure he's fine with it."

"Well, in that case, I'll be more than glad to stay," Lee told her. "Honestly, I hate the cottage just as much as you dislike it here."

"So, your plans of renovating it and moving in are?"

"Well and truly on the back burner for now."

Amelia drew him to a stop and made him face her.

"So why don't we both just up sticks and leave? Together. We can get a place somewhere else."

Lee raised his hand. "Slow down a bit. That's a big decision, and we hardly know one another. Let's not get ahead of ourselves, okay?"

The crestfallen look on her face tugged at his heartstrings.

"But it makes sense, doesn't it?" she pushed. "Then we can forget all about Mother Baxter and Long Meg."

"Now, that does sound tempting."

"Does that mean you'll think about it? Tell me you'll at least think about it."

"I will, I promise." And he meant it. After all, making a fresh start was his intention.

She looped her arm through his and steered him towards the caravan.

"Good," she said, smiling.

"We can talk about it tonight. First," Lee said, changing direction towards his car, "we need to go over to the cottage."

"Do we have to?"

"Yes. I don't like the idea any more than you, but it might be for the last time. You need to get your moped back, remember? And I have some things I need to collect. After that, we have some decisions to make."

• • •

As they drove over to the cottage in Lee's Defender, Amelia was already planning their departure as though they'd beyond question made up their minds. Maybe it was her attempt to break down his defences and get him to commit, but in truth, Lee was quickly coming around to the idea. After all, hadn't he considered this very scenario just last night? Of eloping with Amelia? It sounded stupid when he first ran the idea past himself, but now Amelia was proposing the same thing. And his deadline had more or less passed.

"So, when I think about it, I have no commitments here," she was saying.

She looked over from the passenger seat.

"How about you, Lee?"

He had nothing to keep him from leaving either, he realized all at once. The only friends he had were the very people who'd landed him in trouble: Jacko and Chris. There was his mum, naturally, and not seeing her would be hard. But it wouldn't be forever, and he could always ring her.

"I won't miss the caravan," Amelia continued before he could reply. "It's been my home for over a year, but it was only supposed to be temporary. I will miss Dave, though."

Lee turned the Defender off the track and over the cattle grid and all too soon pulled to a halt close to the garden. Amelia's moped was on its stand next to the front door.

They approached the cottage with an all-too-familiar sense of dread, made slightly more bearable by the thought that they might never have to return to this place.

"Right, give me five minutes to grab my stuff, and then you can follow me back to the caravan on your moped."

Amelia handed him the key she'd kept in her pocket, but the door swung inwards when Lee pushed it into the keyhole.

"Did you lock it?"

"Yes," she replied. "At least, I think I did. I was in a hurry to get away because you were ill."

Lee pushed open the door, and Amelia followed him inside to find a familiar figure waiting for them in the semi-darkness.

"Well, who do we have here?" Jacko Page asked.

PART THREE

And take 13 copper needles and stick one in the brain while saying,
"I am piercing your brain."

GREAT PARIS MAGICAL PAPYRUS
3RD CENTURY

CHAPTER 18

JACKO WAS SITTING IN THE rocking chair, slowly seesawing backwards and forwards. His hair was unkempt, like he'd had several restless nights, and his eyes held a hounded look, although they still appraised Lee with a sharpness that made him blanch.

"Lee?" Amelia breathed close to his ear.

Jacko shifted his attention to her, and his eyes seemed to fog over like she was unworthy of his time. He looked again at Lee.

"Well?" he asked.

"This is Amelia. She's a friend."

Jack seemed to consider this for a moment, nodding as he chewed on the matter. Then he stopped rocking the chair and came to his feet.

"A word, Lee. In the kitchen."

Jacko walked through the door to the small kitchen, and Lee turned to Amelia, saying, "Wait outside, will you?"

"Who is he, Lee? I don't like him."

"He's just a pal. I'll get rid of him."

Then he trailed after Jacko, wondering how he could do just that. He urgently needed to get his story straight.

He found Jacko by the small window, watching through the pane of glass as Amelia appeared in the garden. Lee wondered where he should begin, and he was just about to speak when his old friend spun around sharply. Jacko's eyes blazed, and his mouth spat with fury.

"Which part," Jacko began loudly before lowering his voice and starting again, "which part of keeping a low profile didn't you understand, Lee, my boy?"

"I, erm–"

"All I asked of you was to keep your head down for a few days, wait for the dust to settle, and avoid talking or meeting with anyone else but me. What's suddenly changed to make you think you can ignore my orders?"

"What's changed is that–" Lee tried saying back, but again, he was cut off.

"Because here I am, hoping we can come up with a way out of this clusterfuck, only to find the place empty. And I'm thinking to myself, what the hell has happened to my pal, my partner in crime? Have the police nicked him? Has he done a runner with the loot? And then, low and behold, you come strolling down the garden path without a care in the world with some woman in tow. All fucking loved up, by the looks of it."

"That's rubbish, Jacko."

"Is it? Because that's how it looks to me."

Jacko came closer, and under his coat, Lee caught a glimpse of the sawn-off shotgun Jacko had used to shoot the man in the post office. The sawn-off shotgun Jacko said he was going to get rid of.

Jacko sneered, and he tilted his head to one side.

"Another thought just occurred to me, Lee. Have you had this planned all along? To arrange to meet up with your girlfriend so you can run off together into the sunset with the money? Promise me you're not a double-crossing little cunt."

"Run off together," Lee countered, trying to hide his alarm at how shrewd Jacko could be. "With five hundred quid?"

"What?"

"That's all we got from the robbery," said Lee, remembering to keep his voice down because Amelia was hovering around just outside the window.

"Five hundred?"

"Yes. I counted it. All we have to show for robbing the place and killing that man is the grand total of five hundred and sixty pounds. That's hardly enough to run off to the Costas with, is it? All this was for nothing."

Jacko absorbed this news in phases, his expression evolving from incredulity to anger and finally to a stoical blankness.

"That's hardly the fucking point, pal. It doesn't matter about the bloody lucre anymore, does it? What matters is getting clean away. And you gallivanting around with that floozie out there has thrown a whopping great spanner in the works."

"It's not like that. I didn't have any of this planned. Me and Amelia met by pure chance. Also, pal, I don't split on people, either."

Lee hoped his face didn't give the game away because he started sweating like a pig. Quickly, he tried taking the conversation in a different direction.

"I thought we were in the clear, anyway? You said as much in the text you sent me. And I waited for your call, Jacko. For three days, I waited, and when nothing came, no word of what was happening, what the hell was I supposed to think?"

"Fuck!" Jacko said in an expulsion of fury, and he slammed his hand onto the kitchen counter.

Outside, Amelia glanced over to the window before commencing to pace up and down the garden path.

"Does she know anything?" Jacko asked under his breath.

"Of course she doesn't. Do you think I'm stupid?"

"But if she works it out for herself?" said Jacko, watching Amelia closely. "The robbery is all over the news. If she does put two and two together, then God help me, Lee, I won't fucking hesitate to use this thing to keep her quiet," and he opened his coat to give Lee a full look at the shotgun.

Lee stepped forwards and placed himself in front of Jacko, blocking his line of sight.

"You'll have to put a bullet through me as well," he told Jacko in a steady voice.

"Argh! What a fucking mess!" Jacko snarled in impotent rage and stomped off over the kitchen floor like a caged animal.

Lee let him stew for a few moments, hoping the short lapse in their confrontation might allow tempers to cool.

Eventually, he told Jacko, "I tried sending you a message through Tiny Bob. Did you get it?"

"Not likely. Tiny Bob is dead."

"What?" Lee asked, the bombshell news hitting him like a bolt out of the blue. "How?"

Jacko waved a dismissive hand. "Someone found him brown bread in his bed. The fat fucker finally had a heart attack. He probably had one wank too many. I'm surprised he made it out of his teens."

"When was this?"

"I don't know. A few days ago. Who gives a shit?"

"When was the last time you spoke to him?"

"Before the job. What the fuck does it matter? This has nothing to do with him."

Jacko eyed Lee suspiciously.

"What was your message, anyway?"

"Nothing important. I just wanted to grasp how things were, that's all."

Jacko stopped pacing and leaned back against the cellar door. It creaked loudly.

"Well, things have changed since I sent you that message, Lee," Jacko said, his manner growing subdued now his initial anger was evaporating. "It's a fucking trainwreck, I tell you."

The entire enterprise had been a major disaster from start to finish, Lee figured, so he couldn't see how things could become any worse.

"The police have got a hold of Chris."

But just like that, they did get a whole lot worse.

"Tell me you're wrong."

Jacko gave a dispirited shake of his head. In frustration, he kicked his heel against the cellar door two or three times, making it rattle.

"I'm not. They grabbed him this morning. Chris was hiding out in the flat over Vernon's takeaway. Vernon was supposed to act as a lookout and warn Chris if the Rozzers came around asking questions, but apparently, the takeaway was raided by the drug squad again, and during their search, they found Chris, and Chris blabbed straightaway. The last I heard, they were holding him at Halifax Nick, and he's singing like a canary."

Lee couldn't believe their long-time friend would spill the beans. Surely, after all their years together, he wouldn't give their names to the police. But who knows how people react when under pressure? The upshot of all these fresh developments meant the net was closing, and their escape window was closing with each hour.

On top of all that, he had a suspicious Jacko to contend with.

His friend pushed himself away from the cellar door and joined Lee by the window.

"So, who is she, pal?"

"She's called Amelia."

"You told me that already. But who *is* she?"

"She's just some woman, that's all. She was out walking, and we happened to cross paths."

"What, did you just decide to go for a stroll in the woods?"

"Come on, Jacko. This place is in the middle of nowhere, with nobody around for miles–"

"Duh," said Jacko, pointing out the woman in the garden.

"– and I was going crazy stuck in here. I just wanted some fresh air. Also, when you didn't call, I thought I'd better plan an alternative hiding place in case the police turned up here."

"And did you? Find another bolthole?"

No way was Lee going to mention the caravan, so he just shook his head.

Jacko jabbed a finger against Lee's chest.

"Are you absolutely sure she hasn't twigged on about us?"

"One hundred percent."

"Enough to stake your freedom and her life on it?"

Lee took a deep breath and let it out slowly through his nostrils.

"Totally," he said in a measured voice.

Jacko slapped him on the back, but his tone had no friendliness when he said, "I'll hold you to that, pal. Now, get rid of her. Tell her to go home. The less time she spends here, the better."

Lee felt dizzy with relief and tried to keep the tremor out of his voice.

"Will do."

He moved to leave, but Jacko's following words caught up with him.

"Did you fuck her?"

Looking over his shoulder, Lee replied, "What do you think?"

The first flicker of a smile threatened to spoil Jacko's strained face, but he seemed to lack the muscles necessary for normal smiling, so it was more of a sneer like the mark of a branding iron.

"Good on you. Now say your goodbyes."

As soon as Lee stepped outside, Amelia came hurrying over. Her face was so white it appeared milky.

"Who is that man, Lee? What is he doing here? What does he want?"

Lee held up his hands to fend off the flurry of questions.

"There's nothing to worry about," he told her, steering her away from the cottage door. "Like I said, he's a friend."

"He doesn't look very friendly."

Amelia glanced over Lee's shoulder.

"He's watching us out of the window and doesn't seem happy. I get the distinct impression he doesn't want me around."

"You're being paranoid."

Lee lowered his voice and leaned close like he was sharing confidential gossip.

"He's having problems at home with his marriage. He's in a bit of a mess and doesn't know where to turn. You know what it's like."

Amelia raised sceptical eyebrows and asked, "Is he leaving? You said you'd get rid of him."

"Well, that's the problem. Jacko has nowhere else to go, and so he came here."

Amelia gave a long, slow blink, then pinned Lee with her eyes.

"Are you dumping me? Is that what this is?"

"What? Whoa, no way!"

"Now you've had your way with me, you can't get shut of me fast enough. And then you and your bestie can have a good old laugh about it."

"Amelia, you're being silly. That's a million miles from the truth."

He saw her chin tremble as she fought hard to control her emotions. Lee rubbed both her upper arms tenderly.

"Nothing has changed regarding what we talked about."

"Then tell him to go."

"I can't. He's a mate."

"Is he staying over?"

"Yes, probably. But only for one night. One more night, and then you and me can–"

"You and me can what, Lee? I need you to say it. Or is there something you're not telling me?"

Lee touched his forehead against hers and looked directly into her eyes. "By this time tomorrow, we'll be gone from here. You and me, together. I've made up my mind, okay?"

"Really?"

Amelia's voice was barely a whisper.

"Because if you're just marking time until you get bored of me, then I'd rather you were honest about it."

Lee tilted her chin and kissed her on the soft lips.

"I'm not. Amelia, coming here was the worst thing I have ever done. This place screws with people's heads. It's an unhealthy environment because of all the bad things that occurred here."

He ducked his head, forcing her to make eye contact with him.

"But one good thing that came out of it was the two of us meeting. Call it fate, happenchance, or luck, I don't know. Maybe you were predestined to happen upon me lying in that clearing. But now that we have met, I don't plan on blowing you off. I'm in this for keeps."

A small smile flickered on Amelia's face, and twin red spots rouged her cheeks.

"Now, you head back to the caravan and wait for me there. Tonight, I'll talk some sense into my mate and persuade him to go home and patch things up with his missus in the morning. Once the coast is clear, I'll drive over to yours and we'll be on our way."

They embraced, and then Lee waited while Amelia started up her moped, all the time aware of Jacko watching them and shaking his head.

"You better not be falling head over heels for her, pal," Jacko said when Lee joined him in the kitchen.

"I'm not."

"Because if you are, it will only make things more difficult if we have to…" and he let the rest of the sentence dangle, removing the shotgun and laying it on the counter for emphasis.

"I thought you were getting rid of that thing."

"The gun? I was, but then a little voice at the back of my head told me to keep it. It's a good job I listen to my instincts, right?"

"If you say so."

"Have you still got yours?"

Lee needed to check if his gun had fetched up in his sleeping bag, but for now, he just nodded.

"Good," Jacko uttered. "Now let's see what food you've left me because I'm dying of hunger."

Dweller Under The Roots

• • •

After they'd eaten a meagre meal of baked beans, Jacko snapped open a can of beer and slurped half of it down in one go. He burped loudly and wiped a hand over his chin.

"The food's starting to run low," he told Lee. "We'll need to restock."

"Won't that be a bit risky?"

"Probably. But we don't have much choice if we stay here for a while, do we?"

"But haven't our plans changed? What if the police learn about this place and come for us?"

"All the more reason to replenish our supplies."

Lee felt his eyes widen.

"You mean, if we end up under armed siege?"

Jacko finished the beer, crumpled up the can, tossed it into the sink, and then pulled the tab on a second one.

"It'll be like Butch Cassidy and the Sundance Kid," Jacko said with a sneer.

Lee didn't want to be gunned down like the two legendary outlaws.

Then Jacko laughed harshly.

"Ah, Lee, ye big bollocks," he slurred, the alcohol already having an effect, "I'm just pulling your chain. It won't come to that. As long as your girlfriend stops snooping around, there's no way the police will find us here. I made sure our tracks are covered."

"And what about Chris?"

"It was just bad luck they found him. Look, he doesn't know about this cottage, so when it comes down to it, there's not much he can tell the police. Now stop wetting your pants and show me where you've stashed the money."

Lee showed him the hole in the chimney breast.

"I never spotted this when I checked the gaff out," Jacko said, indicating the hiding spot and dragging out the bags of money.

He counted it and looked quizzically at Lee.

"Are you sure this is all we netted, my boy? I'm positive we grabbed more from the tills. You're not holding out on me, are you?"

"Every last note and coin are in there."

"Maybe I should check down in the cellar and see if you've squirrelled some away, eh? What-do-you-say?"

"There's nothing but junk down there, Jacko. It's dangerous, too," and he pointed at his injured head.

Jacko drank some more and then winked. "I believe you."

He slumped into the rocking chair, making it seesaw, and crammed the money under his coat. After a moment, Lee lowered himself into the armchair and looked squarely at his friend.

"Jacko, we need to talk about what happened at the post office."

"There's nothing to talk about."

"But a man died."

"And? What about it?"

"You said there'd be no trouble. That the old couple running the place wouldn't resist."

"And I was right. They didn't resist. They would have been quite happy to empty the safe for us if it hadn't been for that stupid twat of a son getting in the way."

"But doesn't it bother you?" asked Lee, spreading his hands.

"No, it doesn't bother me, Lee. Why the fuck should it? If he wanted to be a fearless vigilante or a dutiful son protecting his mummy and daddy, or whatever, then he should have seen the consequences coming. I had a big fucking gun in my hands, Lee. What did he think I was going to do? Pat him on the head and say how sorry we were for frightening them all. He came at me like a nutcase, trying to get the gun off me, so I had no choice, and I pulled the trigger."

Jacko slurped more beer and shrugged.

"It was him or me. I killed him in self-defence."

"And that's what you'll say, is it, when the police come for us? 'It was self-defence, m'lud?' We were armed robbers, Jacko. They'll throw the book at us!"

"Stop mithering me, you chuffing berk. You're giving me a headache."

Jacko slapped the can down onto his knee, spilling some of it.

"Now look what you made me do," and he wiped up the spillage and licked his fingers.

He sighed loudly and softened his voice.

"Lee. We're in this together, okay? The police have Chris, and we can do nothing about that. For all we know, he might lead them on a merry dance, stringing them a right old tale. The police thought we'd escaped to Manchester until they nicked him, so that means the focus has switched back here.

That's why I came to join you today: I figure there's less chance of the police finding us if we hole up in one spot. We probably should have done that from the start, and I made a mistake by splitting us up. But we can't go back in time, so we'll just have to make the most of it and hope for the best. If the Rozzers come knocking on the door, so be it. If that happens, we'll have two options: surrender or go out in a blaze of glory. I know which I'll choose."

Fucking peachy, Lee mused. We either end up in the slammer or in body bags.

"In the meantime, we do nothing. That's your plan?"

"Pretty much, yep. I was joking about going out for some food, by the way. There's enough for a few more days; by then, we'll know one way or the other, won't we?"

Jacko finished his second beer.

"Now stop fretting and have a drink. While you're in the kitchen, fetch another for me, will you?"

Lee went into the kitchen. There were four cans of beer left, and at the rate Jacko was drinking, they wouldn't last long. He tugged two cans from the cardboard box and passed the shotgun on the counter on his way out.

Back in the other room, he tossed a beer to Jacko and put the other on the tabletop.

"I'll be back in a minute," he said and climbed the stairs. In the loft room, Lee rummaged around inside his sleeping bag and was relieved to feel the cold metal of the handgun. Pulling it out, he snapped open the cylinder. There were still three rounds inside. He snapped it shut and shoved the gun down the back of his trousers.

Dweller Under The Roots

Then he returned downstairs, flushing the toilet on the way.

CHAPTER 19

AMELIA RODE AWAY FROM THE cottage with her emotions pinballing around inside her head. She was hopping mad, exasperated with the sudden appearance of Lee's friend. Just as they were set to leave all their troubles behind, this scary character popped up. Now their plans were postponed, and knowing what men were like, Lee might shilly-shally around and have second thoughts.

She wasn't furious with Lee. Her ire was directed purely at his friend, Jacko, even though he was oblivious to the ramifications his arrival caused. The story about marital problems may be true, but Amelia was convinced the pair were keeping something from her. Men had their secrets; she knew that from recent experience. But whether Jacko was a friend in need or not, Amelia was in such a rage she didn't really care.

Somehow, she arrived at the caravan without crashing off the road. She parked the motorcycle outside and let herself in. Removing her crash helmet, she threw it across to the couch. Her aim was off, and it shattered a glass vase on a corner shelf.

Amelia bent over at the waist and screamed, pressing her hands to her temple. Deep inside, melodramatic thoughts collided like neutrons, triggering a horrible chain reaction. A fire burned in her stomach, a furious rage that bent her mind out of shape, and the flames grew white-hot, lancing into her heart.

Her hysteria found an outlet in rabid violence. Amelia went ballistic, trashing the caravan. She bounced off the walls for five minutes, smashing furniture and tossing around ornaments. She overturned the dining table, swiped crockery off the kitchen unit, and kicked in the TV screen. Any ramblers passing by outside would have heard a cacophony of crashes and screams riding on the backs of screams.

Finally, she fell to the floor in a heap. Unfortunately, she wasn't spent just yet. Her breathing was out of control, and she could feel her heart racing, producing a series of spasms that snapped her body around like a possessed person. Amelia knew what was happening because she'd experienced episodes like this before, but whereas in the past, she'd been able to manage them, now the seizure ran amok. Her back arched so high that her shoulder blades and the soles of her feet supported her body, and her head twisted from side to side. Her stomach began to swell, ballooning out like a heavily pregnant woman, and she could feel something inside her bursting to get out.

Amelia's mind writhed in turmoil. It felt like her body might catch fire, so she ripped off her clothes, tearing them in the process, and flung them away. She opened her legs and moaned like a person delivering an infant, but when she saw the white, wispy substance floating from between her thighs, she cried out in sheer terror.

Her howl of fear was cut short as more of the strange matter coiled from her mouth, her nostrils, and even her eyes. She saw it swirling like smoke, and the separate tendrils accumulated into one pall. It expanded and grew semi-transparent, now resembling a large and shapeless bubble floating in the air, its taut skin shimmering iridescently. Amelia could see her terrified face reflected back at her.

Something suspended within the bubble caught her attention, something small and scrunched up in a foetal position. Its twisted physique flexed with supernatural life, and the hideous face turned to peer at Amelia. Then the bubble's outer shell turned opaque, obscuring the oddity.

Amelia snapped her legs together, her irrational mind fearing it might try slipping back inside her body.

The air became charged, making the hairs on the back of her arms stand up. A sudden breeze appeared from somewhere, swirling inside the caravan like a mini gale, lifting Amelia's blonde hair away from her perspiring forehead.

She bared her teeth in a grimace as more fiery pains wracked her body. Her nostrils flared alarmingly as a spate of grunting breaths escaped her, and Amelia called out.

"Dave, oh Dave! Make her stop!"

Amelia watched as the shape rose higher until it levitated just below the caravan's ceiling. She hurried away over the carpet and pressed herself against the couch.

The thing started moving again. It drifted directly in front of Amelia, gliding towards the lounge window, and the second its outer shell touched the glass, the entire window shattered into thousands of fragments. Luckily for Amelia, the shards blew outwards, otherwise she would have been cut to ribbons.

The bubble glided through the opening, and Amelia followed its single-minded progress as it disappeared into the woods.

•   •   •

Ryan would never forget the first time Dave Minnock came to see him.

After his arrest for drug dealing in the club, Ryan found himself with nowhere to live. The council put him up for a time in a residential unit, but after several months, they secured him a tiny bedsit on York Street. It was a dump blighted with rising damp, and the alleyway that ran down the back was swarming with mice, but it gave him a sense of independence and freedom. Most importantly, it was away from prying eyes.

Once he'd moved in, Ryan settled into a routine. By day, he would do his community service of scrubbing graffiti off walls and picking up dog shit, and during evenings and weekends, he set about making Amelia's life hell. Ryan orchestrated a campaign of harassment and threats, targeting not only his ex-girlfriend but also her family and work colleagues. He started by bombarding her with hundreds of text messages and phone calls during the wee hours, and when she changed her number, he resorted to waiting outside the office where she worked. To begin with, Ryan begged for her to take him back, pleading for a second chance, telling her he was sorry for screwing around. He promised to turn his life around. When that didn't work, a festering hatred took over, and his tactics changed. Ryan threatened her, and he arranged for some of his old contacts – bouncers from the club – to put the frighteners on her. Ryan shared intimate photos with all and sundry and posted some online. He set up fake social media accounts under her name, including a Tinder account. He drove a wedge between Amelia and her family.

Amelia finished up by quitting her job and moving house, and Ryan lost track of her for a while. He paid online people-finding sites to trace her, but Amelia's details on the electoral roll were out of date, leading to a dead end. He checked out her friends' social networking platforms, hoping she might pop up in their posts, but they had deleted all mention of Amelia. She seemed to have dropped off the face of the earth.

Then Ryan came up with a fresh approach. If he could learn Amelia's smartphone's IP address, he might track her that way. While living together, they'd synced their mobiles like young lovers do, and by working backwards through his settings, Ryan quickly discovered the IP address. By logging onto a lookup tool, he learned who her internet provider was and, from there, the postcodes and locations of Amelia's recent online check-ins, such as internet cafes, shops, and online purchase history. It didn't provide him with a precise location where she lived, but it narrowed the search area down to Hardcastle Crags. Ryan felt he was closing in on her.

Dweller Under The Roots

But then, one evening after a long day spent picking up used condoms with a litter picker behind the park pavilion, there came a knock on Ryan's bedsit door. Reluctantly shutting down his laptop, he'd opened it to find a strange little man standing before him with his hands neatly folded and a beatific smile on his silly chops. Jehovah's Witnesses again, Ryan thought, trying not to sneer at the yellow neckerchief and baggy corduroy trousers.

"What do you want, mister?" Ryan had growled out of the corner of his mouth.

The strange little man hadn't answered; he'd just reached up and very gently tapped Ryan on the centre of his forehead with a bony middle finger.

After that, Ryan must have blacked out because his world turned into a dark and empty void. He could still reason, and feel, and hear, but Ryan couldn't move a muscle. A silky voice drifted out of the blackness, a soft and lilting sound that nevertheless burrowed into his brain like an earworm. He assumed the voice belonged to his visitor, the stranger on the doorstep, because besides his probation officer and landlord, Ryan had no visitors.

The little man in the yellow neckerchief talked to Ryan for a long time because when Ryan came too, he found himself sitting on his couch in the bedsit, and it had grown dark outside. His visitor had left. In his absence, Ryan felt an empty sensation take hold. It felt like his brain had been hollowed out, his memories scoured. The only thing remaining was the simple instruction: he was to have nothing to do with his ex-girlfriend, Amelia. It wasn't a command, more of an arrangement, an understanding. Failure to follow this simple rule would have terrible consequences.

For about a day, Ryan felt greatly confused. Who was the strange little man, and how did he know about Ryan's campaign of revenge? What consequences was the voice referring to?

But then, the following day, Ryan felt rather stupid. Just who the fuck did the odd man think he was, coming in here and warning Ryan off? What could the little fellow do to him? If he ever showed his face again, Ryan would wallop the idiot. That evening, he'd fired up the laptop and dived right back into his vengeful crusade against his ex.

It was the worst decision of his life, worse even than his hair-brained scheme to supply coke to the wealthy patrons at his nightclub. Because within a few days, Ryan experienced a set of startling and, frankly, petrifying visions. So real, he couldn't imagine they were illusions planted in his brain by the oddball visitor.

The first two instances happened while doing his community service. Ryan and his fellow miscreants were cleaning the children's play area in a local park, and he'd briefly wandered away from the others for a smoke when a movement in his peripheral vision distracted him.

Ryan turned and gawped at something lurking under the climbing frame, blinking several times because he couldn't believe what he saw. Standing there was a huge, black, three-headed dog with a serpent tail and a mane of snakes. The sight froze him to the spot. Only when the creature growled from its three salivating jaws and moved closer did Ryan snap out of his paralysis and run for his life. Reaching his

Dweller Under The Roots

colleagues, Ryan breathlessly told them of the three-headed dog, and they all burst out laughing, including their supervisor. Ryan looked back at the climbing frame to see the creature had vanished. Ryan, who'd been so frightened he felt a tiny squirt of shit spurt out of his arse, was struck dumb and didn't speak a word the rest of the afternoon. That night, he hardly slept because every time he closed his eyes, that demon dog was waiting to pounce and rip out his throat.

Two days later, Ryan and his outfit were working to improve the canal towpath next to the car dealership on Old Stubbings. This mostly entailed putting down new gravel and tidying the undergrowth.

Ryan had tried putting the incident in the park to the back of his mind. Either the dog was a figment of his imagination and he was losing his marbles, or it was real and some fearful creature was stalking the neighbourhood. He didn't wish to dwell on any of those two possibilities.

At lunchtime, while everyone else sat on the canal wall and ate their sandwiches, Ryan kept working. Not because he found community service rewarding – being ridiculed by passersby was shameful (he figured that was the whole point). No, Ryan preferred keeping busy because the less time he had to think about the three-headed dog, the better. So he continued hacking at the tall grass alongside the towpath and bagging it in green recycling sacks.

He soon found himself approaching a tunnel mouth where the canal passed beneath a bridge. He could hear roosting pigeons and, somewhere in the near distance, echoing through the tunnel, some builders talking crudely.

There was a godawful stink wafting out from the tunnel mouth. It was like a mixture of raw sewage and rotten food. Considering how much junk there was in the water, together with pollutants arbitrarily dumped by canal-side warehouses, it wouldn't surprise Ryan if all the fish and other wildlife had died.

He went for a closer look and nearly gagged. He paused at the mouth of the tunnel and tried to see into the shadows.

Something was hanging beneath the roof, clinging to the bricks and beams. It looked like a sizeable fungal mass or maybe a massive wasp nest, but then it moved, and suddenly the thing fell onto the towpath, startling Ryan. It came forwards into the light.

Like the other day, he thought he'd flipped his lid because the thing before him was an impossible inversion of nature. This freaky specimen was a mash-up of human and animal because it had a muscular torso with a man's face in the centre, and sprouting from equal points around its hairy body were five goat legs. The monster – and that's what it was to Ryan, a denizen of hell – rolled towards him on its feet like some grotesque spheroid. Ryan started to twitch involuntarily like someone with St. Vitus Dance, and his shuffling steps back tipped him over the side of the canal. He fell in with a loud splash and came up out of the foul water, spitting, coughing, and half-screaming like a killer croc was attacking him.

The sounds of his struggling caught the attention of Ryan's fellow ne'er-do-wells. They came running along the towpath and found him dripping wet and with mud oozing out of his pockets. Again, when he described the nightmarish monster, they had fits. And again, when Ryan turned to point angrily into the dark tunnel, the thing with five goat legs was nowhere to be seen.

Ryan was allowed home early, and on the bus ride, the children and their moms had a good laugh at his expense. Ryan tried ignoring their jibes, asking himself what was wrong with him. Did he have a brain tumour? And then he remembered his visitor the other night and the strange little man's dire warnings.

That evening, a humongous half-human, half-wasp insect the size of a sheep visited him. It had a child's face, six voluptuous breasts, and a wicked sting, and it hovered and buzzed around the bedsit and whispered dire threats all night long. It had knives for claws, and when he checked himself in the mirror the following day, Ryan's arms and chest were covered in lines of blood bubbles where he'd been slashed.

And on it went. Each night and each day, Ryan would see those terrible things that nobody else could see. It was like all the legions from hell had come crawling out of the ground to pry away his sanity, clamouring for his soul. Even when he ceased looking for Amelia and abandoned his plans for revenge, they didn't stop haunting his every moment. Ryan couldn't sleep. He lost weight and had the appearance of a sickly man. He became zombified. He even thought of ending it all and had started researching the best methods for topping himself when, unexpectedly, a chance of redemption came calling.

It was straightforward. All Ryan had to do in return for getting his sanity back was follow Dave Minnock's simple instructions and then recite a few childish spells. Subsequently, the terrible monstrosities would leave him alone.

Minnock had referred to them as daemons rather than demons. The subtle difference seemed to hold weighty significance. Demons were what you dressed up as on Halloween, whereas the tiny change in pronunciation, *Daemons*, conjured something more ancient and satanic.

Ryan didn't care what they were called. He just wanted to stop seeing them, and he'd do anything it took. And the "wee matter" Minnock talked about sounded a piece of cake, although why the hell he needed the task done was beyond Ryan. Minnock talked about "unblocking a channel of dark energy", which meant Jack shit to Ryan.

At any rate, Ryan would indulge the strange little man and do his bidding. Which is how he came to be slogging through the woods carrying a shovel in one hand and a pickaxe in the other.

Ryan was feeling winded, so he paused to put down the heavy tools and get his bearings. He should be nearly there if Minnock's directions were accurate. Ryan was hoping to have the job done and be home before dusk. However, he'd never been this far out in the sticks and didn't want to wander around in circles.

He set off again. A few minutes later, he was relieved when he finally reached the small clearing. There was the stone cross, exactly where Minnock said it would be. Ryan ditched the shovel and pickaxe and walked around it, noticing where centuries of rain had left the surface all pitted and worn. He saw some fool had defaced it by scratching a silly stick figure on the side. Probably a long time ago, Ryan reasoned. Ancient graffiti. Was that all he was suitable for - getting rid of graffiti? The idea made Ryan snigger.

Returning to where he'd dropped the tools, he lifted the heavy pickaxe and started to chop at the hard ground. After ten minutes, his arms were killing him, and his back muscles were feeling the strain. Ryan looked at the results and pulled a face, cursing under his breath. He'd hardly made a dent in the forest floor. There were just a few loose sods of soil and exposed tree roots, and that's all. The ground was as hard as concrete.

Gathering himself, Ryan resumed digging. He alternated between hacking at the ground with the pickaxe and digging out chunks of soil with the shovel. He tried keeping up a rhythm and circled around the base of the cross to expose as much of it as possible.

Pausing in his labours, Ryan pushed at the cross with both hands, rocking it backwards and forwards. The blasted thing hardly moved. It would be easier to use the pickaxe and just snap off the cross at ground level, but Minnock had been clear that it must be fully uprooted, however deep it was planted in the earth.

Wiping sweat from his brow, Ryan told himself it would all be worth it in the end. He'd keep digging 'till midnight if he had to.

He chopped and chopped and dug deeper into the earth. One foot down, then two, and still he wasn't at the bottom. It couldn't go down much further, for Pete's sake.

He tried moving the cross by hand again; this time, Ryan felt it shift an inch each way. Good. Ryan put his back into it, digging with a fury. Not long now, and he'd be free of those visions, and Dave Minnock could take a running jump.

Ryan giggled, and soon, the woods echoed to the sound of his insane laughter.

Finally, he reached the base of the cross. But instead of exposing the bottom edge, he was confronted with a strange sight. The lower part of the stone cross was entangled with tree roots. They were wrapped and coiled around it as though they didn't want to let it go and were intent on keeping it rooted in the earth.

He began slicing through the roots with the shovel's edge, muttering more curses, and then pulled the loose ends free with his hands.

Right, here goes, Ryan thought, and manoeuvered the shovel under the bottom of the cross and pushed down with one foot. When it was wedged as far under as it would go, Ryan heaved down onto the wooden handle with all his weight and felt the base of the cross lift. He forced the shovel under another few inches and pressed down with his body again. This time, the old cross lifted clear of the ground, taking big clods of soil with it, and toppled over with a loud thump. The top of the cross snapped off.

Ryan stood back and looked proudly at his handiwork, clapping dirt off his hands.

Hang on, there was something else here. In the hole left behind by the toppled cross was a large, roundish boulder. It couldn't be a natural feature because it had an iron ring fixed at the top, suggesting somebody had placed it here and then erected the cross over the top.

Ryan thought he ought to just leave it alone. Dave Minnock had said nothing about this; his instructions were to topple the stone cross. On the other hand, Ryan didn't want to leave the task half-done and face a furious Dave Minnock, who had the power to make Ryan's misery ten times worse. For that reason, he took the pickaxe and positioned himself so that his legs were astride the boulder, worked the pointed tip underneath the near side of the rounded rock, and heaved backwards after taking a deep breath.

The boulder came up and then rolled away through the grass. Ryan cried out. Underneath was a human skull. Its black and empty eye sockets bored into Ryan like twin chunks of coal, and its lower jaw had dropped into a fixed grimace. Hammered into the top of the skull was a large copper nail. It had corroded into a yucky green mess. Where the nail penetrated the cranium, the skull had splintered.

There were other bones, too. Rib bones and parts of the vertebrae. And a pair of skeletal hands tied together with rotting pieces of rope.

Ryan lurched away on rubbery legs. He ran his hands through his tousled hair and back down over his face, rubbing at his eyes like he could erase the sight that was burned on his retinas.

"Argh!" he called out unintelligibly.

Ryan stumbled over to the edge of the clearing and used a tree for support. What in the blazes was going on? Dave Minnock must have known what was down there. So why didn't he warn Ryan? And for what purpose was he using him? All this twaddle about opening up a channel of dark energy was nothing but a crock of shit, surely?

Or was it?

Because the hallucinations the strange little man had planted in Ryan's brain felt real enough, as far as hallucinations go. Who the hell knew what other curious and dangerous abilities Minnock possessed?

More to the point, who was the person buried beneath the stone cross?

It didn't matter. Ryan had held up his end of the deal and toppled the stone cross. Beyond that, he had no desire to get involved any deeper. He'd return home and phone Minnock like he'd been told. Then wait for further instructions.

Ditching the tools, Ryan set off on the return trip. He forged a path from the clearing, following a twisting trail into the woods. He walked briskly, spurred on by the prospect of being liberated from his living nightmare. Soon, he broke into a jog.

The afternoon was drawing in, lending the woods a cheerless feel. He'd be relieved to leave this godforsaken world behind.

The trees grew denser and darker. They were crammed in on all sides, squeezing the trail into a thin passage and slowing him down. It didn't take much in Ryan's fragile state to imagine them edging closer, their roots slithering across the ground like vipers.

Up ahead, Ryan noticed a bluish radiance shimmering against the tree trunks. Somebody was approaching with a flashlight, it appeared. Ryan sucked in his breath as the light intensified. Leaving the trail, he thrust his way into the jam-packed lower branches, ignoring the sharp pain. Then he sat down on his haunches and waited for the person to pass by.

The bluish light seemed to flutter and zip through the air, and Ryan didn't think it was torchlight he was seeing anymore because it was accompanied by a stiff breeze, and the air crackled with static. He cringed with fear, convinced he was having another nightmarish vision. Any moment now, one of those hideous monsters would burst out of the trees and scare the hell out of him.

But that's not what happened. The radiance flared so brightly that Ryan had to raise a hand to shield his eyes, and right before him was something at once beautiful and spine-chilling.

A large globule of iridescent light came into sight, floating a few feet off the ground. Ryan gawped open-mouthed. It looked like a giant eyeball, at once opaque and the next transparent. The misshapen sphere paused and seemed to turn and 'look' at him, and he thought there was something suspended inside because he saw a face with corrugated folds of flesh set with narrow eyes. The deviant curiosity scrutinized him for several heartbeats before rotating back around and resuming its journey through the trees.

CHAPTER 20

JACKO GAVE A THEATRICAL SHIVER and looked pointedly at the empty grate.

"It's bloody cold in here," he remarked, sipping his beer and belching loudly.

He was already on his fourth can and well on the way to being intoxicated, Lee observed. Lee, meanwhile, was nursing his first beer and was thinking what a long evening it was set to be.

"Like a friggin' igloo," Jacko added.

Lee, who got the message, pushed himself out of the armchair and reached for the basket of firewood on the hearth. It was nearly empty.

"I'll pop outside and get some kindling."

"Do you need any help?" asked Jacko, making a token effort to come to his feet.

"I can manage."

Jacko slumped back into the rocking chair. "If you insist, pal."

Dweller Under The Roots

Lee stepped outside. A coolish wind blew across from the treeline, and he turned up his shirt collar as he beat a path for the outbuilding. Once under shelter and out of sight, he slipped his phone out and quickly dialled Amelia's number. Silence at the other end of the line informed him there was no signal. He moved to the rear of the building, past the stables, and tried by the open windows at the back. Again, his call didn't connect. Blast. Amelia warned him about poor reception. Lee really wanted to hear her voice.

Gathering several pieces of chopped-up wood from the log pile, Lee retraced his steps over the overgrown garden and closed the cottage door behind him.

Jacko was asleep in the rocking chair, snoring lightly.

Lee looked at his old classmate, casting his mind back to that chance meeting in the school hallway all those years ago. They'd called themselves The Three Musketeers, while others at school referred to them as The Three Amigos, and it was true they'd been tight friends once. But that was in the past, and Lee was done with feeling all sentimental. Loyalty had landed him in this pickle in the first place, and he couldn't risk his freedom because of Jacko Page.

The time had come to cut ties.

Treading softly, Lee approached the hearth and quietly built a fire. Jacko continued to snore as the flames took hold and warmed up the room. Hopefully, the mixture of beer and a snug fire would keep him in the land of nod for some time. Then Lee slipped up the stairs to the bedroom and quickly packed a few things into his overnight bag. Amelia's borrowed parka was hanging on the hook behind the bedroom door, and Lee pulled it on, ensuring the Defender's keys were still in the front pocket. At the last minute, he grabbed Percival the Tramp's book off the shelf and pushed it into the bag. Then he zipped it up, slung it over his shoulder, and tiptoed downstairs.

He came to a halt at the bottom. The rocking chair was empty, and there was no sign of Jacko.

Blast.

Lee glanced around, wondering where the heck his friend was. Maybe he'd woken up and gone into the kitchen for another beer. Making as little noise as possible, Lee padded towards the front door, eased it open, and stole outside. Then he closed it softly and stepped onto the path.

He'd barely moved two feet when something cold and hard pressed into the side of his neck. The sound of a gun being cocked froze Lee's heart.

"Are you leaving?" Jacko's mild voice failed to mask the menace contained in those three words.

The shotgun barrel jabbed harder into Lee, depressing his skin.

"I fucking knew it," Jacko told him. "You're just another backstabber. After all these years, you're nothing but a turncoat, Lee Harris."

Lee slowly raised his hands. He could hardly talk because his throat had closed up. He had to make a conscious effort to speak deliberately.

"I'm not selling you out, Jacko. But the game's up, and you know it."

"What the hell are you talking about?"

"It's over. We screwed up. So I'm out of here."

"That's a load of garbage," Jacko hissed, and out of the corner of his eye, Lee could see a wild look in his friend's eyes. "We just have to hold our nerve for a little longer."

"I'm sorry, pal, but you're wrong."

"No, I'm not. Just use your brain and think it through."

"That's what I've been doing. For days now, that's all I've been doing. And I don't see any alternative but to leave and take my chances."

"It's that bloody woman, isn't it? Jeez, man. You're quitting on me for that woman? I can't believe it."

Jacko laughed mirthlessly, and the gun barrel shook.

Cautiously, Lee turned about and faced Jacko, looking steadily at him. The gun was now inches from his face, and Jacko's predatory eyes squinted along the short barrel.

"What difference does it make," Lee answered in a whisper. "Yes, I'm leaving with Amelia, but it doesn't change the basic facts."

"And what are those?"

"That it's only a matter of time until the police show up. I don't plan on doing a long stretch inside, and I'm not dying in a shootout, either. So, Amelia and I are giving notice. That's the way it is."

"That's the way it is," Jacko mimicked with a sneer. "And does Amelia know precisely what you're walking out on?"

"No, but maybe one day I'll tell her everything."

Jacko shook his head, and then he turned and spat on the ground, mumbling something under his breath.

"What d'you say?"

"I said, in your 'effing dreams," Jacko said loudly. "Your fairytale ending of driving off into the sunset isn't happening. Now give me the keys to your car."

He held out one hand and made a grasping motion.

"Come on, or by God, I'll pull the trigger. I swear it, pal."

"Don't be an idiot, Jacko. You're drunk."

"So don't fucking risk it, then!" he screeched, the fury in his voice shaking Lee. The trees absorbed the words, swallowing them up.

Lee dipped his hand into the coat's pocket and found the car keys. He dropped them into his friend's hand. Lee still had the handgun tucked down the back of his trousers but thought this wasn't the time to play the hero. Not with a sawn-off shotgun in his face.

"Now turn the fuck around and get back inside. Move your fucking arse!"

Lee went up to the doorstep and pushed open the cottage's door. A firm prod in his back propelled him into the room.

"Ditch the bag and sit in the chair."

Lee lowered himself into his seat while Jacko heeled the door shut. Jacko might have been the worse for drink, Lee thought, but he wasn't so plastered he didn't keep the shotgun aimed at Lee the whole time.

"Now, ring your girlfriend and get her over here. And don't give the game away, pal."

"The signal out here is bad. It comes and goes."

"Just do it."

Lee fished out his phone and dialled. Again, there was no tone.

"Nothing," and Lee held out the phone.

Jacko snatched it from him and held the handset to his ear.

"Bloody backwoods," Jacko said. He threw the phone back over to Lee. "Try sending her a text."

"What shall I put?"

"Just tell her to come over. Keep it short."

Lee typed out a quick message, showed it to Jacko for approval, and hit SEND.

"What now?"

"Now we wait for her to arrive, don't we?"

"And then?"

Jacko didn't answer Lee. He just looked at him with empty eyes.

"You're going to shoot us? Just like that? Do you think Amelia won't be missed? Killing the pair of us is the surest way of attracting the attention of the police."

Jacko waved his hand dismissively and bent over to scoop his beer can off the floor. He drank the final dregs and then tossed it away angrily.

"You can have mine," Lee offered, holding out his beer.

"I don't think so, pal."

It was clear Jacko was reacting to events on the fly and hadn't thought any of this through. Either that was the beer addling his brain, or he really didn't care what happened to him. Lee, in contrast, felt a panicky feeling start welling up inside.

All he could do was wait and hope for an opportunity to act. Otherwise, the night was heading for a bloody climax.

The opportunity came in an unexpected way just a few minutes later.

Jacko had pulled a chair out from the small table and positioned himself where he could see out the window as well as keep watch on Lee. Meanwhile, Lee was trying to find ways to distract his friend long enough to pull out the handgun and gain control of events.

In the next instant, a bright blue light lit up the inside of the cottage. It shone through the window and underneath the front door, bathing everything in a flickering, bluish tint. In the same split-second, the house seemed to lift an inch off the ground and then slump down again, causing dust to come trickling down from the roof beams. Jacko, whose attention was fixed on the light, didn't seem to notice the bizarre phenomenon. Lee wondered if they'd just experienced a minor earth tremor, but he had no time to dwell on the notion because Jacko had leaped from his chair and was backpeddaling away from the window.

"It's the fucking police!" he screamed. "The bitch has called the police!"

Lee came to his feet and yanked the gun from his trousers, but instead of pointing it at his friend, he found himself ducking out of sight in case a hail of bullets from police sharpshooters came through the walls.

Amelia wouldn't phone the police. Lee told himself that even if she'd worked out who they were, she wouldn't do that.

But the police were right outside. The flashing blue lights all around told him he and Jacko were surrounded. Even as he thought this, the blue strobing luminescence grew more dazzling. It blazed through the window. They must have searchlights atop their vehicles, Lee reasoned.

"The bastard fuzz! They're not going to catch me!" Jacko raged.

He ducked down and then scurried below the window frame.

"I'll fucking die first!"

Before Lee realized what his friend was doing, Jacko had yanked open the cottage's door. Lee saw Jacko silhouetted in the blue light, with the sawn-off shotgun raised to his shoulder and pointed outside.

This is it, then, Lee concluded. This is where it ends.

The next moment, Jacko's jaw sagged open, his eyes enlarged, and his knees buckled. All the strength appeared to leave his friend because Jacko dropped the shotgun and his legs collapsed from under him. In slow motion, his body folded in on itself. He slipped down the doorframe and stared wide-eyed at something waiting outside.

CHAPTER 21

From his position, Lee couldn't see beyond the open doorway. He was glad because whatever was out there frightened his friend so badly that it skewered him to the spot.

Then, something long and slender snaked over the threshold, slithering like a tentacle towards Jacko's outstretched foot. Lee watched dumbstruck as it looped around his friend's ankle and started to pull. Jacko screamed. A panicky whimpering and moaning followed his cry, and Jacko kicked and thrashed with all four limbs as he tried pulling back. A bizarre game of tug-of-war ensued between Jacko and the thing holding his foot.

The tentacle – or whatever the heck it was – gained the upper hand as Jacko was pulled inch by inch through the doorway. In desperation, he grabbed the door handle and looked at Lee with pleading eyes.

Lee understood perfectly that if Jacko were dragged through the doorway, he'd never see him again. He didn't know how he knew this; he just did. And despite their differences, Lee couldn't let that happen to a fellow human being. Even one as reprehensible as Jacko Page.

Lee sprang forward and gripped Jacko's coat collar just before he disappeared. Lee still had the handgun in his other hand, and he aimed it outside. But when he saw what lurked beyond the cottage door, the shock was so big that Lee felt like he'd been hit in the solar plexus with a sledgehammer.

The entirety of the overgrown garden had come alive. Bathed in blue light, it moved like a living carpet of vines or a nest of wriggling serpents. Hundreds of plant and tree roots crawled towards the cottage entrance, pushing and sliding over the ground. A few reared like cobras about to strike their prey, while others rose from the ground and whipped back and forth.

At the centre was a small child, her fearsome visage a mass of crawling earthworms. Her hair writhed with more roots, so she resembled the mythical Gorgon. All around her bare feet, the roots battled in a crazy, impossible, unnatural desire to reach Jacko and drag him to his death.

The tendril holding Jacko continued to pull. Lee nearly lost his grip on the coat collar, but it helped snap him out of his state of shock, and he redoubled his efforts to save his friend. Lee stamped down on the root, and when this didn't cause it to let go, he pointed the handgun at it and fired.

The weapon kicked brutally, hurting Lee's wrist, but at such close range it was impossible to miss. The shot ripped into the root, nearly disintegrating it, leaving only a few hairy sinews behind. Jacko jerked his leg back, snapping them, and then he was free. They both sprawled inside the doorway.

The root whipped in the entrance like an octopus' tentacle seeking its prey, and white foamy liquid squirted from the severed end. Then it slithered away and was lost amidst the hundreds of roots swarming forwards. Lee clawed his way up the doorframe on shaky legs and slammed the door shut, but several roots had already crossed the entrance, stopping the door from closing. They thrashed in the narrow gap like they were possessed with malevolent fury, which was an insane but accurate analogy. With all his strength, Lee pushed with his shoulder against the wood, but the roots were impossibly strong, and they flicked their tendrils at his face and hands, stinging Lee's flesh. He watched through the gap as the child in the garden approached the cottage, passing slowly through the carpet of living plants. Whatever unnatural phenomenon was going on, this person was the foci. He could not allow them inside the cottage.

"Help me, Jacko! I can't hold them!" Lee looked around, but Jacko was crawling away on all fours. The last Lee saw of his friend, he was heading through the kitchen door. A few seconds later, Lee heard the cellar door rattle open, and heavy footsteps pounded down the stairs.

Sounds over his head told Lee the roots were on the roof, and when he heard them slithering down the chimney, subzero fingers clenched his heart.

In desperation, Lee pointed the gun through the gap and fired twice into the writhing mass. He saw pieces of roots pulverized into shreds, and he'd be damned if he didn't hear them screech in pain, and they pulled back briefly. Lee seized the moment to slam the cottage door shut and drag the table across as a barricade.

Dweller Under The Roots

He stood there, drawing in massive lungfuls of air and trying to steady his frazzled nerves. Lee's foot knocked against something on the floor, and when he looked down, he saw the end of the tendril that he'd shot off was still alive. It squiggled over the flagstones towards Lee, driven by some supernatural desire for revenge. He kicked it away, seeing it skitter across the floor.

More noises from the fireplace reminded Lee the roots were worming and bellying their way into the cottage. There was no time to linger. He needed to vacate this hellhole immediately, and there was only one way out. He threw the empty handgun away, picked up the sawn-off shotgun, and fled into the kitchen.

The cellar door was flung wide open, and Lee paused at the top in indecision. Lee knew there was no alternative, but the idea of going down there filled him to the brim with terror. But when he heard the kitchen window start to fragment, he raced down the stairs at full throttle.

"Jacko! Where are you?" he shouted once he reached the bottom.

He could barely see a thing. Lee swatted his arm from side to side until he found the pull cord. Pale light washed over the root cellar. Lee did a quick search, ignoring the overripe produce, the sharp smell of vinegar, and the cobweb-shrouded shelves. Jacko wasn't anywhere in sight. Then Lee thought he heard scuffing sounds from the narrow passage at the back. He swiftly passed the rows of containers and glass vessels and approached the small wood door.

As before, the door latch was stiff with rust. It took several strong tugs before it turned, and the door sprang open. Cool air wafted from the opening.

When he and Amelia had explored this part of the cellar, the passage beyond was dark and unfriendly, and they'd needed the flashlight to find their way. That wasn't the case now. The candles set in their recesses all burned brightly, burnishing the passage in golden light.

Lee didn't question this. He didn't ponder who had lit the candles and when, but just accepted it as another strange occurrence to add to all the others. Nor did he puzzle over the exposed tree roots that were now twisting with life from the walls and roof like tactile feelers.

Lee briefly thought of racing back up the cellar stairs and trying to escape from the cottage that way. But he felt sure the kitchen would already be choked with plant life, and he had no desire to fight his way through it. Consequently, he had no choice but to run the gauntlet along the passage.

Lee moved forward while bent over at the waist. The roof seemed lower than before, and he could feel his head brush against the roots. Lee cringed as they sought to curl around his scalp or probe into his ears. He could feel movement all around and saw chunks of soil fall away from the bare walls as more tree roots wormed through, drawn by his presence. Once, one particularly long tendril wound around the shotgun, and he had to snatch the weapon free.

Under his feet, the hard-packed ground suddenly became all sticky. Not pausing, Lee stole a glance down and saw yellow slime covering everything. It glistened in the candlelight and sucked at his shoes as he trod through it. Bile rose from his gullet, and Lee clenched his teeth to stop himself from being sick and frantically swallowed several times.

"Jacko?" he called again. "JACKO! – oh, Christ!"

Lee stopped dead. He'd reached the shallow cave on his right containing the slugs' breeding ground and stared horror-struck at the sight that confronted him.

His friend must have taken a wrong turn and blundered right into a trap. Jacko was entangled in a web of tree roots covering the cave mouth. They ensnared his whole body and penetrated his mouth, his eyes, and between his legs, harpooning him and skewering him like a bug. Then, the slugs had come slithering from their giant nest and started to feast on him. They weren't normal-sized gastropods anymore; they were supersized creatures, each at least two feet long, with sharp mandibles that chewed and masticated Jacko's flesh. Worse of all, even more abhorrent than this underground feasting, was the realization that his friend was still alive and conscious. Jacko's slime-coated body spasmed in agony at each bite, and his fingertips reached towards Lee in hopeless despair. The tree roots wormed deeper into Jacko, shredding his insides and adding to his torture.

Lee couldn't bear to watch his friend being eaten alive, and he brought up the shotgun's barrel. He aimed at Jacko and started to squeeze the trigger. At the last second, he hesitated. Jacko's jaw was moving, attempting to speak around the length of tree root lodged in his mouth.

"Run," Jacko gagged. "Run."

Lee shook his head to dislodge the tears in his eyes, then turned away. He ran from the cave and over the mass of slug goo covering the ground. He could hear his breath ratcheting in the back of his throat, like a trapped cry.

More slugs crawled down the walls, and as he passed, the little eyes on the end of their twin antennae turned to follow him.

The passage jinked in a dogleg to the left and right and came to a dead end. In front of Lee was the ladder he remembered from the other day, and above his head, the trapdoor. Lee scrambled one-handed up the rungs and pushed against the trapdoor with his back.

It didn't budge; belatedly, Lee remembered that it was bolted on the outside.

He moaned in despair.

Looping one arm through the top rung and holding the shotgun, Lee pushed against the wooden slats with his free hand, and when that didn't work, he banged against it with the heel of his hand. The trapdoor rattled in its frame but refused to open.

Lee dropped to the earth floor. Rustling noises from behind had him looking over his shoulder. The tree roots appeared around the dogleg bend, waving in the air like a multi-tentacled creature from hell. A narrow furrow appeared in the soil close to his feet, widening into a crack. In the candlelight, Lee saw a fresh root sliding through the dirt like an advanced guard to the army of living, subterranean plant roots that, even as he watched, were edging closer and closer.

Lee scrambled back up the ladder just in time before the root snaked out of the earth and made a grab for his feet. He frantically kicked it away. It fell back like it was momentarily stunned before rising like a snake-charmers viper. Again, it struck out, and this time, gained a purchase on his trouser leg. Lee yelped and tried to shake it free, and in the struggle, the root touched one of the lit candles. There was a sizzling sound and a smell like burnt hair, and the root let go of Lee's leg and cringed away severely singed.

Lee knew the pause in the assault would only last a few seconds because the mass of plant life was almost at the end of the passage. Taking the shotgun, he pushed the business end right underneath where the bolt should be, shielded his face, and, praying that it was loaded, he pulled the trigger.

The noise of the discharge was deafening inside the confined space, and it reverberated around Lee's skull like someone was striking his head with a rock. Wood splinters flew in all directions. He peered through the gun smoke, willing it to clear quickly.

The trapdoor was split apart by a hole as big as his fist. He could see the bolt on the other side was bent out of shape and hanging off one screw. Lee pushed with his back once more, and this time, the trapdoor lifted clear and fell back against the outbuilding's inner wall. Lee was up and through in two bounds and then ran past the animal stalls and out of the building.

Behind him, the roots burst out of the square hole in the floor, grasping and grabbing at the air in vain.

CHAPTER 22

RYAN REMAINED IN HIS HIDING place for five minutes, fearful the iridescent sphere might return. He tried not to dwell on the supernatural encounter. His head was already in a fragile state, and if he spent too much time considering what it all meant, the speck of sanity remaining to him might go out like a guttering candle.

When he was sure the coast was clear, Ryan rose from his crouch and forced his way through the branches. Then he resumed his brisk walk along the trail in the opposite direction to that taken by the floating entity.

It was getting hard to see in the poor light. More than once, Ryan nearly lost his footing. Ryan forced himself to slow down and navigate more carefully, telling himself his terrible ordeal was near an end and that it would be stupid to take a tumble and turn his ankle. He'd be safely back in his bedsit and sitting pretty in another hour.

The walking trail sloped down a bank. It twisted around a thicket of young saplings and finally arrived at the tourist car park. The small patch of gravel was empty at this time of day, which suited Ryan. If his probation officer got wind of him sneaking around the woods late at night, it might land Ryan in trouble. He wasn't under a curfew, but the less the busybody knew, the better.

Exiting the car park, Ryan emerged onto the narrow country lane and headed towards Midgehole. Very few people lived this far out, so only a few farmhouses dotted the landscape, their lights just starting to come on. Ryan picked up the pace again. As soon as he was home, he'd be straight on the blower to Dave Minnock with the good news, and if the odd fellow kept to the deal, very soon, Ryan would have his life back: one free of sinister visions.

He was soon striding down the centre of the road with a confident swagger.

As he walked, he considered his future. The way Ryan saw it, he had two choices. He could carry on searching for Amelia; he was closing in on where she was living, he felt confident of that. Ryan also thought Dave Minnock might be the key to tracking her down. Then, once he had her address and phone number, he could continue hounding her and maybe even step things up to another level. From Ryan's twisted perspective, she was the root cause of all his problems - the police raid at the club, his arrest and sentence, as well as the daemons that haunted him. Therefore, she had it coming, and Ryan looked forward to dishing out some payback.

His second choice was to drop the whole thing. Harassing Amelia had been fun at first; it had given him a thrill to call her in the dead of night and listen to her trembling voice or to catch her as she left work and follow her down the street.

But with no ultimate endgame other than making her life miserable (Ryan, like most jilted men with a grudge, was a snivelling wimp with as much backbone as a jellyfish), he soon grew bored. As time passed, and Ryan limped through his days doing community service, coming home to a cold bedsit, and eating microwaved pot noodles, his appetite for retribution dwindled. And when the bad dreams and visions started messing with his sanity, Ryan frequently asked himself: was it all worth it?

Perhaps he ought to take Dave Minnock's advice, find a proper job, get his life back on track, and forget he ever met Amelia.

Amelia who? Ryan laughed out loud. Yes, taking that approach was much nicer.

Screw her and screw Dave Weidro Minnock! Ryan was the master of his fate.

Ryan got his skates on, already planning for the next chapter in his life.

After twenty minutes of walking downhill, he passed through the tiny hamlet of Midgehole, which comprised one row of houses. In the gathering gloom, the large bulk of the burnt-out mansion across the field caught his attention, and Ryan stopped dead. He listened carefully because he thought he'd heard children's laughter. He must have imagined it because the children's home closed in Victorian times, and the borstal that followed was shut down by the authorities several decades ago. So, who the heck were the running figures in the gardens? And why were they wearing petticoats and buckled shoes?

Dweller Under The Roots

Ryan faced over the field, watching them dance and play. After a short time, a handbell sounded, and the children – all girls, by the looks – ran across a terrace and through the entranceway of the abandoned building. All but one. One girl hesitated and turned to wave at Ryan, and stupidly, he raised a hand to wave back. Then, the last straggler followed the others, and Ryan, somewhat puzzled by the encounter, turned to continue his walk home.

He never saw the bus come out of the dark and hit him in a head-on collision.

One of the passengers on the Number 64 bus was Dave Minnock. He, with everybody else, alighted and milled around in the roadway. Several people went for a closer look at the pile of bloody mush under the front wheels. One lady crouched and held the young victim's hand, whispering to him, but it was apparent to all those present that he wouldn't make it. Meanwhile, the bus driver was sitting on the roadside wall, shaking his head and mumbling about seeing a dog with three heads bound across the road. By the end of the day, he'd wind up strapped to a bed and heavily sedated.

Dave hung around for a short time, feeling satisfied with his handiwork. A lifetime of careful study and application across different occult disciplines was paying dividends, even though there were still many branches of the metaphysical realm he hadn't yet mastered, primarily the more mystical pantheon of Sumerian and Babylonian rituals. Dave wouldn't consider himself a magus until he had command of all the secrets of ceremonial magic. But so far, everything was going to plan. He'd spent years preparing for this night and would achieve his first objective in just a few hours.

Of course, Dave recognized that he couldn't have done this alone. A whole cast of actors had played their part, most of them – but not all – oblivious to the role they had in his grand drama. The planets, indeed, were correctly aligned, figuratively and astrologically speaking.

When he caught the distant sound of sirens floating in the evening air, Dave peeled away from the crowd of onlookers and headed uphill. The night wasn't done by any measure. He still had tasks to execute and certain rituals to perform. Even then, this was only the start, the realization of a covenant he'd made over half a century ago when Dave learned about his heritage and ancestral connection to the past. The future held so much more promise.

As Dave left the road and struck out across the large stretch of moors, a tiny but persistent sliver of doubt resurfaced in his mind. No matter how well he'd prepared and laid the groundwork, there was always an element of the unknown, that unexpected happenchance that might still harm things at the last moment.

The one aspect Dave couldn't control was the arrival of a stranger in their midst - Lee Harris, whom Dave had only partially succeeded in manipulating.

The unknown component. A factor beyond Dave's command.

The chap had proven mentally strong and resistant to nearly everything Dave had thrown at him, except for the carnal kind.

Dweller Under The Roots

Dave Minnock was feeling uneasy, which was a new experience for him.

CHAPTER 23

LEE FLED FROM THE COTTAGE like the Devil himself was on his heels – which he might well have been. He sprinted out of the outbuilding, leaping over more roots that wriggled across his path. Everywhere he looked, the land seemed to stir with life: the ground bristled with moving plants, and the trees shivered and creaked, leaning close like gossipy women. He angled around the side of the cottage, giving the front garden a wide berth (luckily, there was no sign of the child or the unearthly light), and bolted towards the Defender. But when he was still fifty yards away, the car started to shake on its axle because the earth underneath was rising and breaking open, tilting the Defender over. A large tree root pushed from its subterranean world into the upper world, groping like a blind creature before curling over the car and crushing its roof like some extraordinary boa constrictor summoned from hell. The sound of rending and popping metal filled the air, and Lee skidded to a stop and witnessed his car being dismantled before his eyes.

Dweller Under The Roots

A rumbling from over his shoulder spun Lee about, and he looked in wide-eyed awe as the cottage was shaken loose from its foundations, the walls shedding mortar dust and bricks, the crooked roof splitting open. New shoots of ivy slithered up the walls like part of a time-lapse film. Creepers and vines twisted around and through each other, so the old building was wrapped in a cocoon of greenery in less than a minute. One of the chimney stacks fell over in stages like a tower built from children's wooden blocks, crashing through the outbuilding's roof and adding to the noise and violence.

Lee sped around the opposite end of the cottage, rocketed down the crooked path, and dove headlong into the woods.

Coming this way probably wasn't the greatest idea. The country lane would be safer. It would also take twice as long. And after what just happened to Jacko, Lee needed to reach Amelia's place as urgently as possible.

But a shortcut through the darkening woodland meant a shortcut through a small corner of hell because he'd merely swapped one nightmare for another. To his left and right, the serried ranks of slender trunks and bigger elms and oaks jostled and bumped together as they crowded forwards, and sinewy roots burst out of the ground, seeking to trip and impede.

He could barely see his way in the twilight. Tree trunks reared up out of the shadows, no longer the silent, eternal sentinels of old but now hostile adversaries intent on stopping him. Branches and barriers of interlaced underbrush slashed Lee's face and ripped the sleeves of the parka. Several times, he collided with trees as he ran the gauntlet of this lethal obstacle course.

Lee's heart was beating rapidly in his chest, thudding in tempo with the heavy stomp of his footfall. The experience in the cottage and the secret passageway had left him shaken, and he hoped never to witness anything close to Jacko's gruesome death again. Still, he was keyed up. Adrenaline flooded his veins, providing an extra boost to his body, matched by a gritty resolve to face whatever came next and escape with Amelia.

Lee still had hold of the shotgun even though the chamber was empty and he had no replacement ammo. It was an encumbrance, so he tossed it into the undergrowth and ran a mile a minute, using his forearms to shield his face and hack a path through the branches.

The woods tried to mob him, crowding in like a gang of muggers. Green stems sprouted from the sides, and Lee felt them on his shoes and ankles as they sought to arrest his flight through their world. It was, Lee thought, like Mother Nature was fighting back. If he screwed up and took a misstep, Lee doubted he'd have time to get to his feet again because the plants and roots would swarm all over him in moments. The woods seemed to intuitively twig onto this (no pun intended: it wasn't the time to be witty) because the ground under his feet was shaking, and Lee could hear it splitting in hairline cracks.

He grimaced with the effort of running. He had a painful stitch in his side.

Somewhere in the distance, Lee thought that he heard a faint scream, together with barking dogs and men's gruff voices. He tried not to think of the story Dave Minnock told them about Mother Baxter's death. If he did, he might give in to hysteria.

The woodland path emerged into the clearing. Lee barely paused, but he managed to snatch a brief look around. In the semi-darkness he saw a deep hole in the earth, but he couldn't see what, if anything, rested at the bottom. Next to the hole, the stone cross lay flat on the ground. Nearby, he spied a discarded shovel and pickaxe. Lee had no idea what it meant, and he didn't linger for long. He ran across the clearing and onto the path again.

All around him now, there were hundreds, maybe thousands of glowing mushrooms and spores lighting the way. Their luminosity reflected off the plants, creating a tunnel of light just like in his dream. More multi-coloured fungi clung to tree trunks. The woods still moved and rippled with supernatural energy, but the trees and roots cringed away from the pathway, almost like the incandescent radiance repelled them. Lee twisted his head from side to side, entranced by what he saw.

A feeling came over Lee just then. A weird sense that he wasn't fighting single-handedly against the powers of darkness. That something was helping him. If it hadn't been for the glowing toadstools and mushrooms keeping the vegetation at bay, Lee was convinced it would have overflowed the path and turned him into a human/plant hybrid. Lee thought of the ley line that ran through the woods and cottage, the ancient corpse road, and he wondered if this was what he was seeing, lit up. Lee was grateful for any help, in whatever form it came. Discovering a second wind (or maybe a third, after the adrenaline boost), Lee bounded along like he was a teenager, and within a short time, the pathway dissolved into a broad pasture as it left the trees behind.

Ahead of Lee was the valley with the stream running down the middle, and on the plot of land was Amelia's caravan. A light inside beckoned Lee. He hurried forwards, but his euphoria lasted only a handful of seconds because his heart sank when he saw the shattered window and the curtains flapping in the breeze.

"No, no, no," Lee lamented.

He closed the gap, staggered past her moped and up the steps, and pushed open the caravan door. Inside, it looked like a bomb had gone off. The furniture, the television, and all Amelia's belongings had either been smashed to pieces or upset. Clothes lay scattered all around. Lee ran from room to room, calling out her name, but it was the same throughout the caravan; except for the ceiling lights, everything was destroyed, and there was no sign of her. Somebody had been here, vandalized Amelia's home, and taken her away.

Lee returned to the lounge and sank onto the couch, holding his head.

Who would do this? And why?

Through his splayed fingers, Lee noticed a white stain on the carpet. Leaning over, he touched it. His fingers came away all sticky, and Lee was reminded of the slugs down the cellar and the foot-track spell he'd trodden through.

It must all be connected.

Connected to Mother Baxter and her infant daughter, Long Meg.

But connected how?

Dweller Under The Roots

Lee came to his feet and stepped across to the wreckage of the window, and as he stood gazing out, his eyes were drawn up the steep hillside to the tunnel entrance. It stood out like a mouth against the purple twilight sky.

That's where he would find the answers; Lee felt as sure as anything.

CHAPTER 24

LEE TOOK HIS PHONE AND quickly found Amelia's number, and then rang her more in hope than expectation. He was surprised when the call connected and momentarily flirted with the idea she might answer. But his run of bad luck showed no signs of abating because he heard Amelia's ringtone sound from somewhere within the caravan. Lee sullenly poked around until he found her handset amidst the pile of clothes.

Perhaps he should ring Dave Minnock and ask for his help. Lee could be wide of the mark about Amelia's whereabouts. She'd been having trouble with her ex-boyfriend, so maybe this Ryan fellow had something to do with her disappearance. Dave might know. But it was a moot point; Lee didn't have Dave Minnock's number, and Amelia's mobile phone was locked.

Also, Lee knew he was stalling and putting off the inevitable.

He had to check out the old pit workings.

Dweller Under The Roots

Putting both phones into the parka's pockets, Lee entered the kitchen. After checking that it worked, he took down one of the magnetic strip lights and slipped it down his waistband. Thus primed for exploring the mine, Lee left the caravan and hoofed it across the grass, past the old supports to the trestle bridge, and then started up the slope. He didn't wish to give away his approach using the light, so he had to climb in the dark. He also reasoned he'd need to save the batteries for later.

The higher he went, the more hazardous the ascent became. Losing one's way in the darkness was also a possibility. He tried using the glow from the caravan to guide him, but after he'd gone a certain distance, this just became a pinpoint of light against the black earth.

Lee stumbled around, using his hands for support when the hill steepened. Rocks were scattered indiscriminately, and some came loose when he placed his weight on them. He took several tumbles, which knocked the wind out of him and left his body bruised and scratched. At least the vegetation here didn't try and kill him – that phenomenon seemed confined to the woods.

Lee sensed that he may have drifted too far to the left – the mine's entrance was just beneath the summit near the hill's right shoulder – so he crabbed-walked sideways. After an indeterminate amount of time, the grass gave way to stones and scree, which at least meant he was on the right track.

Higher and higher he went. A gusty wind buffeted him, trying to dislodge Lee. It was just another method Mother

Nature employed to try and finish him off – the list was growing longer.

Just as Lee grew concerned that he'd indeed gone wrong, the land levelled out, and he stood upright. The moon appeared briefly from behind scudding clouds, lighting the slope and revealing the boarded-up mine entrance a mere six feet away.

Hallelujah.

Lee approached the wooden obstruction and soon found the section he'd left prised open and, after a short pause, squeezed through.

The weak moonlight from outside illuminated the tunnel entrance. Lee blinked several times to let his eyesight adjust and refamiliarize himself with his surroundings.

Everything was as he remembered. The doorway to the blacksmith's workshop was on his left, and the steel rail lines ran away into the darkness. Lee craned his neck and peered towards the curved roof; he pictured hundreds of bats suspended upside down, their slitty eyes watching him (contrary to popular belief, Lee knew bats weren't blind). All he could see were shadows and more shadows.

The moon disappeared behind the clouds, and the tunnel sank into darkness. The wind vibrated through the wooden slats in a high-pitched hum, lending the tunnel a suitably atmospheric feel.

Taking the magnetic strip light, Lee turned it on. It cast a bright white glow that reflected off the damp walls. As before, he had the impression of being swallowed down some monstrous throat. Cautiously, Lee started forwards, minding he didn't stumble over the rails.

Dweller Under The Roots

As he walked, he listened intently. He wasn't quite sure what he expected to hear. Voices, maybe. Or Amelia crying for help. Perhaps Long Meg's terrible cackling. Lee shivered and berated himself; thoughts like that weren't helping.

But, other than the wind and his footfall, there was nothing. Even the former fell away as he progressed further into the mine.

As he advanced, the tunnel shrunk, the walls and roof closing in. Lee was convinced it was narrower than when they explored earlier, but he told himself that was either imagination or the strip light making the tunnel appear different from torchlight. He paused momentarily and reached his arms out to the sides; he could almost touch both walls with his fingertips. Above his head, the timber roof spars sagged like they'd grown tired of bearing all that weight for a century and a half. He had to guard against bumping his head against them. After another five minutes, the tunnel boiled down to a thin tube descending shallowly through the hillside, making him hunch over.

Presently, he emerged into the large chamber, and Lee stood erect. The old steam locomotive was still in place, with its tender and carts. Across the way was the second tunnel they'd chickened out of exploring.

It was frigid here, much colder than where he'd just come, and he could see his breath like a comic-strip speech bubble. Lee walked to the middle and turned around in a tight circle, holding the light aloft. The walls around him were sheer and cut in smooth vertical planes of granite that dully reflected the light.

Lee was contemplating whether to call out Amelia's name and hope she might hear (he still had no concrete evidence she was here – just a feeling), but he weighed up the risk of alerting their foe. He was still internally debating what to do when a sound that froze the blood in his veins reached him. It was a high-pitched and familiar chittering noise, the same sound he'd heard coming from the woods that first morning. It swelled out of the smaller tunnel across the chamber to undulate and swirl around the vast cavern.

Lee knew precisely what it signified. He wondered how easily he'd come to accept the recent paranormal happenings. In the past, he might have questioned if he was of sound mind. But too many inexplicable events had occurred for him to dispute them.

Here he was listening to the cry of some long-dead person - the wise woman, Mother Baxter.

Her cry was a challenge, pure and simple; a test of his fettle and his love for Amelia. A weaker man might have abandoned Amelia to an ungodly fate and fled from this place. But Lee knew if he succumbed to craven instincts of self-preservation, he'd never sleep easily again.

He stepped around the locomotive and crossed the cavern. Mumbling, "Oh, boy. Oh, boy," repeatedly to himself, he stole through the black orifice.

Immediately, Lee felt the weight of some terrible torment drag him down. It clung to him like a heavy shroud. He sensed that a thousand trials and tribulations awaited him at the end of this passage, wherever it led, and he was under no illusions that he'd probably not see another day. He was entering Mother Baxter's lair, trespassing into her realm.

Dweller Under The Roots

Still, he trudged on.

The passage angled downwards more steeply than the first tunnel. The light revealed dark brown walls and stone steps rounded smooth by water or the passage of many feet. Lee passed an old, hand-drawn cart piled high with gear that told him this was still part of the pit workings, not some natural subterranean crawlspace. He could see little to his front because the strip light wasn't focused like a flashlight; it cast a suffused glow that created contrasting shadows beyond its leading edge. The light jumped and bounced off the rough-hewn walls, creating a jerky world of light and dark.

Lee came to a sudden halt.

He could hear something. A clip-clopping noise, coming closer.

Footsteps.

Lee held his breath and peered into the blackness, wanting to see who approached, but at the same time hoping the footsteps would fade away. But they didn't.

Then he saw a man clambering up the steep incline, his body folded over with the effort. He was wearing loose clothes, and on his feet was a pair of clogs. His face was grimed with streaks of dirt, making his eyes stand out. On his head was a leather hat with a lit candle attached to the front.

The man didn't appear to see Lee, who hastily stood to one side as the fellow passed. Behind him came more figures, including several children, all similarly dressed and with candles on their headwear. They didn't speak; their laboured breathing and heavy footsteps were the only sounds. The line of people clomped by without acknowledging his presence, and a freezing chill frosted Lee's skin like it was midwinter.

Lee pressed his back against the wall to allow them through and then turned to watch as they plodded up the slope. After a few seconds, they disappeared into the shadows. The sound of their steps melted away.

Instead of being blown away by the encounter, Lee felt strangely numb. It wasn't easy to codify what he'd just seen with his own eyes. Best if he didn't over analyse it, Lee told himself. Keep moving. Don't waste time dwelling on distractions. Stick to the plan.

What was the plan?

Find Amelia and get the hell out.

Pushing away from the passage wall, Lee resumed his descent.

The passageway infiltrated deeper into the hillside. The air was stale, but at least it was breathable. Lee reasoned that there must be other openings leading to the outside. He didn't think there was a danger of pockets of poisonous or combustible gases after such a long time, but he was only guessing. He surmised that death by asphyxiation or noxious fumes was the least of his problems.

Lee had lost all track of time and how far he'd come, but after what felt like an age, the narrow passageway levelled out. He saw a familiar bluish light just ahead, around the next bend. Slowing down, he covered the final stretch in deliberate steps.

Lee found himself on the rim of a vast grotto, bigger than a cathedral. Enormous stalactites and stalagmites looking like sharp fangs gave it the impression of a colossal jaw about to snap shut on him. The blue light revealed a small waterfall gushing down a rock wall and feeding a narrow stream of crystal water. Lee had read about Hades and the River Styx from Greek mythology and reckoned this was a close approximation to that nightmare underworld. This impression was reinforced by what he saw at the centre of the grotto.

Some great, shrouded form stood as still as a statue on a raised rock dais, framed by two pillars where stalactites and stalagmites had joined together. The figure was at least twenty feet tall, and even though the face was hidden under a hood, Lee could see from its bowed posture that the figure was slumbering. Or waiting.

Four skeletal arms – two on each side of the body – were locked in position like a praying mantis. Between Lee and the grotesque abomination were dozens of stunted figures made from dried-up, twisted tree roots, looking in the bluish light like half-human/half-plant mutants. They waited on their haunches like silent sentinels, guarding their queen.

Lee's attention was drawn back to the tall figure on the dais.

It had to be Mother Baxter in all her glory; he recognized her from the old sketch the miner had drawn. The blue light radiated from behind her, casting blue beams to all parts of the grotto, like some otherworldly laser show. Lee then noticed one more thing. A tiny, crumpled-up body was on the ground before Mother Baxter, and even at this distance, Lee saw the infant's arms and legs, the emaciated husk-like body, and the malformed features.

Despite the terror welling inside him, Lee felt an unbearable sorrow in his heart. This was the child, Long Meg. Born during a thunderstorm, deformed and beset with the cackling sickness, without friends for her short life and long thought to have escaped the lynch mob to subsequently wander the woods and moors for over a century and a half, but all the time lying dead in this forlorn place beneath the earth. Beneath the roots.

Lee stood in the small opening to the passageway with his eyes bolted on the scene. He felt as weak as a kitten and could barely move because it was like he was shackled to the ground. It took a superhuman effort to flick off the strip light and slowly return it to his waistband.

Other than the waterfall, not a thing stirred. Lee wondered if Mother Baxter and her acolytes might be hibernating or trapped in a frozen limbo. Time might have turned them to stone, like in the petrifying well at Knaresborough. As this thought flickered through his head, Lee doubted he'd be let off so easily. Nothing about this promised an easy ride.

His attention was drawn back to the waterfall again because, through the cascading liquid, he'd seen something out of place. He screwed up his eyes and then drew in his breath.

Behind the waterfall lay Amelia's slumped body.

• • •

Ever so carefully, Lee lowered himself from the passage to the grotto floor. The waterfall was perhaps a hundred paces away, a short two-minute walk there and back. But to reach it required Lee to pass through the ranks of mutations and right by the slumbering harpy.

Dweller Under The Roots

From this distance, Lee couldn't tell if Amelia was conscious, unconscious, or dead, so he might be gambling everything on a lost cause.

Drawing on inner reserves, Lee started across the grotto.

He tried keeping his breathing low and rhythmic, his footsteps light and with no sudden movements. Did the mutations have eyes and ears? Or could they feel vibrations through the ground? Lee had no blasted idea, but if the roots that attacked him and killed Jacko were any indication, he had to assume they had some form of intelligence. Either that or Mother Baxter and her child were directing them.

Lee neared the first of the crouching hybrids. He could see more detail. The thing vaguely resembled the human form with a torso and a domed, bald head. But its spindly legs and arms contained a mass of stringy roots that twisted down to the ground, where they joined more extensive roots that, in turn, snaked across the cavern to Mother Baxter. Lee tiptoed past the hybrid, and then the next one, and the next, his whole body tensed and ready for potential attack.

As he drew closer to Mother Baxter, Lee studied her bowed form with a blend of fascination and horror. Her shroud was ripped into shreds and blackened with decades' worth of dirt and soot, and it gathered on the ground like a pool of sludge, hiding her lower body. The elongated skeleton arms had fingers made from hairy roots that tapered to thin points. She smelled like something from the grave; she was cloaked in a musky and cloying stench, a miasma that infiltrated Lee's mouth and nose with each shallow breath. Lee shivered on the inside.

As Lee approached, he had to step over one of the thicker roots on the ground. As he did, the thick stem flexed and fleetingly became semi-transparent, allowing Lee to see veins beneath the hard surface. Perhaps the roots acted as umbilical cords feeding Mother Baxter's adherents nutrients and energy.

Slowly, Lee circled the tall, slumbering witch with his senses on red alert. Then he slipped past one of the limescale pillars with a sigh of relief, leaving the last of the hideous mutations behind. A few seconds later, Lee was behind the waterfall. He saw Amelia was wearing tattered woollen trousers and a pullover like the miners. Lee gently shook her shoulder.

She stirred and mumbled something.

Thank God she was alive. Unconscious but alive.

Lee leaned forward and whispered in her ear, praying the sound of the water masked his voice.

"Wake up, Amelia. I need you to wake up."

Her eyelids fluttered open momentarily, closed again, and then peeled open once more. Her eyes appeared glazed and unfocused. By the looks of it, she'd been given some potion to knock her out.

"Lee?" Amelia murmured sleepily. "Where are we? What are you doing here?"

"Hush. You must be quiet, alright? Do you think you can stand up?"

Amelia said something incoherent and then rolled back over like she wanted to go back to sleep.

She was in no state to walk, at least not until she'd come around a little more. He'd have to carry her. Lee went down on one knee and worked his hands beneath her legs and back and then straightened up, his muscular frame easily bearing her slight body. Amelia shifted in his arms and snuggled her face under his chin. For now, at least, she was better off asleep; that way, she wouldn't have to see the horrors inside the cave. But carrying her would be challenging once they were in the narrow passage.

Turning about, Lee edged sideways from behind the curtain of water and looked out over the underground expanse. Mother Baxter and the hybrid mutations remained motionless.

Lee took a moment to consider if they could find another way out of there. He supposed dozens of small fissures must lead down from the surface. The water cascading down the rock wall had to be coming in from somewhere. Yet when he looked up, following the flow of water back, Lee saw that it poured all the way down from the grotto's roof towering above them. Lee quickly judged it was too high to climb, even with a fully conscious Amelia.

Okay then, it was back the way he'd come.

If he could make the trip once, he could make it again.

Carrying Amelia in his arms, Lee began the return leg, once more planting his feet as noiselessly as possible on the uneven ground. They went by the pillar and around the raised dais, across the front of Mother Baxter's statuesque shape, and cautiously through the resting hybrids.

They'd almost made it to the passageway without incident when the one thing Lee dreaded the most happened. A deep grating noise, like the sound boulders make when grinding together, made the hairs on the back of Lee's neck stand up. He looked over his shoulder.

Mother Baxter was rousing from her long slumber. Her head came up with majestic slowness, like an Easter Island statue coming to life. The hood fell away, allowing Lee the privilege of looking upon her exquisitely frightful face.

Lee was granted an audience with a shrew from the bowels of hell.

CHAPTER 25

MOTHER BAXTER'S HEAD REMAINED ENCASED in the set of branks. Lee cringed at the sight of the gruesome torture instrument she'd been made to wear, with its bridle-bit wedged into her mouth to prevent her from talking. Her lower jaw – what was left of it because her face and skull were emaciated and covered in weeping sores – was wet from excessive salivation. From the crown of her flayed head grew twin branch stumps.

Through the iron branks caging her head, a pair of glacial eyes blazed with hatred, their intense blueness seeking Lee out. He felt her penetrative stare inside his head like someone was scratching at the inside of his skull with crooked fingernails.

The four skeletal arms moved up and down in that horrible scarab-like clockwork-toy motion the petrified miner had once described, making a horrendous creaking sound like an old woman's arthritic joints. With the movement, Mother Baxter's shroud fell away, uncovering her half-formed and scarcely human body. Her rack of ribs was gnarled and yellowed with age, housing something black that throbbed and pulsed, pumping dark blood around a network of veins on the outside of her skeleton. Remnants of pale breasts hung like hessian sacks, their nipples oozing gelatinous milk. She had no legs, just a backbone coiled on the ground like a serpent.

Lee could barely breathe, feeling like a deep-sea diver who'd run out of air. His eyes misted over, and he tottered weakly, feeling his strength drain. He stiffened the muscles in his legs in a last-ditch effort to remain standing.

Suddenly, the air inside the cave started to vibrate with a peculiar buzzing, like something was being fired up. Lee could feel it in his chest and diaphragm. Then he watched dumbfounded as Mother Baxter slowly rose into the air, levitating on an invisible column of air, and her arms spread wide.

The most hideous of bellows rumbled up from deep inside her, a throaty bass sound that elongated into a high-pitched howl of pain and distress. The air inside the cave oscillated, trickles of dust and stone showered down from the high roof, and the ground under Lee's feet shook so severely that loose pebbles bounced around like magic beans. Mother Baxter's screech became so loud that if Lee hadn't been carrying Amelia, he'd have clamped his hands to his ears. It finished with that terrible chittering sound, like a thousand birds chirping in the trees. Long after she stopped screaming her rage, Mother Baxter's awakening rang around the caves and tunnels, rebounding back and forth.

She towered over them and slowly raised her arms, and her army of acolytes rose like ranks of believers climbing to their feet after morning prayers. Lee watched as their uplifted faces shone from the blue light that lanced across the cave. A murmur, almost a sigh, escaped their mutant lips, and then they turned to look at Lee and Amelia.

For a handful of heartbeats, there was total silence in the cavern. Then there was bedlam. Screaming and gibbering, the hybrid mutations snapped free of their umbilical cords and stampeded over the cave floor on hands and feet, looking like rampaging apes or scuttling alien arthropods. They swarmed towards the two human interlopers.

The muscles in Lee's legs suddenly snapped back to life, and he spun around and bolted for the passageway. Amelia's deadweight barely slowed him down because fear gave him wings, and he scrammed over the cave floor with feet that hardly touched the ground. Right on their backs was the horde of screeching mutations.

Lee reached the tunnel entrance with seconds to spare. He threw Amelia inside and then jumped up after her. In a flash, he had her over his shoulder in a fireman's lift and was racing down the passage. Lee risked a fleeting look back and was gladdened to see the mass of mutations hit the entrance in one big clump so that the tunnel entrance became plugged with their bodies. The shock of their impact made them fall away badly dazed, and when they recovered, the creatures tried again. The tunnel was too narrow to allow them to pass through more than one at a time, which raised Lee and Amelia's chances of survival from zero to minuscule.

Amelia's fingers suddenly clenched painfully at the flesh on his shoulder, and then she screamed because she'd come awake only to see those mutants chasing after them.

"Lee, put me down! Put me down!" she hollered.

"Can you run?" Lee asked between gasps.

"They're getting closer! Oh, God!"

"Can you run, Amelia?"

"YES!"

Lee slowed down just long enough to deposit Amelia onto her own two feet, and then he pushed her to the front and propelled her forwards down the tunnel with his hands on the small of her back. Lee was inches behind her.

The passageway grew steadily steeper from this point, and running uphill with a horde of ravaging mutant hybrids hot on their heels was like something from his worst nightmare. Lee didn't like to dwell on what would happen if he and Amelia were run to ground: they might be devoured or strangled with loops of roots around their necks, or they might end up one of the hybrids themselves, destined to serve Mother Baxter and Long Meg.

The blue illumination from the cave dwindled, forcing Lee to switch back to his light. He dared not risk a second glance back; he could tell from the sound how near their pursuers were to catching them.

A moment later, they stumbled across the abandoned hand-drawn cart.

"Quickly, Amelia," Lee shouted above the din, "help me push it."

Together, they grabbed the handles and, with some effort, managed to propel the cart down the slope.

"Let it go!"

They released the cart simultaneously, watched as it careered down the narrow passage, and then overturned with an almighty crash, spilling its load in all directions. The cart collided with the first mutant, ripping it to pieces. With shouts of triumph, Lee and Amelia were elated to see it was now blocking the crawlspace. The second mutant scrabbled at the cart with its tentacle-like feelers but could not squeeze through the slender gap.

"We beat them!" Amelia shouted jubilantly.

Lee looked at her cock-a-hoop expression and gave her a high-five, thinking he ought not to warn her the mutants knew every nook and cranny of the pit workings and would quickly find another route. They couldn't linger here for long.

"Let's keep moving," he urged.

They jogged ahead, and the ear-splitting hollering gradually faded. Several minutes later, they reached the large chamber holding the locomotive.

"What now?" Amelia asked.

"Now, we get the hell away from here."

"I know, but there are things I need to tell you, Lee. About me and Dave Minnock."

"Minnock? I don't understand?"

The harsh light shining on Amelia's face made it impossible to hide her distraught expression.

"I'm sorry, Lee. I'm so sorry for everything."

Lee wrapped his arms around her and squeezed her slender frame.

"I don't know what you think you've done, Amelia, but none of this is your fault."

"It is, though," she wept. "It's all my fault."

"Look, why don't we get out of this horrible place first, and then you can tell me what's on your mind. I'm sure you're getting all confused—"

Lee broke off mid-sentence and looked around.

"What's that noise?"

An abrupt whooshing sound reached them from the second tunnel, the one leading outside, and in seconds, it grew so loud that it felt like a full-blown attack on their senses.

"It sounds like rushing water?"

"Like hell it's water," Lee answered. "Duck!"

From the opposite tunnel came a swarm of dark, flying creatures. The bats, oh God, they'd forgotten about the colony of bats. Thousands of the flying vermin swooped straight at Lee and Amelia like a murmuration of starlings, and they just had time to fling up their arms before they were battered around the head and shoulders. Tiny teeth and claws dug into the back of Lee's hands, and when he swatted his arms, they felt heavy, weighed down with furry little beasts. They chirruped in their peculiar high-pitched tone, and their wings beat frenziedly, disturbing the air.

Disregarding his own interests, Lee pulled Amelia close and started swatting away any bats that sought purchase on her head and upper body. He swung his arms about like a madman and caught himself shouting and swearing for the bats to leave them alone, pointless as that was.

Then it dawned on Lee that the swarm of flying creatures was moving on, flapping on a course that took them spiralling towards the high roof and away from him and Amelia. Within seconds, they'd flown away, leaving a few broken bodies behind.

Amelia was bent over at the waist and spitting on the ground.

"Are you hurt?" Lee asked as he caught his breath.

"No, just covered in bat shit."

She pointed at his bloody hands.

"How about you?"

"They're only scratches, to add to all the others," Lee insisted even though they stung like heck.

He took Amelia by the elbow.

"Come on."

They trotted around the locomotive and then along the final stretch of tunnel that would lead them outside. Weak daylight buffed the steel rail lines up ahead, turning them golden. How long had they been down in the pit workings? It only felt like an hour or two since he'd left the cottage. Nothing seemed to follow the same rules; even time was playing games with them, Lee figured.

"What do you think startled the bats?" Amelia asked as they jogged along. "They were in a mighty hurry."

Lee didn't like to offer an answer.

She shivered violently and asked, "Those creatures that chased us, Lee? What in the world were they? And the other thing in the big cave. My memory's hazy. All I can remember is something bad happening at the caravan–"

"I saw the mess."

"–and the next thing I knew, you were shaking me awake in the cave. I don't know how I got there or how I ended up wearing these clothes. Then you carried me away while I was half asleep, but I caught a glimpse of..."

Amelia's sentence trailed away.

"Try not to think about it."

"It was her, wasn't it, Lee? Mother Baxter. And her daughter."

"Amelia, we don't have time for this right now. Let's just concentrate on clearing out, agreed?"

He saw her nod and grow pensive.

Lee switched off his light and returned it to its place. In front of them was the boarded-up exit. They made a path for the prised-open section, passing the blacksmith's workshop.

"You go first."

While Lee waited for Amelia to slide through the breach, he ventured one final look back into the mine. It was eerily quiet now which, rather than give him hope, left him feeling uneasy. Frowning, Lee turned away and bent over as he crammed his body between the wood slats.

A low, early-morning mist lay over the valley floor like a satin blanket, hiding the caravan. The tops of some of the taller trees poked through the white veil. In the distance, heather-crowned moorland stretched to the horizon. There was no sign of the hybrid monsters or their queen.

"We should fetch your motorcycle. We'll stick to the main road and ride back to Hebden Bridge. Then, once we've composed ourselves, we go far away. I don't know about you, Amelia, but I never want to see this corner of the world again."

"Then we can talk?"

"Yes, then we can talk. I also need to get some things off my chest."

They proceeded down the slope and soon entered the thick, gauzy mist. They could feel it brush against their skin like soft kisses. It felt good after the greasy patina left behind by the half-world deep below.

Lee felt Amelia's hand slip inside his own, and he gave her fingers a tiny squeeze.

The soupy mist grew thicker the deeper into the valley they went, and visibility was soon down to a few feet. It swirled across their paths in the breeze. Lee drew to a halt.

"What is it?" Amelia asked in a whisper.

"There is no breeze," Lee said back, thinking aloud.

"So?"

So, what was making the mist swirl so much?

With little warning, Mother Baxter came flying out of the haziness, her arms working like spring-loaded appendages. The set of branks was gone, somehow ditched now that she'd broken free of the grotto, allowing her to bellow her fury from her bloody orifice. She swooped down, and the tip of her backbone whipped at Lee's head like a scorpion's tail. He wheeled away with hardly a second to spare and watched in terror as Mother Baxter swept past, turned in mid-air, and returned for a second pass. This time, she swooped so low she was only feet above the rocky slope, taking Lee by surprise. The tailbone of her spine hooked the hood of his coat and lifted him clear of the ground.

Lee cried out in panic as his feet left the earth. Mother Baxter tried to climb higher, but Lee's weight was too much to bear, so she spun around and dropped earthwards instead.

Lee saw she meant to dash him against one of the old bridge supports and break his legs, so he lifted his arms straight up and felt his body slip out of the parka. He fell six feet to the ground, folded his legs, and rolled.

The impact expelled the air from his lungs, and he groaned in the grass. He must have hit his head on something because the world was topsy-turvy for a few seconds. Through his out-of-focus eyes, he thought he saw Amelia racing over to where he'd come to rest.

"Get up, Lee! Get up! She's coming back!"

Lee clambered to his knees, then gained his feet with Amelia's help. He looked around, but all he could see was white mist.

"Where is she?"

"She's circling us. Look!"

Lee followed Amelia's finger and saw a flying shadow through the wispy veils.

"We'll never make it to the caravan. If we use the moped, she'll pluck us off anyway. We'll have to head up the valley and try using the rocks and undergrowth for cover."

Lee thumped the heel of his hand against his head to clear it. Then, praying they weren't going in the wrong direction towards the woods, he led Amelia to the bottom of the slope, on constant alert for another attack from Mother Baxter.

She'd stopped that awful howling, but they could still sense her circling them. She was probably biding her time for another pass.

Lee hoped the mist might conceal him and Amelia – assuming Mother Baxter wasn't psychic or had x-ray vision. The problem was, if they were to escape up the valley, they would eventually come out above the mist and be in full view. But they had no choice. He'd worry about that when the time came.

Lee's thoughts were interrupted because the brook was just ahead of them. They picked their way over the wet rocks, heading upstream.

"There she is!" cried Amelia, and she pulled Lee down as a dark shape swopped just above head height.

"Move over to those rocks on the far bank," Lee told Amelia, indicating a set of bulky shapes just visible in the haze. "The big ones jutting out of the slope."

They splashed through the cold water, tottering on the broken streambed. On the other side, a narrow sheep trail twisted through the heather and gorse. They hurried along it and sought shelter in the shadow of a collection of boulders, pausing to gather themselves.

"Why won't she leave us alone?"

"Because she's hunting us, and she won't stop until she's either captured or killed us both."

"But why is she doing it?" Amelia implored, close to tears.

Lee had no answers. They were also quickly running out of options because they couldn't go on like this, being harried from spot to spot until they grew exhausted.

They pressed on upstream. The mist thinned out as they gained the higher ground, and Lee noticed a dark crevice where high bluffs straddled both banks. He shepherded Amelia across, pushed her inside, squeezed in after her, and then put his finger to his lips.

The crevice was slick with spongy, wet moss, and drops of condensation dripped on their heads, but the important thing was they were out of sight. Lee could hear Amelia's harsh breath in his ear, but gradually her breathing quietened, and a hush settled over them.

Lee pressed his forehead against the rough stone in front.

If they got out of this alive, he swore he'd never go to the countryside again. From now on, he planned on a life in the city, a million miles from the boonies.

Suddenly, a shower of small pebbles tumbled down from the top of the crevice, bouncing off their heads. They both looked up instinctively. A long and bony appendage stretched deep into the fissure, lengthening as it folded open, and then jabbed towards them with fingers made from roots.

Amelia screamed hysterically as they fastened onto her blonde hair and commenced to snatch her from the hiding spot. She was hoisted up the inside of the chimney-like crevice, and Lee grabbed her legs and pulled in the opposite direction.

It was like a repeat of the struggle between Jacko and the tree roots, but whereas Lee had saved his friend that time, he doubted he'd win on this occasion. The tight space restricted his movements, and it was clear Mother Baxter was too strong for him.

Any second, Amelia would be wrested out of his hold like a fisherman landing his catch.

CHAPTER 26

AMELIA WAS FIGHTING FOR HER life. Lee put as much effort as he could into pinning Amelia's legs with his arms, but he could feel her slipping from his grasp.

Then, out of the blue, Mother Baxter released her grip. Amelia dropped into the crevice, landing on her feet alongside Lee. The two of them were stunned into silence by the sudden turn of events. One moment, it seemed she'd be taken away to face certain death, and the next, she was free: dishevelled, her hair a mess and her face stained with tears, but alive.

Lee was the first to recover.

"What happened?"

"I don't know," Amelia responded in a shaky voice. She had a thin trickle of blood running from her hairline down her forehead, where it collected in one eyebrow. "She just let me go."

Lee fleetingly wondered if Mother Baxter had abandoned the fight and returned to her underground lair. It was a short-lived flicker of hope snuffed out when all hell broke loose. A cacophony of noise battered their senses as Mother Baxter commenced yelping and howling like an animal in extreme distress, her shrill voice conveying pain and fear. Whatever melodrama was playing out was music to their ears, and they grabbed the opportunity to squeeze out of the crevice and make a run for it.

They'd only taken a few steps when they faltered and stared openmouthed at the sight that greeted them. Mother Baxter was atop the crag and writhing with apparent agony. Her elongated arms flapped about, broken in numerous places, and her backbone flicked violently from side to side, sending stones flying and reminding Lee of a viper in its death throes. She twisted her neck about, and Lee saw a big copper nail hammered so deep into the top of her head that it had passed through the roof of her mouth, then into her tongue, and finally out from beneath her lower jaw. Blood and gore ran in rivulets down her features.

As Lee and Amelia watched, the skin on her head peeled apart and fell away in chunks, sloughing off the bone beneath and discarding her lips and eyes in the process until all that remained was a skull with eyeless sockets like chunks of coal.

Then, Mother Baxter started to crumble. Beginning with her head, then her appendages, and lastly, her backbone, her body disintegrated like a speeded-up film of a skeleton falling apart with age. She was reduced to dust in less than a minute, which blew away on the breeze.

Lee scrambled up the face of the crag, followed by Amelia. At the top, he walked over to where Mother Baxter had been moments ago, unable to comprehend what they'd just witnessed. He needed to be sure.

"Be careful, Lee."

There was nothing left of the sorceress. All signs that she'd ever existed had vanished.

"She's gone," he whispered to himself.

"Lee," called Amelia, and when he turned around, Lee saw she was looking out over the blanket of mist at some distant point on the far skyline. A figure stood atop one exceptionally high precipice, silhouetted against the bright sky. The person held a pair of staffs planted in the ground and watched them silently. Lee immediately recognized him as the person from his astral vision, the Dodman of old, marking out the ley lines with his marking staves like The Long Man of Wilmington had millennia ago.

"Who is he?" Amelia asked under her breath.

It was like a light had come on inside Lee's head, furnishing him with the straightforward answer.

"Percival," he muttered.

"The tramp? How can it be him, Lee? He died long ago."

Lee said nothing. He just watched as the Dodman raised one stave and pointed with it down the misty valley.

"What's he doing?"

"I think he's trying to help us, Amelia."

At the bottom of the deep valley, the thick cloak of mist started to roil and twist in majestic waves. They watched as it parted along the entire length of the gorge, like something out of the Bible, the two sides pulling apart and leaving a clear gap down the middle where the stream was. Lee and Amelia experienced a tiny shuddering under their feet and looked on as a crack appeared at the base of the valley, a narrow rift in the ground alongside the watercourse. It grew into a long, slender breach stretching to the caravan and into the distant woods. The shaking subsided, and the splitting of the earth halted.

Lee felt Amelia loop her arm through his, but strangely, he himself felt unafraid. He couldn't take his eyes off the spectacle.

Now the mist was curling over like slow-moving breakers on a beach, twisting and sliding into the breach, drawn down into the opening like something was sucking it into the earth. When the last of the tendrils vanished, the ground shifted again, and this time the slender crack closed and disappeared, leaving no trace behind.

"He opened the ley line, put her down there, and closed it again. Trapping Mother Baxter forever."

"You're positive that she's gone for good?"

Lee nodded.

"I don't know how I know, Amelia. I just do. It's over."

With the mist gone and the morning sun rising higher, the valley and woods looked like any other pleasant spot on an autumnal day. They turned their attention back to Percival the Tramp, who stayed to watch them for a moment. Then he nodded solemnly, turned around, and walked away over the rocky skyline.

• • •

Now that the danger was past, they felt safe returning to the caravan so Amelia could collect some overnight items. Lee waited outside next to the moped. He did not need to return to the cottage; the stolen money was immaterial, and although he didn't say this to Amelia, he wasn't one hundred percent certain it would be safe in the woods. Maybe one day, in the future, he might return. Coming back could help with the healing process and allow him to set things aside once and for all. On the other hand, maybe he wouldn't. It might be for the best to end this chapter right now.

As he stood in the sunlight, his face upturned, Lee thought about Jacko. He considered what had become of him. Lee could only pray his friend was dead and not living some eternal nightmare, with his flesh and bones grafted onto the living plants and knitted together to form a subgroup of some new species. Perhaps that's what the mutations in the grotto were: people who found themselves lost in the woods and on the moors only to wind up victims of Mother Baxter.

There were too many imponderables.

Too many unanswered questions.

Lee turned at the sound of footsteps. Amelia came down the stairs holding a sports bag. As soon as she reached the bottom, she burst into tears and ran into his arms.

As he held her tightly, Amelia told him everything. She explained more about her ex-boyfriend, Ryan, and how she'd turned to Dave Minnock for help, not realizing until it was too late the things she'd have to do in return. By then, she was in too deep and couldn't back out of Minnock's scheme. Lee listened in astonishment and dread as Amelia told him of Minnock's duplicity, how he'd masqueraded as a kindly gent, only then to reveal his true identity. She learned of Minnock's background, heritage, and ancestral links to Mother Baxter, which set him on a life-long quest to redress the wrong done to the wise woman and her child and seek retribution. Lee suspected even Amelia didn't know the full extent of Minnock's plans nor his uncanny abilities. He liked to think had she done, she would have refused to draw Lee into Minnock's plot, such as setting the foot-track spell, seducing him that night in the caravan, and all that had followed. But Lee didn't honestly know how unwittingly she'd been played by the little occultist. Amelia had been desperate, after all.

Besides, Lee was in no position to judge.

They climbed onto the moped. As they rode away, Lee swore he'd tell her about himself once they settled somewhere far from here.

• • •

Dave Minnock stood at the centre of the small clearing and stared dejectedly into the empty burial spot. Dear Mother Baxter's mortal remains had vanished, just like her metaphysical presence had been banished from this realm.

He asked himself once again: how could things have gone so wrong?

Dave had spent decades planning for this day and travelled worldwide to seek knowledge of the dark arts. He'd studied ancient texts and conducted rituals and rites to understand the many esoteric mysteries of the hidden and malign forces known only to mages and shamans of the past. He'd seen and done tremendous – and oft-times, wicked – things during that period, all for a greater purpose.

But now, all his plans lay in ruins. And it had happened in the most unexpected of ways.

Dave Minnock had been thwarted not by Lee Harris or the silly girl, Amelia, but by that interfering old vagabond, Percival the Tramp, the foolish oath who'd wandered the byways of England, collecting ridiculous fairy tales from the uneducated country bumpkins. Percival, who heard of the legend of Mother Baxter in these parts and appointed himself custodian of secrets and gatekeeper against her return.

Now, Mother Baxter is in purgatory and seemingly trapped forever.

Or perhaps not.

Dave Minnock knew a reckoning was coming for his failure, but there was one final thing he could try. One last-ditch attempt to put the wrongs right.

Dave had only attempted the Rite of Transference once before, in a hotel room in Paris twenty-five years ago. On that occasion, he'd made mistakes, the ritual went wrong, and Dave had spent six months in a Swiss rehab clinic. But since then, he'd learned so much. Since then, he'd acquired necessary wisdom by adopting more cautious disciplines as set out in his rare copy of the 1563 edition of FALSE MONARCHY OF DEMONS – one of only two copies that existed (the other was in a sealed case at Angkor Wat, Cambodia)

Dave moved around the clearing, kicking away leaves until he'd exposed a big enough piece of bare earth. Then he scratched a series of symbols and sigils into the ground.

Stripping to the waist, he sat cross-legged and anointed himself with oil in the sign of an inverted cross.

When he was ready, Dave began the rite.

9 MONTHS LATER

LEE DROVE AS FAST AS possible through the city streets, ignoring the speeding signs and red lights and banking on luck that he didn't have a collision. Thankfully, the roads were quiet, which was partly down to the late hour as well as the terrible weather.

It had started raining late in the afternoon, just about the same time Amelia's labour pains began. The weather steadily worsened for the next few hours while he fretted over his fiancé. The rain intensified, and the wind howled around the building, rattling the windows of their third-floor apartment and threatening to send plant pots crashing off their balcony. According to the lady on TV, the fluke spring storm had appeared from nowhere, blowing off the Irish Sea. She'd forecast gale-force winds and thunderstorms through the night.

Lee had telephoned the hospital and explained his wife's condition. They advised him to keep a note of her contractions and to bring her in when they came every five minutes and lasted about sixty seconds. Amelia reached that point shortly after midnight, and despite the downpours and the buffeting winds, Lee walked her outside to their car and set off through the stormy night.

It was a hair-raising but thankfully short journey, and they reached the hospital without incident. Amelia was whisked inside to the maternity unit, and by the time she was squared away in a private room, her contractions became more and more painful. The midwife popped in to check on them both every quarter of an hour and to monitor the baby's heart. Meanwhile, Amelia walked around the small room, breathing through her mouth.

Shortly before three in the morning, Amelia's waters broke, and she gave birth to their first child very soon after. As the infant was delivered, a peal of thunder crashed outside.

The rumbling faded, and there were several moments of tense quiet as the midwife fussed over the newborn. Then she passed the child across to Amelia.

Both parents smiled at their daughter, feeling proud, emotional, and happy.

Lee noticed something odd about Amelia's hands. Where she held the baby and stroked its scalp, her fingers looked peculiarly long and misshapen, covered in fine hairs.

To Lee, Amelia's fingers resembled plant roots.

And their newborn didn't cry like a normal baby.

It cackled with quiet contentment.

MARK HOBSON
FEBRUARY 2023 – JANUARY 2024

AUTHOR'S NOTE

This is a work of fiction. The plot and characters are products of the author's imagination. Where real persons, places and incidents have been incorporated to create the illusion of authenticity, they are used fictitiously. Inspiration was drawn from the following nonfiction sources:

Cavendish, Richard. *The World of Ghosts and the Supernatural: A continent-by-continent tour of the occult, the unexplained and the mystical around the world*. Waymark Publications, 1994.

Lancaster Brown, Peter. *Megaliths, Myths and Men: An Introduction to Astro-Archaeology*. Blandford, 1976

Lipscomb, Suzannah. *A History of Magic, Witchcraft & The Occult*. Penguin Random House, 2020.

Neil-Smith, Christopher. *The Exorcist and the Possessed: The truth about exorcism.* Chapel River Press, 1974.

Schiff, Stacy. *The Witches - Salem, 1692: A History*. Weidenfeld & Nicolson, 2015

Sullivan, Jack. *The Penguin Encyclopedia of Horror and the Supernatural.* Viking Penguin Inc, 1986

Watkins, Alfred. *The Old Straight Track*. Abacus, 1974.

Mark Hobson

ABOUT THE AUTHOR

Mark Hobson is a writer and historian. His works span numerous genres, both fiction and non-fiction, ranging from post-apocalyptic survival thrillers and crime novels to books on various military history subjects.

Dweller Under The Roots is his first folk-horror novel

You can follow the author's Facebook page at:

facebook.com/yorkshirescribbler

If you enjoyed this book, please consider leaving a review on
Amazon or Goodreads

Mark Hobson

WORLD QUAKE

It was a day like any other. People setting out on the commute to work or taking the kids to school or chatting to their friends in the park. Normal. Routine. Nothing to mark it apart.

By lunchtime, everything they had ever known, every aspect of their lives, would be changed forever – marked by the most catastrophic series of global disasters to strike the planet in over 6000 years.

MANKIND STANDS AT THE GATES OF EXTINCTION

The world is being ripped apart by a great geological cataclysm. Cities crumble and entire continents disappear beneath the sea as earthquakes and mega-tsunamis lay waste to the land. For the human race there is no escape and nowhere to flee. Millions perish.

From the rubble, a disparate group of survivors emerge.

A school teacher hell-bent on finding his pregnant wife.

A scientist with the fate of the world in his hands.

The workforce of a power plant who fight to prevent a nuclear meltdown that would poison a nation for millennia.

While the politicians hide in their bunkers beneath London and Washington, these ordinary people will have to fight to stay alive in this new world, an existence blighted with violence, cruelty and death as they journey across a devastated landscape.

They must ask themselves profound questions about their own morality while humanity descends into chaos.

A new epoch in Earth's history is underway.

THIS IS THE AGE OF DEATH

ABSOLUTE PAGE-TURNER, AND A BRILLIANT, BRILLIANT STORY.
A FRIGHTENING VIEW OF WHAT MAY AWAIT THE WORLD.
THE AUTHOR PAINTS A DEEPLY-RESEARCHED AND GRAPHIC PICTURE OF A POSSIBLE SCENARIO OF AN EXTINCTION-LEVEL EVENT.
WOULD MAKE A BLOCKBUSTER FILM.
AVAILABLE FROM AMAZON ISBN: 9798795916309

WORLD QUAKE 2

The old world is gone forever.

The Great Cataclysm has left the planet on its knees, and over 2 billion people are dead. Now the dust has settled, and all of mankind's greatest achievements lay in ruins, from the modern metropolis of New York to the grand old cities of London and Paris and the ancient pyramids of Egypt – everything is destroyed.

EARTH IS UNDERGOING A GRAND RESET

With nature holding sway over the fate of the world, the survivors strive to overcome the catastrophe that has broken their lives and threatens the very existence of the human race.

Scott Cook and his companions have somehow endured, but at a cost. Seemingly stranded, they unexpectedly find themselves presented with a choice: remain where they are and risk dying from hunger and disease, or join a group of young people on a dangerous odyssey across a mysterious land.

In America, Kenny Leland is saved from certain death, only to find himself accompanying a mad president hell-bent on a perilous mission.

And beneath the mountains and glaciers of Switzerland, scientists in a top-secret subterranean laboratory take desperate measures to prevent the world from falling into the abyss as a new threat emerges.

THE GREAT TRIBULATION IS AT HAND

OUTSTANDING.

I BECAME CAUGHT UP IN THE CHARACTERS AND SCENARIOS FROM PAGE ONE.

A TERRIFYING BUT ADDICTIVE STORY.

THE DEVELOPMENT OF THE CHARACTERS IS MASSIVE.

BREATHTAKING… I CAN'T WAIT FOR THE NEXT BOOK.

AVAILABLE FROM AMAZON ISBN: 9798387952166

Mark Hobson

GREY STONES

Carter Middleton returns to his childhood home in Yorkshire to bury his father and to reconnect with his estranged family. Yet, after fifteen years away, he quickly learns that the old bitterness and feuding that first drove him to leave is still as deeply rooted as ever.

Others in Stansfield Bridge make it clear they want him gone too. His arrival stirs memories from the past, of events best forgotten, of secrets they would prefer kept hidden.

Jessica Bates has also come home. Years earlier, her mother left their caravan one evening and never returned. Her whereabouts remain a mystery to this day. Now Jessica is determined to get to the truth, whatever the consequences.

An act of brutal violence brings Carter and Jessica together. With steely resolve, they set out to investigate, soon unearthing terrible decades-old sins and revealing a darkness at the very heart of the community.

They soon discover that everything comes at a cost. Life is cheap in the countryside.

Set against the hard and unforgiving landscape of northern England, **GREY STONES** is a shocking tale of betrayal, revenge, loyalty and grief.

A SMOULDERING BUILD-UP TO A DRAMATIC AND TERRIFYING ENDING.
NOT A RUN-OF-THE-MILL MURDER MYSTERY... I FOUND IT A GREAT READ.
WOW! WHAT AN AMAZING STORY.

AVAILABLE FROM AMAZON ISBN: 9798548418586

A MURMURATION OF STARLINGS
TWO STRANGERS. ONE SEEKING REVENGE. THE OTHER REDEMPTION

Twelve years ago, Francis Bailey was locked away and left to rot in Britain's most notorious prison: found guilty of the worst kind of crime – the murder of a young child. A crime that he did not commit.

Finally released on appeal, he returns to his home town in the Yorkshire peaks to rebuild his life. Unable to land a job, stigmatized by society and branded a dangerous lunatic by a corrupt police force, he soon realizes that his only course of action is to prove his innocence to the world by solving the case that still haunts the small community.

But the truth lies hidden behind a wall of silence, where the bent copper who sent him down is shielded by people at the very top. When it comes to justice, truth is irrelevant.

Liam Brennan is a man haunted by his past. Living on the streets, he is a drunkard and a deadbeat.

Dangerous people are searching for him. Former colleagues who want him dead. Because Liam knows too much about their dark and violent history. There is nothing they won't do to ensure their secrets stay hidden.

Forever in fear that his whereabouts may one day be discovered, his life is one long mess of drunken brawls and petty crime.

When Francis and Liam's paths cross, they form an unlikely bond and together set out on a tortured quest seeking truth and absolution. Either they must conquer their demons and prevail, or be crushed by the horrors they carry with them.

BUT NOW ANOTHER CHILD IS MISSING, SNATCHED OFF THE STREETS. TIME IS RUNNING OUT.

A JAW-DROPPING CRIME NOVEL
AVAILABLE FROM AMAZON ISBN: 9798840016992

Mark Hobson

WOLF ANGEL

AMSTERDAM OCCULT SERIES
BOOK ONE

The City of Amsterdam is gripped with fear.
A series of brutal murders have left homicide detectives baffled. With no motive or clues to work with, they find themselves probing blindly through the city's dark and violent underworld. But Inspector Pieter Van Dijk is not convinced this is the work of one lone psychopath.
Drawn deeper and deeper into the shadowy heart of the case, he unearths a terrifying history of family madness and occult conspiracy echoing across the decades.

BRILLIANT... GRIPPING... A WELL THOUGHT OUT AND WELL-WRITTEN BOOK.
A DARK STORY WITH LOTS OF ACTION.
THIS ISN'T JACKANORY.
THIS IS SIMPLY A GREAT READ WITH ALL THE ELEMENTS TO KEEP YOU TURNING THE PAGE.
GRITTY DRAMA... WITH THE SUPERNATURAL ELEMENTS CLEVERLY WOVEN IN.
INTRIGUE SOAKS OUT OF THE BRICKWORK OF AMSTERDAM'S ALLEYWAYS.

AVAILABLE FROM AMAZON ISBN: 9798696036946

Dweller Under The Roots

A STATE OF SIN

AMSTERDAM OCCULT SERIES
BOOK TWO

Three psychopaths are haunting the streets of Amsterdam this winter.
A doctor, who leaves his patients horribly disfigured.
A hunter from South Africa, determined to add to his collection of human trophies.
A kidnapper, who keeps his victim locked away in a small metal cage.
When Dutch cop Pieter Van Dijk answers what he thinks will be a routine call to investigate a case of arson, little does he realize the chain of terrifying events that are about to grip the city with icy fear.
Fresh back from a break of rest and recuperation, and trying hard to deal with the aftermath of a brutal case, he soon finds himself plunged deep into a new nightmare. What links the three crimes? Just who is behind them? And why does he feel that this time the answers hinge on his own past?
From the snowy alleyways of Amsterdam to the frigid shores of the North Sea, the hunt to put a stop to the rampage of murder and bloodshed soon becomes a race against time. Because one thing he has learned over the years is that Amsterdam is a city of shadows, hiding the worst in human nature.

A GRIPPING CRIME DRAMA.
THERE ARE SEVERAL HIGHLY DISTURBING SCENES THAT GAVE ME CHILLS.
VERY HIGHLY RESEARCHED AND WOVEN TOGETHER WITH LAYERS OF HISTORY... VERY WELL WRITTEN.

AVAILABLE FROM AMAZON ISBN: 9798724812566

Mark Hobson

NOW MAY MEN WEEP

ISANDLWANA
A Story from the Zulu War
JANUARY 1879 – ZULULAND

Lord Chelmsford, commander of British forces in South Africa, leads an invasion into Zululand. At the head of his main spearhead column, he expects a quick and decisive campaign against a poorly armed, ill-disciplined force of tribesmen. To achieve this aim he has with him the veteran soldiers from the 24th Regiment, 'Old Sweats', as they are referred to, men with years of campaigning behind them.

Just days into the invasion Chelmsford's force sets up camp beside a strangely-shaped crag, barely a few miles from the safety of the British Colony of Natal.

The battle that develops in the shadow of that mountain, with British redcoats fighting hand-to-hand with their Zulu foe, will become the stuff of legend.

It is a story punctuated with acts of incredible courage and heroism and moving sacrifice, a human drama that will shock the world.

ISANDLWANA!

I FEEL LIKE I'M PRESENT AT THE BATTLE OF ISANDLWANA.
PAGE-TURNING EXCITEMENT... RIPPING YARNS 21ST CENTURY STYLE!
CAPTURES THE TERROR... GRIPPING MOMENTS OF ACTION.
A CRACKING READ.
AVAILABLE FROM AMAZON ISBN: 9798666828472

WHAT READERS ARE SAYING ABOUT MARK HOBSON'S BOOKS

I COULDN'T PUT GREY STONES DOWN... A GREAT READ
GREY STONES

THIS IS A RARE BOOK. THE FLOW OF THE STORY KEPT ME ADDICTED
GREY STONES

HAD ME HOOKED FROM THE VERY BEGINNING... THE WRITING IS EXPRESSIVE, AND TAKES THE READER ON A ROLLERCOASTER RIDE OF OUTRAGE, HORROR AND SYMPATHY
A MURMURATION OF STARLINGS

THIS IS A GREAT STORY AND SERVES AS A GREAT SETUP FOR THE SERIES
WOLF ANGEL (AMSTERDAM OCCULT SERIES BOOK 1)

MARK HOBSON BUILDS UP THE TENSION NICELY WITH RARELY A DULL MOMENT
WOLF ANGEL (AMSTERDAM OCCULT SERIES BOOK 1)

YOU HAVE THE INGREDIENTS FOR AN EXCITING THRILLER... GREAT READING
A STATE OF SIN (AMSTERDAM OCCULT SERIES BOOK 2)

HAD ME GRIPPED FROM THE START, I HIGHLY RECOMMEND THIS BOOK
A STATE OF SIN (AMSTERDAM OCCULT SERIES BOOK 2)

Mark Hobson

WELL WRITTEN AND VERY FRIGHTENING... WELL-DEVELOPED CHARACTERS AND A GREAT STORYLINE
WORLD QUAKE

A REAL PAGE-TURNER OR FINGER-SWIPER
WORLD QUAKE

LOVED THIS DISASTER NOVEL, WELL RESEARCHED WITH LOTS OF ACTION
WORLD QUAKE

YOU FEEL YOU ARE THERE WITH THE SOLDIERS, FEELING THEIR FEAR AND PAIN... ABSOLUTELY BRILLIANT
NOW MAY MEN WEEP

THIS IS A MASTERFUL RETELLING OF THIS STORY... ONE IS DRAWN TO THE INEVITABLE CONCLUSION
NOW MAY MEN WEEP

Printed in Great Britain
by Amazon